HUMANE

Stonehouse Publishing Inc. is an independent
publishing house, incorporated in 2014.

Cover illustration, *Shifter* by Trish Sewell.
Cover design and layout by Anne Brown.
Printed in Canada

Stonehouse Publishing would like to thank and acknowledge
the support of the Alberta Government funding for the arts,
through the Alberta Media Fund.

Government

National Library of Canada Cataloguing in Publication Data
Anna Marie Sewell
Humane
Novel
ISBN 978-1-988754-24-6
First Edition

HUMANE

A NOVEL BY
ANNA MARIE SEWELL

HAZEL: DOG THIEF

So, here I am with this damn dog.

I mean, I literally got up in the morning, threw out my boyfriend, drove out to the Humane Society and stole a dog.

What happens now? I ask him, in my head.

He gives me a slight grin, swipes his tongue along his teeth, *Well, that depends on you. You ready to get to work?*

To work? I—don't know what you mean—weird skin crawl feeling snakes down my back.

Yes, I do believe you do. His eyes are orange/yellow/brown, and way too close. I shoulder check left, away from the glare. This is freaking me out, and I'm getting mad; but I've got nothing in the bag for this situation, and can only muster teen-level truculence.

How can I know?

Oh, you know. Spider laughs and it raises every hair on my body.

I know?

I reach for the Timmy's, playing for time. Just like that, he ducks his head to intercept the motion, grips my hand in his mouth.

Hey! I jerk free. *Cut it out! I'm driving here!*

He rolls an eye.

Okay, then. I shake my head, as if that's going to shut up the voice—his voice.

I've got to pay attention to the road, Spider.

Wuff, he says in disgust, and curls against the bucket seat, turning his head toward the window.

And shouldn't you be riding in the back, dog?

He turns his head, curls one lip to show me the teeth—*Very big, very sharp teeth*, snickers the voice. *The teeth ride up front, human.*

I have to think for a minute, have to take this back. I am in the driver's seat here, am I not? For a moment, I see us as if I were the driver in the oncoming lane—woman and her over-entitled dog—

Well, don't shed all over the upholstery, I manage. And then I have to laugh. This is ridiculous.

What's funny?

I just stole a dog. I'm imagining what the police would say if they stopped me. 'The dog told me to do it, officer. Well, I mean, first of all my granny—my dead granny—told me to get the dog, and then the dog—'

I lose it and start laughing in a panicky way. Like that, Spider whips his head around and grabs my coat sleeve.

Steady, he says in my head. And for the first time, there's a whiff of kindness, some sort of tone I've only ever heard from Gran, and I guess from Dad. Suddenly, I'm blinking tears away. *What the*—I don't cry over Dad anymore, it's been way too long. And he never liked crying anyway. *Hold your own counsel*, he'd say, low and controlled.

The stuff he held in, too much, and it got him in the end—but I shake my head, focus on driving. Spider has had the decency to let go and look away.

We roll through the rain-slicked streets, the faint slap and squeak of the wipers on the Jeep's windshield a slow counterpoint to all the things I have no idea how to say.

Now he speaks up, as a certain acridity invades my space.

Hey, crack the window, would you? Guy could use some air. Stuff they feed us there.

And there we are, heading home, like the first scene in some American cop-buddy movie, the part where the mismatched pair has the first glimmer of connection.

CONNECTION

I am sleeping.

I walk and I walk, and I smoke.
 The light has bled out of the sky.

I am not lost.

'It's not like it's even related. Totally different. Maybe that's it.'
 I find I'm muttering aloud, and I don't even care. Maybe I am
crazy. No matter. Let any fucker try to stop me tonight.

**I know just when I am; and this where that I am is every bit as fasci-
nating as I saw in the glimpses that I dared to take.**

'It's not—' I continue, talking to some invisible listener, (if you want
to make it sound even a little bit like I'm okay,) '—It's not like they
are the same sort of death. Fuck. Frankie wasn't a cheap whore murdered in a fucking alley.'

**They told me not to do this, they warned me, do not even look. And I
did not speak back. To speak back is not for the young. But I considered, which is what every person must do.**

'Frankie was good. Frankie was super. Just ask him, Frank could always say what he was born for, what he was up to, why he was doing what he was doing. He was so full of shit sometimes, but he always could say…'

I consider the stories of how humans came to Turtle Island. Remember? A star woman looked Between, and fell down here. And look at everything that follows from that!

I'm crying, but it doesn't matter. The wind wipes my face, adds some sour rain.

'But these others, they don't … do they even have a single goddamned clue as to why they're born? Do they know? Do they care?'

Me, I did not fall here. They cannot say I did. I looked around before I came here. I studied Her, and I studied her territory, Hills of the House of the Beaver People. There are few beavers here.

I glare at the empty darkness.

'Why the fuck do they throw themselves away like that? And why should I have to try to pick up the fucking pieces?'

This Amiskwaciy is full of Star Woman's descendants. They have woven themselves into other families of their kind, humans of strange and diverse origin; but I can see them, the ones who hearken back to that story.

I think of Mrs. August, her overstuffed, sagging body and her slow, selfish mind. The way she talked, ill-educated, patently stupid—

And, if—when—they find out what I do, I will be able to answer truly that I am truly true (what fun this language offers—truloolooloolooloolala!) I am truly true to our true promise to help them, the humans.

'But she loved her kid, didn't she?'
    I hate myself for the question. But I've seen it all over, people

who say they love their kids, but they go on about themselves, ignore those same kids, act powerless to try to make a different choice, powerless to open up a better possibility for their kids than they have.

'Fuck! Why can't they change it?'

She cares. She is a medicine for the illness of this place. And She is weeping. I consider not to sing, la la, for She is weeping. And I have come. I can help.

I feel like... I don't know... I'm chain-smoking, my boots have cracked all the cold slick puddles from here to the Kingsway, and there is no solution.

Something looms ahead, big, moving.

I stop.

Look sharper.

I am sleeping, in Shinguak's arms. Just a nap, not a nest, and besides, this shinguak stands alone, so I think she is glad of my company. Other than me, it is just ravens and chickadees and squirrels, she says, she hasn't seen my kind in too long, seed and branch, too long.

No, it's just the big ragged pine in the hospital parking lot. The rest of the wind has died down, but up in the pine top, there's enough to make it shake and move.

'You,' I say to it, 'Pine. Shinguak. You're supposed to be Wise. What the fuck do I do?'

I am sleeping, resting, waiting for the call I trust will come, the answer to my prayer, that I will see and hear and know that I am in the right where, where She is, in Amiskwaciy.

And suddenly, like I'm pulled to it, I turn toward that ragged great tree. There's just a dirty small boulevard apron round it, dirty, gravelly, no grass.

'Look at you!' Suddenly, that tree makes me madder than anything. It's so clear. This is all that's left, this shitty, shifty, skinny remnant. This tree is me.

I hate this tree. I find myself running. I slam into it, full shoulder, like I'm going to roll it over.

'Where is Justice?!' She screams up at me.

Stupid, Hazel.
    Of course, I cannot uproot a pine.
    Of course, it hurts.

'Justice! Justice! Justice!' This woman screams.

Impact hurts, and it hurts all the way down as I slide into a heap in the dust and grime and gravel.

This one shakes Shinguak and I awake; and I hear her call, answer to my prayer. This one cares. Through this one, I can help Her. Shinguak shivers.

I lean my head against the bark-stripped wound on her side, probably some driver in a hurry, careless of this awesome, awful, lonesome being. And we just lean like that together, in the dark, and I breathe the sharp, good smell of pine—Shinguak.

Shinguak was the name of the man who saved my father from the church schools. How fitting that I'm crashed out here with the only pine tree between work and home.

I consider this one. Does she nest? I drop needles.

A couple of needles float down, knocked loose by my stupid charge, I guess, and I brush them sheepishly off my shoulder.

'Sorry,' I say, patting the pine tree. 'Sorry, Shinguak.' Grandma always talked to trees that way, like they were neighbours and friends.

Maybe sometimes, it occurs to me, they were her only friends.

I consider. This one does not know I am here. But she cares about Shinguak, enough to apologize. Yes. This one. I will help her. And she will help me. And I will bring her what she asks for. Justice.

I shake my head. I am not solving anything sulking under a pine tree. I'm just mad and weary, and I should go home. So, I do.

And I go to bed.

And that night, in the wind and the creaking darkness, I get that dream. Grandma, standing there, firm and strong, telling me what to do.

Simple, right? Everyone knows (who knows anything about dreams) that you shouldn't resist the message you get in a power dream; and more than that, you should never ever talk back to your Nokomis, if she makes the effort to turn up in your dreams.

Thing is, I'd never had a dream of that kind before, only heard about them. Had come to think maybe power dreams were a thing of the past; gone like Dad, gone like the connections to the cousins, all those ties severed when he moved off the Rez, out into the world beyond, married out and all. Maybe I was too mixed to get power dreams.

But then there was Grandma, her blackish eyes laughing, smoking a tailor-made and sipping on coffee.

Nothing beats Alpha, she said, chin pointing at the can of condensed milk on the table. *Some say Carnation is good condensed milk, but Alpha, that's number one.*

She crinkled her half-moon eyes at me, and that detail stood out so sharp, that I *knew*—just like Dad always said 'you just know'— that this was a power dream. So, maybe I'm not too mixed to dream.

You're human, aren't you? Grandma growled, gruff as a bear. *You have to stop thinking about 'mixed' or whatever else. If you're human, you can dream. Anyone who tells you otherwise is full of shit.*

Good old Grandma, never pulled a punch.

Why, then?

Why am I having this dream?

She blew smoke at me. I could smell it. *You're looking for the way to make things right. Seeking justice? Then do what I say. Hazel, get that black dog you'll find at the Humane shelter.*

How do I know they won't have adopted him out? Even in my dreams, I'm a bit anal, and I knew I had a jam-packed work schedule coming in the morning when I woke up. I didn't question the mission, just the details and timing. Weird, the things that can come through into your dreams. Or out the other way.

Oh, he'll be there, drawled Grandma, and tapped out her cigarette. With each tap, she grew more ethereal, 'til the light and her image both winked out. I woke up with her voice in my ear. *Last kennel on the West wing. They've named him Spider. Stupid name.*

'*Should I change it?*' I asked.

Knew I was awake because Josh answered, 'Change what, babe?'

He was looking at me with his concerned-horse face, eyebrows peaked up high in the middle, lips up-curled in the world's sugariest smile. He was so on his way out.

And he and Grandma had given me an opening to tell him.

He didn't take it too badly, considering it's not every day you wake up and get thrown out before coffee.

Okay, truth. I offered the man coffee.

I pushed off the bed, told him, 'It's over, Joshua.' He got up, reached for me, I took a stance, ready to roundhouse kick him. He knew I trained hard. He knew how I felt about being touched without permission. He just stood there. I gathered up his clothes, threw them on the bed.

'No,' I said, both times he tried to say something. And he got this really frantic look on his face, but he shut up, and I stalked out. When he came into the kitchen, I offered him coffee.

I waved my cigarette at him, too, a banishing move he took as invitation.

'*It's bad for you, Hazel,*' he hissed as he struggled into his jacket. Not the most emphatic exit line ever, but Joshy wasn't such an emphatic guy. Which, if I were to get all self-analytical, would tell me something about me. I could find a man who doted on me, and ditch him, and even accuse him of being auto-set to bland compliance. *Not really true*, I told myself. *Mean besides.* But to wake up all smiling like that, completely unaffected by the most powerful vision I'd ever experienced? He did not know me.

I'm not a visiony kind of girl. Or hadn't been before that night. But in every cell, I could feel the truth of what I'd seen and heard. I felt changed. And to this new me? He just smelled wrong.

Truth? Didn't want his concerned-horse face nosing into my doings. Starting with that morning.

Weirder truth? I could still smell Grandma's tobacco, and worse, I swear there was a drop of what looked exactly like Alpha condensed milk on Joshy's forearm, and he swiped it with his finger and licked it off, and didn't even notice what he'd done.

I looked out the window at the rain, didn't watch him leave.

Drank some coffee, got dressed—black jeans, fleece jacket, trail runners, nothing raspy. It's a bush thing; nylon is just too loud, never could get used to it.

It was raining and I hate the rain, but I park my Jeep just in front so it's never more than a short bastard sprint from porch to car.

Tuned the old-fashioned radio to the harder-edged of the two old-fashioned classic-rock stations in our city. It was an AC/DC kind of morning, the scream, crunch and yammer of Australian hard rock fitting right in with the vistas through which I drove.

Amiskwaciy is not big. That's the thing; it's a centre for all the lands round it, but it's not too big for all that. It used to be unwieldy, but now it's more what you'd call *right-sized*.

It helped a lot that the gardeners made over a lot of the land into multi-use. It's funny what you can do when your life depends on it. Funny the changes we can make—some of us.

***

So here's a few facts about Amiskwaciy. It sits in the Canadian prairie, in the parkland that is not actually prairie. People who say it's a prairie city have no real idea of what it is. It's a city of dust and toughness. A civic poet—yes, we have civic poets—once called it *Dirt City*, and got drummed out of town for his arrogance. We know we are, but you don't get to pick on us for it. We're like any big, brawling family. We don't want to see that, to the rest of the world, we're just one small thing. To us, we are everything.

We've had to be, over and over again throughout our history. *Wicihitowin*, that's what we're built on, the Nehiyawak concept of working together for the common good. Not communist though, not by a long shot. We have an inbred sense of individualism and even though that is delusional, we prefer to bask in the delusion. The ones who talk too loud about how it's such a *community*—well, we roll our collective eyes at them. As if they know what we are.

Does it matter that I didn't grow up here?

I grew up just outside of town, out past Big Bend, past the Gnarly Hills, in the agrarian wonderlands that were the Breadbasket of the World during the first reign of King Wheat. These days, under King Kamut, or Red Fife (or any number of names that sound pretty cool actually) the agrarian wonderlands are doing just fine again.

Did people move back out from the urban crush, become farmers like their settler immigrant ancestors? Nope, that so rarely happens except by crisis. The famine happened here, and the Plague. In Jai Hind, all those people declared illegal needed a place to come. So, we made a deal—and by we, I mean the government—and we got Delhi Tech's land-healing expertise, and also all those unwanted millions, who repopulated our countryside. Together, we built Up-Top, the massive geothermal battery that runs this town. We're still adjusting to it—a change like that, it's a whole long story, but the upshot that matters is, Amiskwaciy is a brown city, a city where the faces of the races of the world all show up.

It's a bit of an adjustment, for a girl who grew up being nearly the only colour in the small redneck town. Me and my sibs, and the kids from the Chinese café family; we were it. There was still the Rez, pretty much right across the tracks, but even then, people didn't move from there into the small towns. They moved into the cities if they left the reservations.

Smart.

But that is not our story, we're not from that Rez, not Nehiyaw. We're a mix of Anishinaabe and Mi'gmaq. And Polish—and anyhow, it doesn't matter. What matters is that these days, Nish-beige is as normal as anything here. People whose heritage is all kinds of mix live here now. I don't stick out.

Mind you, back when I first came to Amiskwaciy? Let's just say I was a bit puzzled by the lightness I felt. Took me years to work it out; what I felt was the loss of the burden of being *the Other*. People just saw another person, not a label. They were free to like or dislike what they saw, and it was personal. And mostly, person to person, people default to live and let live, if you don't crowd them too much.

I try not to crowd people.

I keep my own house, like Mom would've said. It's painted salmon pink, if you can picture that—my daughter Frankie's choice, the year she turned sixteen. She had a summer job with one of those student companies and got us a deal, so I agreed to take a chance on her choice of colour. I'm used to it. It's a two-storey wooden house. I've got a solar array on the roof, pitched just right more by accident than design. Northern roofs are supposed to be pitched to let snow slide off.

When it snows. We get the prairie-dog winters more often than not these days; those ones where there's not much snow, and the classic surprising January rain is a series, not a one-off. Summer is longer, fall is brighter. Spring still sucks. It sulks into being, taking forever to get itself out of bed. Then it mopes through a week or so of grit and gumbo mud, and bang, it goes flat out into summer.

And we have mosquitoes.

We didn't for a while, when we were stupidly trying to eradicate them. What are we like? Greedy, shortsighted, and so on. Not that I like mosquitoes, but they turned out to be a keystone, and we had to restore them. Now they're once again just part of the irritation that is summer in Amiskwaciy.

Don't talk to me about twilight strolls.

People don't stroll at twilight here without a reason. Here in the old part of town, too often that reason is the oldest game in the books.

You'd think we could have solved drugs and prostitution. But they seem to be particularly adhesive to our society, a legacy of the bad old resource extraction, unibrow industry days. So, at some hours, the girls—and some sad boys, too—hunch and flex and try to own the decision to let their bodies be for rent.

***

On the morning after the vision, in the indifferent light of a rainy day, I had the streets in this part of town to myself, and that suited me just fine. It had been a rough couple of days, actually. I had been wondering, for the umpteenth time, why I'd let myself get talked into trying to help the Augusts.

I mean, I don't even like them.

I don't like their whining voices, their sloppy, poverty bodies, the marks of habitual alcoholism. And I don't like myself for so strongly disliking them. They're Indigenous. I'm Indigenous. Shouldn't my inside knowledge of our hideous history mean I've got some kind of empathy for them? Why was it so hard to listen to them talk, and not think of it as a spiel, designed not to help their murdered daughter, but to paint themselves as victims? Like her death only mattered because it happened *to them*.

Driving through the rain, my grandmother's voice echoed in my head. *You want justice for that woman and her family? Trust me. Get the dog, and then listen to him. Work with him. Pay attention to what happens.*

Was I crazy? Maybe. But, if you've never been visited by the spirit of a beloved ancestor, how can you know what it's like?

I wouldn't have thought I'd get a vision like that. I'm not the type.

Then again, I'm not the type to go around punching pine trees, either. And I'd done just that the night of the vision.

I glanced down at my right hand, the little scuff across my knuckles; flexed my arm, feeling the bruising up in my shoulder. I'm pretty fit, and I was pretty mad when I hit that tree.

Not mad at the tree.

Just frustrated. Everything swirling in my head. All the deaths. All the miserable stories I got to transcribe over the years. All the youth I passed daily, knowing they were throwing themselves away. All the times I thought of Big Frankie, who wanted to live, who lived with a purpose, who contributed, and whose life got cut off.

And these same sad fuckers looking to me for help? They just oozed in my office door and dumped their misery on me. They hadn't the human perception to even consider that I might've lost people too. It might not be easy to hear their pain. I might hurt too.

Yeah, I was raging, in a full-blown self-pitying rage against it all. And I ran at a pine tree in a parking lot, body-slammed it and screamed at the sky, 'Where is Justice?! Justice! Justice!'

And the wind sighed in the pine branches, and I sat on the ground crying. And the wind sounded like voices. So I gave my head a shake, got the fuck up off the ground, and went on home.

And that night, the vision. And this morning, before I could think myself out of it, I was rolling up into UpTop, to the Humane Society's big, blue building to see a man about a dog.

***

The shelter was quiet when I got there, just opened for the day, with all the doe-eyed staffers (girls, not a man in sight) still nursing their Starbucks. I cradled my Timmy's tight, as if the heat would burn off the slight shiver that hit me when I asked the reception gal could I see the dogs in west wing?

I don't know why I asked. Holdover from another lifetime, asking permission for every damned step I take. Because the world needed me to be fucking polite and a credit to my race?

She waved her cup at the sign, softened that with a Joshy-style lip-tilt, and said, 'Sure, go ahead,' because she really does care that someone cares for those cast off loser dogs. Nobody takes a job there unless they do.

Spider was waiting for me, though you sure couldn't tell if you didn't know him. Which I didn't, so I took his turned back and pointed stare at the corner of his cell as a bad sign. Second I cleared my throat, though, he stood and turned in one fluid move, and looked at me gravely with those yellow eyes of his. Swear the bastard nodded. Swear I nodded back.

***

And then I looked around sheepishly to see if anyone had noticed. There wasn't anyone else in the wing. I needn't have worried.

'Well, big fella,' I said, 'this is gonna sound strange, but I'd like to take you home.'

Of course, the process takes a little longer than that, usually. Application, fee, meetings to determine compatibility, paperwork blah blah, but when the doe-eyed staffer came back to check on me and Spider, he was a different dog. He shimmied up to the wire cage-front, whining and panting and trying to lick me through the wire.

Say 'it is him', said the voice in my head, *the dog you lost. The dog who was stolen from you. You came home from work and he was just gone.*

I looked at that dog and I swear he winked. *Gone!*

Like I was reading a script, I repeated just what the voice said. 'Stolen. Gone! My own beloved dog! My Spider!'

'No kidding?' *squeaked* Doe Eyes, 'His name really is Spider?!'

'Really truly,' I said, winking at that dog. No way he was going to run the whole scene, even though I could hear him growling in my mind, *Not my name!*

'We named him that,' said Doe Eyes, 'because when they brought him in, he was so sad. The first thing he noticed was this big orb-weaver. He was terrified!'

'That's my Spider,' I crooned. It was no weirder than anything else that had happened. I even managed a chuckle, like a fond-and-still-slightly-shocked owner reunited with her weirdly beloved mutt.

Which I was, in short order. Signed, sealed, delivered, Spider was legally mine and sitting in my front passenger seat, once again ignoring me.

'Well, what now?' I said it out loud, not at all used to him speaking in my head.

He indicated, by pointing with his big pointy snoot, that I should turn down a little side street. Yes, I did as he directed. Why? It seemed natural enough at the time. Made as much sense as the rest of the morning. What happened next? Guess.

He had the decency to look embarrassed, and kicked at the scruffy crud under the edge of the shrub, shoving his business further inboard. I stood by the car and scowled at the old brickwork wall behind him. Welcome to a whole new normal.

***

I consider where are Hazel and Spider? I call this one Hazel, now. Hay zel. zel. Zzzel is a good sound. To hold a vision for them. Now I must find them again. That is part of why my elders say we don't go into their cities. There are too many of them, crammed too close together.

But I consider. And I ask another Shinguak. He offers me hospitality.

Here, he says, the one called Hazel makes her nest. He does not consider she will change it. She has kept her nest there, seed and branch; her hands set him in place. Then he tells some crazy story about his seed times. Shinguak is puzzled by humans. But he does not fear Hazel.

She is like her name, a bitter tree, bitter and thin and tough.

I rest with Shinguak and learn the names of Hazel's family, sort how they tie.

I learn Francesca—Fran, shes, ka, like the calling of birds—but they call her Little Frankie, to sort her from the one gone to spirit, that they call Big Frankie. I consider, Big can be a word for when they expand beyond their bodies? I think about this through long time, but to one side. Here, I sort Little Frankie and Missy—she has another name too; perhaps it is for ceremony only—they are sisters. Hazel is their mother.

I learn Devin; he is seed of the Frankie they call Big. I love Devin.

I love the Frankie they call Big. The elders say we must hold all we meet in the light in our hearts, and that this is the thing they call Love. So, how many can you hold? How many can you love? It is a lot of considering.

Of course, I love Her. She holds me in the light of Her heart.

For Her, in Amiskwaciy, I rest with Shinguak, I count the names of the ones tied in—Hazel, Missy, Little Frankie; Devin; Jim, and we call him Spider, and he is angry until he admits that it is right for us to do so; and I consider that there are the ones tied to them, they move through this story, too. Like Maengan. Like Her. But I let Her stay hidden.

I watch Hazel in my heart.

***

So, I've got a dog now.

And I've got a case. Did I mention I work as a detective? It seems like a stupid job, sometimes, even to me, and it's *my* job. Actually, I trained as a transcriptionist, first for medical records, and then for court records, and I'll tell you what, even though so much has changed in Amiskwaciy, too much still hasn't. Even in a brown city, where globalization shows on most of the faces if you're paying attention, even here, there's still no balance. Still, too many Indigenous faces in the line-ups, in the poverty wards, or just dead. Too many stories too tediously the same, and transcribing them was not changing anything.

But detective? I might be stupid, might actually be stupid, to think that I can do any good as a detective.

I guess it's a good thing Big Frankie is dead, and can't snark at me about what kind of a sensible person goes in for detective? He was always full of ideas of how I could live my life better. Too bad his own life ran out on him. Fuck. Whatever.

He's gone. And I don't hang around Sandra—why give her the chance to pick up where Big Frankie left off?

What matters is, I've so far resisted the weird urge to take the dog to work with me. I can get used to him padding around the house like he owns it, but my office is mine.

***

I sit in my office and I deal the cards, and let my thoughts sort themselves out while I challenge the deck. Solitaire, real cards, the slip and click of them as comforting as the oldest memories, Mom in the kitchen dealing. She called it Patience. Not my strong suit, patience, but somehow, dealing the cards, I can sink into my hind mind and mull.

So far, to no avail.

Who killed Nell August? It seems simple, but it's not. The cops reported that she was 'known' to them, in a 'high risk lifestyle'—ie, a hooker, and their inquiries have led nowhere.

And they have more cases every day, and so, cursory inquiries leading exactly nowhere: *very sorry August family, but we can't give you more closure than that.*

To the cops, the subtext goes, it's a story as old as the streets, and the ending is just what it is. I don't know why, but there is something about it that just doesn't sit right with me.

Shit, I don't even like the Augusts, if I'm honest. They're not nice people. It's too obvious, the way their own dysfunctions contributed to Nell's bad ending. So, it's not for Delphine August's whiney sake that I'm still doing this. And it's not for the money; she can barely afford my fees. Her whining about that was almost enough to make me turn down the case, if I'm honest.

Fucking victim queen. *Boohoo, she can't afford more.* I saw the truck they drove up in, and I figure they're not the poor Rez-billies they portray. I don't care about that, really. Not my problem if they're assholes who figure it's their right to screw people by playing the old stereotype for all it's worth. Maybe they do have scores to settle. Maybe I'd do the same in their shoes; but I like to think I wouldn't pull that shit on a person who's also Indigenous, even if I'm also part Slav and not about to pretend I'm not. I clearly am not part of the oppressive overlord system, me in my crappy office with my beater Jeep and my salmon-pink house in a cheap part of town… and I'm bragging, not complaining. I'm okay with what I've made of my life so far. History is rough for a lot of us.

And it's old. And I don't give a shit about it. I barely give a shit about this case.

Just like they don't give a shit about their daughter, except as part of *their* victimhood. I could be wrong. That doesn't matter either, really. What matters is maybe I can find out who killed Nell August, and if there is any way to bring them to justice.

The cards slide and click, patterns fall into place, the deck slowly aligning.

Maybe I'm wasting what slight talents I have chasing this useless story about a throw-away person who ended up just like you'd expect her to, dead in an alley.

Why do I care? I care so much that I bruised myself thrashing a tree, wound myself up into a visionary state, and on my dead grandma's advice, stole a dog who, it turns out, can talk to me telepathically. Which—although it is oddly satisfying to have this physical evidence, 'Actual Proof,' as the Nichiren Buddhists say, of the Animist/Indigenous perspective that recognizes soul and sentience far beyond the human—does me exactly zero good in trying to solve this case.

But I work the deck into order, and I know I'll keep on sifting the deck of facts on Nell August's murder.

For sure, nobody else is trying to, and honestly, it's at least one small hit back against the steamroller history of girls, women, boys, throwaway people, gone with no accounting. Why haven't we been able to stop throwing our own away?

MISSY/HAZEL: NIGHT WITNESS

Missy sits at Hazel's computer all night, the night of December 8th. They are going on about how John Lennon was shot back in 1980 on December 8th. She remembers her mother crying about it, and saying that she felt foolish crying about it, cause John Lennon was so far from their world, and anyway he sure didn't know them, did he? Together, huddled in quilts under the creaking eaves, they pondered the image from the magazine, his cracked and bloodied little glasses.

She realizes that her memory wasn't of *that* December 8th, which was.before her lifetime, so it was looking back at December 8th from some vantage when she was young enough to huddle with her mother under quilts, back on the farm. However delayed, the tragedies of the world stage still reached up in a one-way gesture to them, then as now.

Tonight, social media witters on about John Lennon, and Missy thinks about how he beat his first wife, and how he admitted to anger management issues and issues with sexism. She thinks about Yoko Ono, the weird performance artist second wife, widely accused of controlling Lennon, causing him to walk away from his famous band. She wonders, though, if Yoko has memories of bruises that the rest of the world never knew about.

The other death in social media is some metal musician who went by Dime-bag, a druggie nickname, glorifying illicit narcotics. Missy feels the familiar rage surging at the spectacle of all these people mourning for a wife beater and a druggie.

Today, though, is also the day John Trudell has walked on. She compares the dignity of those who write notices of his passing with how the others who share his death-day get noticed. Trudell is remembered with grace, and with a quiet, profound respect.

That is how she thinks of him too, the man who walked through so many fires, and who did not die in a hail of bullets, nor of an overdose, but simply was worn thin by his nearly seven decades of work, finding grace in deadly situations.

She knows whom she would want her sons to emulate, if she had kids.

And who taught her about John Trudell? She smiles faintly to herself, remembering her mother and Big Frankie and Auntie Sandra, talking about the history of the American Indian Movement, agreeing for once on what they thought.

'John Trudell was a truly spiritual man,' said Sandra.

Big Frankie, older brother, adding, 'Even though everyone talks about Leonard Pelletier and Anna Mae Aquash; Trudell's whole family was killed in a suspicious house fire, and he still kept his dignity.'

And her mother, nodding, smoking by the window, murmuring 'mmhmm, mmhmm.'

John Trudell. What would he have to say about the long work of the many gentle souls who pressed, for long years, to raise awareness about the extent of the violence, about the ways the rape of the earth walked hand in hand with the rape and murder of women and girls.

'Oh, Mother Earth,' Missy sings, and does a search on MMIW. Down the rabbit hole, but she can't resist paying witness. 'Oh, Mother—'

Missy turns at the clicking of the door. Her mother, home, and alone. She has a moment of dismay—what to tell her if she asks why Missy is here? Hazel doesn't make a big deal of it, though; Missy can tell she's surprised to find her there, but a stranger wouldn't think Hazel was reacting at all, would miss a lot of the little tells.

'Hey,' Missy says, 'what's up?'

Hazel crosses to her, peers over her shoulder. 'You reading the CBC?'

She smells strange, a slight odour that does not land in any sort of recognizable category; Missy doesn't ask about it, just moves to get up from Hazel's chair.

'Sit, sit,' says Hazel, resting a hand on Missy's shoulder just for an instant. She's seen. 'I'll bring another chair.' But Missy gets up and gets another chair. Her mother's chair is her mother's chair.

Hazel rummages in the cupboard, then she's back with a box of crackers and a cup of coffee. 'It's a little old,' says Missy. Hazel shrugs, settles in her chair, almost absentmindedly opens the box of crackers, and starts crunching them loudly as they read together through the CBC's Twitter feed.

'They are doing,' Missy says, 'twenty-four hours of tweets, of the two-hundred fifty-two known "open" cases of missing and murdered women.'

'And children,' says Hazel, because the first face she sees is Cheyenne K, five years old. Hazel remembers when the kid went missing, and the way the search for her petered out.

Her cousin Bets, living in Regina, scoffed at the time: 'They won't bother looking much longer. It's just another brown kid, who cares?'

And yet, someone cared enough that at least the name is familiar. She perches on the front of the chair, drinking her coffee reflexively. They scroll through, reading the names.

Lisa S, 29. Laura B, 18. Women and girls from sad backgrounds, some with diagnosed mental illnesses, some with children and families of their own, many involved in street sex trade, many others known to struggle with addictions. Will Loreen's name go in there, they wonder? Because of course, people were charged with Loreen's murder.

They hunch together through the long dark hours, reading and witnessing. Mandy P, post-graduate in environmental studies. Angela W, 13 years old, last seen dragged drunk and nearly passed out from the back of a cab; it was Treaty Day and of course, everyone in her community was drinking.

'Of course,' sneers Hazel. Missy blinks back tears, almost overcome by the thought of her mother's fierce protection. Hazel worked on-reserve, and never failed to puncture any talk of the reserves as nostalgic homelands, as places of safety. Not for her family. And that's a loss, because Missy knows she doesn't know a whole branch of her family, because the reserves are not their family home. These people? These tragic victims? Also people they do not know, most of them.

But there's Shannon's daughter Sherry, disappeared August 23, 2003. How could it be that Shannon is the mother of a disappeared?

Missy studies the face of the journalist and filmmaker. She expected to hear Shannon's reporting on someone else's tragedy. She expected to hear Shannon raging against the injustice, but on someone else's behalf. She expected Shannon up in the fight to stop the murders, but she did not ever think of Shannon as a statistic. Beautiful Shannon, articulate, friendly, smart and accomplished, her daughter vanished. Unbelieving, Missy sits blinking in her chair, swallowing gulps of air trying to choke this down and get to grips with it, to take in the truth that even Shannon is part of this.

'What do we even know?' she mutters.

Her own mother sits beside her, drinking a beer now, face stiff.

***

Hazel: Shannon. Sherry. I remember then, that day my own daughters were almost taken. A moment's carelessness, I left them in the car while I ran in to get ice cream for them. They could still eat dairy, back then. Left the car door unlocked. It was full afternoon, lots of people running around the park, people everywhere.

Some locals walking by intervened when a man opened the car. Saw him getting into my car with two little girls and stopped him. He could've been the last one known to have seen them alive. I could have lost them, like that, in an instant, to a man I never even saw.

Five minutes in the middle of the day, forever.

I want to break the bottle in my hand and cut someone with it, some asshole in a suit who'll say it is wild, bred in the bone of those people, that they can't help themselves. Who'll talk as if the man opening the car door to steal children is the victim of the wild, musky lure of them. They were six and nine, then. I held them so close, then.

Not perfectly, but close. I trained as a medical transcriptionist, so I could work from home. And when I went out, I made sure it was family watching them. George's mom, for whatever reason, stuck around in our lives. No, I never asked her why. I didn't want to know whether or not it was guilt. She'd pushed him into proposing, pushed me into accepting, wanted us to 'do the right thing,' him to 'make an honest woman of me,' and then it was her son who ran off with Édith the Embryo.

So, maybe it was guilt.

But it was also racism, I could tell, on some level. She wanted to monitor her son's girls for signs of wicked blood, of wildness. She kept saying things, they kept telling me what she'd said, often laughing, but it wasn't funny. By the time Missy was twelve, I'd had enough of George's mom.

Missy was old enough, I figured, to take care of Little Frankie when I needed to go out. And I needed to. I sure wasn't going to be one of those martyr women, drying up at home 'for the sake of her kids,' all the while seething with resentment that they were keeping her from having a life. Fuck that. I had a life.

Too much of a life, maybe. Maybe I don't blame my girls for pushing away. But they got through school. And I never brought home sketchy people who might hurt them.

They did amazingly well, really. Sometimes I can't believe how proud I am of them—Missy, working at the hospital to put herself through grad school; Frankie, on full scholarships.

They're doing fine. Just fine. It burns me up to know that that doesn't mean they're safe.

Look at what happened to that Loreen girl, in Manitoba. It was all over the news.

The good Loreen. Doing everything right. Post-secondary keener. Her long blonde hair and fitting-in eyes, her clean, middle-class teeth, earning her PhD studying the epidemic of missing and murdered indigenous women and girls. Murdered.

Maybe I should've asked my girls how they felt about that.

But I gave up asking, gave up just transcribing people's misery, set myself up as a detective.

And look at me now.

***

Missy clears her throat. Hazel blinks, and sees that she has taken her daughter's hand, and that she is gripping tightly, pressed deep against the heat of her skin, the heavy silver rings burning her, too.

'You want to tell me?' Missy asks, softly, her too-old eyes holding Hazel's stricken gaze.

'No.'

''Kay then,' she says, and doesn't let go.

Winter turns to spring, and Missy still feels her mother's fingers crushing her own, hard love.

DEVIN: LIGHTNING STRIKES

Three lightning strikes along the wall.

Devin stands quiet, watches the priest trace his nicotine stained finger along the first, scratched into the brick in a flurry of sharper, thinner marks.

'What do you suppose did this?' asks the priest. 'Chisel?'

Devin shrugs, puffs out his lips. 'Would a person hear that?'

They consider the noise, effort and dust of carving these marks with a chisel in brick.

'Maybe,' allows the priest. They both know it depends when it happens; some hours, nobody hears anything on this street.

'What do you think it means?' Devin asks.

The priest looks down where his little dog is dirtying her white coat in the low shrubberies along the wall. He leans down, then takes a knee. The little dog is snout deep in smells, oblivious to them or their concerns, on her own quest.

The priest rubs his fingers through leaf litter, where brick dust has settled.

'Don't know. What do you think?'

'I think,' says Devin, 'there's some things I want to show you.'

'Oh yeah?'

Devin nods.

'Huh,' says the priest, scrounging his smokes out of his vest pocket, resting one on his lip and lighting it one-handed. At the scrape of the lighter, the little white dog reels herself in and lands by his boot. He nods to her, pushes himself upright, then lifts one hand slightly, 'Come on, then, kiddo. Better show me.'

They trudge back to the parish house, two tall men and one small dog, a cold late spring wind beginning to flick at their edges.

Inside, the priest strides to his office, sweeps papers into a pile, and jiggles the mouse to wake the computer. He pops up a browser window and steps back.

'She's all yours,' he says, and goes out to the kitchen, calling back over his shoulder. 'Tea?'

Devin doesn't answer, doesn't have to, the priest is gone.

When he returns, the priest has shed his vest, and bears a tray laden with a surprisingly prissy pot and two incongruent chunky mugs. He puts it down, turns to Devin.

'Well,' he growls, 'let me see what you've got.'

Devin shows him.

'Huh,' says the priest as Devin scrolls and clicks through the pages. 'What makes you think there's a connection?'

Devin clears his throat, rubs a hand through his hair, nervous; he ducks his head a couple times, fast, making that little noise in his throat that the priest knows so well. The kid has thought long and hard about this, just needs a moment to remind himself why he has come to his conclusions.

'Well, see,' says the kid, 'what these men have in common.'

The priest frowns at the screen.

David Lancaster, 53, financial analyst from Sherwood Park, murdered in a north end motel.

That was a weird one, brutal, notorious when it happened, and still under investigation. The priest remembered the news around that one, Lancaster's family loud in their horrified protestations that they knew no reason why David would be in that motel. The truck they found outside the murder room, registered to Lancaster, was unknown to any of them. They talked about conspiracies and plots, the sort of talk that got them bumped onto online and broadcast shock-jock shows, but to which the police maintained a stolid silence.

Devin, the priest sees, had a few other tabs open, so he clicks to another.

Laine J. Mogren, 39, from the west end, dead in the river, his Lexus resting below the Capilano Bridge, described as a simple accident, but for the one line that Devin highlighted for him, how the car appeared to have somehow jumped right over the guardrail, leading to speculation as to how fast he must have been driving. The impact had broken him up pretty bad.

'Huh,' says the priest, and reads the last one.

Stephen McAllister, 39, oilfield worker, Fort McMurray 'til the fire, then a little town south of there, dead in a fiery crash just off Highway 63.

'What's weird about this one, kiddo?' says the priest.

Devin ducks his head again, clears his throat, darting glances around the room. The priest, wily, takes the cue to remember the tea, and steps over to pour them both a mug, chamomile in deference to his bitchy stomach. The kid likes his straight, but the priest stirs in two spoonsful of honey, sighing as he inhales the steam, his back still to the kid.

'Well—' says Devin, and the priest turns, passes him a mug.

The kid blows on his tea. 'Well—' He puts down his mug, picks it up again.

They hold silence for a minute, Devin at the desk, the priest at the small table, each man leaned against his own edge. Devin sips, rolls it around his teeth, swallows, sighs.

Then he squares up and stands tall, a high school boy giving his report.

'The thing is, for him it was just the timing at first.' He looks around, and back into the priest's eyes.

'Timing?'

'Yeah,' sighs Devin. 'I didn't tell you when I found the first lightning bolt. Or the second. One is random. Two could just be imitation. Three,' he settles into his rhythm, on a point they've covered before, 'three is a pattern.'

The priest nods, sips. The clock he keeps on the wall, battery-operated quartz from the 1980s, ticks loudly.

'So,' Devin continues, 'when I found the third, I started thinking, why would someone make marks like that? What are they keeping track of? I thought about what if it had something to do with—' he swallows '—you know, the *women*.'

The priest nods, sips.

'So, I looked a little further.'

The priest nods, sips.

'And I couldn't find much about women dying at the right time, not for all three.' Devin looks into his cup, purses his lips as if he's about to drink. 'But these three men, their deaths were all written up and posted on Facebook by the same person. They had that in common. So why?'

Now he takes a drink. 'And the other thing they had in common was they were... really messed up. Everyone knows about Lancaster—'

'Huh.' The priest remembers the constant coverage of that sensational, bloody murder.

'But those other two, why were they written up? They were just car wrecks.'

The kid starts to pace, just from the desk to the doorway and back, in a tight little loop.

'So, I looked into these guys from a couple other angles. You know, thinking about the women made me do it. And I found out something. Mogren had been in that John rehab program the city ran a couple years back.'

'The other two?'

The kid nods his head.

'Yep. But also,' he adds, 'that truck from the murder scene? The one registered to Lancaster that his family doesn't know anything about? Well, turns out that license plate number, just like Mogren's and McAllister's, was listed on John TakeDown,' he says, stopping to click over to a different tab, this one full of vivid colour and edgy graphics.

The site title, John TakeDown, is scrawled in a vicious hue of red-violet, throbbing behind the head of Miranda Jones, the blazing young métis firebrand whose public actions certainly raised awareness and ire.

'I thought that site was taken down?' says the priest.

'Yeh,' says Devin, 'this is an archive someone screen shot and pasted onto a blog. They haven't shut that down yet. Anyhow, there it is,' he says, tapping a photo of a red pickup, the license plate number enhanced. 'Rumour is, Lancaster's family were a big part of shutting down John TakeDown.'

The priest takes a deep drink. He knows Devin's source for the rumour, but the kid says no more, so he says nothing about it.

'So, what we have is?'

The kid sums it up, resuming the school report pose.

'We have three men known to use, to frequent … uhm, you know.'

'Mhm.'

'All dead, violently, on the dates the lightning bolts got scratched on that wall. One by murder, Lancaster. His family convinced something deeply conspiratorial is at work, insisting the truck found at the scene and registered to him was not his. It's listed as a plate on John Takedown.

One by vehicular accident, McAllister, on a highway notorious for crashes, but on a night when the 511 says highways were bare and dry. No witnesses. A motorist came upon the scene about five AM and the fire was mostly out and there was nothing to be done. People in his online book of condolences wrote *'We loved Stephen. He was fighting his demons with faith. We all pray he is at last at peace.'*

The priest's snort is almost inaudible, but the kid flicks him a look. *Faith.*

'And then Mogren, presumed either accident,' Devin looks up. 'Or suicide.'

The priest nods. Of course, that is the subtext of the mention of the speed at which the car leapt from the bridge.

'Mogren had attended a John school. So, he got caught. People in the online book of condolences say they loved Laine, that *he was fighting his demons with faith*, that *they all prayed he was at last at peace.*'

'So, did Lancaster have an online condolence book?'

'I had to hunt around a little, but I found it.'

'And—?'

'*We loved Dave, he was fighting his demons with faith, we all pray he is at last at peace.*'

Devin draws in a sharp breath. The priest looks a question at him, he fires one back.

'You conducted one of those funerals, didn't you?'

'Mmhm. Mogren's.'

'Any chance you can remember who all came, Father?'

HAZEL: NEWS

Spider brings me the paper this morning. Funny on two counts. One, Spider is obviously not the sort of dog who brings papers and slippers, who sits cosy at your feet while you sip your tea. Two, I don't even read newspapers anymore. Like the rest of the normals, I get my news online. The hipsters, of course, have revived newspapers, and I don't like to admit they have anything to crow about. Hipsters. Pfft.

But there is something about the absolute dry clarity of a newspaper. In print, hard copy, it's more real, a substance you can touch, look at, move here and there. No matter which way you turn it, the news is bad. Acquittal, the verdict in the latest murdered woman case. How can that be?

I light a smoke, move out onto the verandah, glare at the morning, and drink my coffee. The rest of the news is the usual, politics, innovation, the ongoing reclamations, business of the nation. Yada yada. My work has never seemed less inviting.

DEVIN: NOTES FROM A FUNERAL

The priest remembers feeling like an idiot, sweating in his vestments, waiting for the first of the mourners to arrive.

He knows there is so little most people want from him these days. He listens to them when they come to make arrangements, and he hears how much they don't say. They don't talk about God, most of them, not with any sense of personal conviction. If they want God, they mostly want to know, will he tell them when to kneel, when to stand, when to move? Will He take care of the person they couldn't hold on to? And will His servant say good things about their lost loved one in his sermon?

Sometimes, the assurances he offers are as hollow as their eyes. He is not burying saints, he knows. But he also knows he is often burying people whose family, in the things they say and don't say, reveal that the death is a relief as much as a loss.

He remembers Mogren's funeral as one of those. Laine Mogren's passing was a relief to some of his hard-bitten, downcast family. Now they can stop waiting for it, stop worrying, stop trying to save him from the worst. Now, the worst has happened.

'Father, I'm sorry. Maybe I'm getting carried away—'

Devin's wondering if he is actually an idiot, trying to solve a mystery that doesn't exist, making some family's tragedy into his own role-playing diversion.

Devin questions himself a lot. The priest just looks away smiling, warmed by a feeling that he imagines is as close to parental as he's likely to get. That's always followed by the moment he remembers Cendrine and the child he wasn't ready for, the penance he owes to God and Life for as long as he now shall live.

'It's okay, Devin. Just let me think back. There's something about that funeral…'

The priest remembers the first mourners coming in. Cody, one of Devin's friends, is helping Robbie, who directs traffic with the ease of long practice. The family were grateful for the offer of ushers provided by the Church, especially when the priest emphasized that there was no additional money expected. He has become adept at implying that the ushers are part of a community outreach for addicts trying to straighten out. It's not exactly untrue. It's just that Robbie and Curtis have been doing this for so long that they're well past as straightened out as they'll ever be.

Curtis had been in hospital for dialysis, and Devin had somehow convinced Cody to volunteer.

Skeptical, the priest remembers being surprised at how well Cody had done, how gently and gracefully he'd shown the paltry crowd to their seats.

'Cody!' the priest cries, breaking the silence.

Devin's round, slightly pug-nosed face is a natural for expressing surprise. His eyes flare open.

'Cody? Oh no. What did he do?' He's already condemning himself for recommending Cody. The priest holds up his hand.

'God be blessed,' says the priest, 'Cody did fine. But he packed up the guest book and I never realized, because the family never asked.' The priest leads the way deeper into the old rectory. 'I don't know if it will help at all, but I happen to have the guest book.'

As he pulls it from its dusty resting place, he remembers that he'd thought it just one more pathetic detail. The family had fought over whether to have a reception. The 'no reception' faction had won. But someone had bought a guest book, and with no other option, put it by the church door. Cody had discreetly indicated it to people as they entered, and people had signed it. And the priest had said nothing about it being out of place. And then it got left.

When nobody from the family called asking for the guest book, the priest had Robbie call a couple of the numbers they'd variously left. Nobody had cared to respond.

So now he opens the strange and tawdry thing and passes it over to Devin. The round-faced boy reads the names, blinking at one of them, reading it twice.

Three times is a pattern, he thinks.

***

So, I am here now. We are all here now. It has to be healed now, in this time, in this place. There is no other time, no other place. Ri ri ri ri, I sing in pine branches, make them bounce a little, the chickadees laughing as they ride the boughs. Ri ri ri. I hold in my heart that this small work might be worth while. Hazel can help him find Her.

HAZEL: NEW NORMAL

How long have I had this dog now? One month?

I look up at the pine branches, swaying a bit on a touch of higher-up breeze. I've left the door off the latch and Spider ambles out, suggesting we go for a walk.

Hey, I say as I get up, *So, if I say we've been together for one month, is that seven, from your point of view?*

I like to say stuff like that, just to make him roll his eyes. Also, to show him that, even if I don't get how it happens, sometimes I can take the initiative and speak silently straight into his brain. The new normal.

We do actually do some pretty normal stuff. We watch comedian/commentators on the Youtube. We binge watch (*The Crown,* if you have to know). I hook him to me with the blue leash (*Aren't dogs colour-blind?* I asked him. *Not me,* he snapped, so I got the blue leash) and we go to Tony's for take-out. We don't do the dog park by the river too often. It freaks out the coyotes too much, and we're not in it for the freak factor. Mostly we live like the normals. As if there's nothing weird about me having a dog. As if it didn't freak out my fearless elder daughter the first time she met him.

MISSY: NEW NORMAL

'Mom? Mom? You here?' Missy pokes her head round the door. It's unlocked, she must be here. 'Hey, Mom—?'

'Wuff!'

How had she not seen the black dog lying on the living room rug? He's standing now, head to one side, measuring her. Missy freezes, both hands gripping the door.

'Mom?' Her voice is ridiculously trembly. Missy is not scared of dogs.

She hears Hazel before she sees her, coming down the stairs, muttering under her breath. Her hair is rumpled, her arms full carrying a box. She puts it down on the leatherette armchair. 'Too much to ask you to help, I suppose,' she scoffs.

'Mom!'

Hazel jumps. 'Missy!'

Missy boggles. Her mother had not been talking to her, but to the dog, bitching at the great hairy beast. *It's no big deal,* she tells herself. *Mom has a dog now. Okay. So what?*

'Nice dog,' she says, recovering first.

'Um,' says Hazel, and she looks guilty. Missy feels the little clench in her stomach. What has her mother done now?

'Come on in, my girl. Come in.' Hazel turns a frown on the dog. 'Sit, dog.'

The dog doesn't move, except to swing his head away. Hazel huffs.

'Spider. Spider, sit.' Hazel seems almost to be pleading. 'Come on.'

The dog blinks at Missy, lowers his haunches back down to the carpet.

'His name's Spider,' she explains to Missy. Missy steps in further, shaking off the unease. It's just a dog, and a nice looking one at that.

'Can I pet him?' The dog wags the tip of his tail.

'Spider,' says Hazel. *My daughter, Missy. Miranda, but you don't need to know that.*

'Hi, Spider,' says Missy, moving forward slowly, calmly, not fearful, just respectful, the way Grandpa Bill and Auntie Sandra taught her back in the farm days. 'You sure are handsome.'

The wag becomes a thump, the yellowish eyes warm on her, and the dog grins, waves a forepaw toward her.

'Aw, look, Mom, how cute. You wanna shake, boy?' Spider holds his paw out like a foreign dignitary, grinning, tail thumping. Missy takes his offered paw, and he bobs his massive head at her. She pets him, and he leans into her, looking up through his eyebrows at her as she runs her hands through his luxurious ruff.

'Wow, Mom, he's gorgeous. Where's he from? Is he Joshua's?'

Hazel says nothing, and Missy straightens from petting the dog, looks around, sees the slight changes around the room, the absence of Joshua's token things. 'Aw, Mom…'

'He's mine,' says Hazel, defensively. Her voice is so tight.

Missy takes a deep breath. *Not again*, she thinks. What can she say? Focus on the dog. 'So… where'd you… where'd he come from?' She's not sure she wants to know, but this is at least new.

'The Humane Society,' says Hazel.

'So…'

'Coffee?' says Hazel, already pouring. 'Or did you come for something in particular?'

'No, no, sure, sure,' says Missy. So, her mother doesn't want to talk about it. She sighs.

Hazel puts the coffee down hard. 'Look, Miss,' she says, shoulders high, voice tight, 'nothing happened with Josh, okay? Nothing bad. Look at me.'

Missy looks at her. Hazel stands with her hands on her hips, her head back. She turns her palms out, swivels her bare, unbruised arms. 'Nothing like that, okay?'

Missy looks down. She doesn't know where to look, her eyes stinging a little, and feels the resentment coming up. It shouldn't still be this way. She shouldn't still feel like she's got to protect her mother. She never did have to, really, she tells herself. *Not your job*, she hears Frankie's voice in her head.

'So…?' Missy picks up her cup, brings it to her lips. The coffee's no longer really hot, it's been sitting in the pot a while. She drops her gaze to the oily film on top, takes a drink. 'So, you got a dog?' She tries to keep *the tone* out her voice, but she knows Hazel hears her suspicion that there is something off here. That this dog will turn out to belong to some man, for whom Hazel has thrown over the first of her boyfriends that Missy actually liked.

'So I did,' says Hazel. She lights a smoke, steps to the window and opens it wide, her concession to Missy's health-care admonitions against smoking.

Missy looks down. She's gripping her hands together, squeezing the cup. She deliberately unclenches and drops one hand. The dog pads over, sniffs her free hand, sits down beside her. He rolls an eye up at her, kind. She reaches out to pet him. How is it that dogs understand emotions so well?

'So, well,' says Missy, keeping her voice light, 'What brought this on?' Poor word choice, she knows. Spider bumps her hand with his snout. *Keep petting me,* he seems to say. She looks down at him, distracted, and returns to running her hand along his smooth fur. It's soothing.

Hazel sighs. 'Well,' she says, 'believe it or not… I, uh…'

Here it comes, thinks Missy, braced. *Joshua turned out to be a stalker, so I got the dog to protect me.* But when Hazel continues, it's not anything she would've anticipated.

'I had a dream.'

Missy stares at Hazel, dumbstruck. Spider bumps her hand, she keeps petting like a reflex. 'A dream?'

Hazel nods, staring at her cigarette for a moment. 'Yeah.' She looks at the dog, who's gone still under Missy's hand. 'Your great grandmother came to me and said, *Get a dog, they're good company*. And it seemed like a good idea, and so I woke up and I went to the Humane society, and I got this dog. And, he's mine, and I am fine, and I guess,' she adds, rushing on, 'I'm tired of my girls being mad at me for my choices.'

Missy looks at her mom, who's staring at the dog, who's staring at Hazel, who's uncharacteristically stopped short in her nascent rant. She's just standing stiff-legged, arms crossed, up against the wall with her cigarette burning in the ashtray unheeded.

'He's beautiful, Mom,' says Missy, sincerely. 'Really beautiful.' The dog butts her again, thumping his tail. 'What kind of dog is he?'

'No idea,' says Hazel. 'They figured he had some wolfhound in him.'

'It would explain the size and the hair. What a gorgeous coat.' She gazes at the dog's curling black pelt with its under-brindling of warm cinnamon, the white blaze on his chest, the eyebrows marked in lighter too.

Hazel has picked up and finished her smoke, ground it out in the cut glass ashtray. She sips her coffee, still standing, leaning against the counter top. 'Yeah, well. I figured it was time for a change.' She looks away, out the window. 'You like him? He sure likes you.'

Missy smiles down at the dog.

'He's so gentle, Mom. What a gentleman.'

She doesn't see Hazel's expression, but she hears the tiny huff. Hazel turns it into clearing her throat.

'Say,' she says, 'You want to take him for a walk with me? He's still getting used to the neighbourhood.'

'Sure,' says Missy. This day has taken an entirely unexpected turn. Walking out through the afternoon light, she keeps stealing glances at her mother. Hazel looks nervous. There's more going on, she's sure of it, but Missy figures it's best to keep quiet. Whatever happened with Joshua, she'll never get Hazel to tell by asking her.

***

'You ever think,' says Little Frankie later, as they sit on her balcony, 'that maybe it's none of our business now?'

She's drinking lemonade, her legs already bare, as if summer arrives earlier for Frankie than for anyone else in the world. Missy shakes her head.

'But I liked Joshy, Franks. Finally, she seemed to have picked someone who wasn't a complete loser.'

Frankie sighs. 'I don't want to talk about Mom's man problems. You've got to let it go. We can't fix her.' She looks at her sister, and her voice softens. 'Hey, Miss, I know. I liked Josh, too. He was even good looking. And not too stuffy for a pillar of the community type. Treated Mom alright, didn't get up her nose?'

'So it figures she'd fuck that up.'

'Aw, Miss.' Frankie pats Missy's knee.

Missy pulls her knee away, snorts. Then she shrugs. 'Well, hey,' she says, 'at least the dog is new, right?'

'I know. I can't believe it,' says Frankie. 'Mom got a dog. I'm almost tempted to go see this for myself.' Frankie shifts in her chair, like a cat seeking the best of the sun. 'Tell me all about him. What is this dog like? He's a *him*, of course?' Frankie quirks one eyebrow, grins at her sister.

'Of course.'

Missy tells Frankie about meeting the dog as the sun eases down through the new leaves, cutting warm angled shadows over the neighbourhood. A mourning cloak butterfly, out late, tipsily dances past Frankie and away on its own trajectory. Everyone has their path.

***

I consider Star Woman planned it, too; maybe she didn't so much fall as jump, trusting that the ground would appear. And thanks to Muskrat, well, she was right.

I look. I see Her. Heart light of love I see. I look for lines to weave these people together for Her. I do not know how to heal the waters. I know Her. My elders might consider me foolish. But I say, I watch the rest of my generation losing ground, moment by moment. They do not even want to sing ri-ri-ri with me.

We guard the waters. We are getting weary. I have seen too many of my kin curl into their nests in despair, burrowing down, hardening their hearts, disappearing. I will not give up. I will help Her. To reconcile, re re re re rididididi! I do not know what that means. I know Her. And these.

I am getting good at singing with chickadee. We sing in the tree. I watch with my heart open. My Frankie turns her face toward the sound of our singing and shines the light of her smile.

HAZEL: GHOSTS

We just do our jobs, best we can.

My grandma was a hardworking Anishinaabekwe. She lost her status after Grandpa died, when she remarried a non-status guy. She had to move into the city, wasn't official anymore. But anyone could see who she was by her tan, her continental-shelf breasts and slender-ankled legs, her black half-moon eyes and the sound of the bush in her words.

That was back in Ontario, back in the days of pass cards and Treaty cards and Indian Agents and bizarre-ass stuff like that; back when women were pushed from their traditional place into the place dictated by what Missy called 'That Dead Old Euro-Imperial Patriarchal Sexist Shit,' in an undergrad paper once. I laughed at the title. Not sure Grandma would have. Quite possibly not. She might not have had the distance to laugh.

She did what she had to do to support her kids. Cleaned houses for people who felt they were maintaining order by giving her the sort of job the Indian Industrial Schools imagined for girls—maid, cook, servant of the colony. Did they ever even see her clear mind, her deep well of humanity and humour? Maybe she would have laughed just a little at Missy's summation of her situation vis a vis the old government.

She did like to laugh and she was magnificent when she did. I was five when she died and Dad became the oldest in the family. That's the way he broke the news.

'I am the oldest in the family, now. Your Grandma is dead.'

I ran outside and wandered around the yard bewildered, found the rope we'd strung between two trees for a game, and pressed my throat into it. I needed the roughness of the twisted strands against my skin, the weird pressure. What did 'dead' mean?

I hadn't expected it to mean that when she came back to me many years later in a dream, I'd obey her without question.

Not out of fear. I didn't fear her, because my dad told me, told us all, about ghosts.

'Ghosts,' he said, pouring the last of his tea into the big mug, 'can't hurt you. They literally have no physical substance. How can they hurt you?'

There'd been some stupid horror movie on TV, and we'd watched it for a while, then hadn't wanted to go to bed when he told us it was time.

Here's a great thing about my dad. He could see we were scared, so he made tea. Black for him, some kind of herbal blendy thing (stale, leftover from Mom) for us, and told us about ghosts, and how to deal with them.

'You just have to look at them straight, and tell them to go. And there is nothing they can do to you. Physically. Where they get you is, if you let fear take hold of your mind, they can get in and convince you to hurt yourself. But look at them straight, tell them to go. Tell them this is your place.'

He'd sighed. 'It's not their fault. They just have unfinished business, or something keeping them here. But that's not yours to take care of. Don't let them trick you. Just tell them, *you have to go*. Don't be mean. Don't get mad. Just tell them.'

And he made us each take a turn practicing looking at the kitchen door, telling it, 'Listen, Ghost. You don't belong here with the living. This is my place and you have to go now.'

And when I said it, I actually felt a little braver. Brave enough to go up the stairs, into the dark. We all went.

But then I was scared. We were all scared, lying there. We looked at each other, screwing up our courage, and then we tiptoed back down. He heard us coming. He turned off the little TV, and showed us what his mom had taught him: *picture yourself climbing into a sleeping bag of light. And then you zip it up. And then you are safely held in the light.*

Maybe we still looked doubtful, or maybe because it was the Space Age now, he added, *Last of all, you picture a helmet of light, of energy, that you put on your head. You pull the visor down, and you can't be touched by ghosts, or any bad spirits.*

I used that technique for years, and slept just fine. Can't recall when I forgot to keep in practice. Now I'm the oldest in the family, and I've let a ghost talk me into getting a talking dog.

***

I consider. I would not have been able to reach her if she hadn't been taught about dreaming, once. Even if she didn't do it anymore. I consider it is like a twig on the body of the soul, once it grows, it is there, ready to move.

DEVIN: TRANSFERENCES

Devin itches within his skin, walking as fast as he can. He shakes his head from time to time, like a bear beset by bees. He wonders why he listens to them at all—those girls and their overly confident voices. Maybe he's caught by that self-assured tone and wonders if just maybe, one of these times, their confidence will be well-founded. It would make a change.

This time, it was Taylor at the centre of the group, calling him over.

'Devin, sit down,' she purred. 'We were just talking about you.'

Devin frowned, his shoulders up.

'No no,' she said instantly, 'really. Come on. This is right up your alley, so to speak. Maybe you can help us.'

She's known him all her life. She knew he wouldn't be able to resist 'help,' even though her drawl and her posing contradicted her, signaling that they didn't really need help. They were clearly never in any trouble, at least so far as they were concerned. These girls dished it out.

'Now, Devin,' she sounded so sincere, tilting her head just slightly. Her friends tilted their heads in perfect unconscious sync. 'We want, all of us—to know what you are. Em says you're clearly Trans and Sal says you're Asexual like them, but I think you are like me, Gender Fluid. Am I right?'

She intoned the capitals, as if these states of being were titles.

Devin just turned and walked away, straight out the doors into the cool clearing wind.

He holds his head high and he walks without stopping until he reaches the priest's house.

The priest hears his tread on the porch steps, then the pacing, and puts on the tea. He doesn't go out to the door though, not 'til Devin offers his particular light-handed knock.

'Devin,' he says. 'Good to see you. I was just about to have a cup of tea—got time to join me?'

***

'She was still looking at me straight, Father,' says Devin. 'That's what really got me. Usually, when she and them—' he blushes, looks down and around and away, then squares up to it

'—usually, when they're going to try to bully or embarrass me, I can tell. She gets this look, you know?'

The priest nods. He does indeed know.

'But she was just looking at me as if we were friends. And… you know… like a woman… looks at a man,' he finishes in a rush, his face burning red. The priest finds his hands restless, and decides to build a smoke.

'Anyhow, Father, then she said that, about being *gender-fluid* as if it's a prize or something. She's always–' and Devin stops himself, always too conscious of kindness, too careful of transgressing on his own inner ethical voice.

'Devin,' says the priest, 'it's not gossip nor cruel to speak honestly of what people say or do to you.'

'Words have power, Father,' says Devin in response.

'Yes, you are right,' says the priest. 'You are right.'

He stands up, lights the smoke, lets the first puff run up into his eyes so that he has a reason for the stinging in them. He'd thought he was well used to Devin's aching purity, but here he is, surprised by the way the kid can reach right down to the forgotten core of innocence. No, not innocence, he thinks as he wrenches the crooked window up a couple inches to let in the breeze. Devin immediately shoves the rock in place. The window is so warped it has to be forced open and closed, but Devin has always insisted on wedging it, 'because things can shift and fall, Father.' What's the word for that knowing beyond innocence?

'So, anyhow, Father, she tells me she's become gender fluid now. Like I'm supposed to know what she means by that, and like I'm supposed to … well…' He scrunches up his round face, tosses his head a little '… you know, like she's looking for me to give her my approval or something.'

The priest pours the tea, looks around for the honey, which he has left in the kitchen. He steps out to get it, and Devin finds the nub of his troubles.

'That's what freaks me out, Father. She mostly ignores me, they all do. But then she talks like she knows me. Like they all know me. Like it's obvious I'm some kind of authority on all this gender stuff that is going around, Father. And I'm not. I'm just me. I'm just Devin, who I am, how I am.'

He speaks without stuttering now, and the priest hears the echo of his ferocious father, his mother, and the people who somehow managed to shield and shepherd this remarkable soul, who gave him some of the tools he wields so powerfully, as yet without awareness of all their power. Devin doesn't see what others see, his own singularity. He doesn't understand how his power bothers others, but he feels very clearly that there's a danger in how they look at him.

'It's like the Salem Witch craze,' says Devin. The priest nods. 'I mean, suddenly every one of them has to be experiencing gender dysphoria. And that's not statistically likely, Father.'

The priest knows better than to say 'Well, the Bible says—' but he thinks it. He's lost a lot of faith in the power of quoting the Bible, but it has been rooted out by plain faith in life and in integrity, which turns up in the most unlikely places and faces, and confirms that there is a Master Plan. So, he just grunts—'Uh-huh.'

'Inexorably,' declares Devin, his round owlish face glowing, 'we are dimorphic and that is how we reproduce. Fact of life. But so is carrying capacity. It makes sense that there should be a bunch of people who express as other, who are born not to bear more of us, so we don't over-populate, and so that everyone's life has meaning and purpose, not just the ones who engender kids.

'And Father,' he says, 'I know Taylor is just a f–f–' he stutters, bats a hand in the air, like a bear bothered by bees, '*fashionista*—whatever is the latest trend, she's on it. But Father, some people say this gender erasure craze is… what you might call the End Times.'

'The End Times?' The priest wrinkles his nose a bit at the phrase, with its whiff of American evangelism.

'Yeah. The end of this society. We've lost the will to procreate, because we don't believe we deserve to go forward. We are punishing ourselves for failing Life. Father, I don't want us to have failed.' His round face is bleak. 'But look at what we do…' Devin waves his hand again, pacing now and angry.

'We take a world of wonders and turn it into pop culture trends, narcissism and destruction. Look at what happened before Up-Top…'

While the boy rants on, the priest thinks about scripture, about Simon Peter being called a rock on which to build the Church. And the Church had grown and prospered, had divided and ruled the world for centuries. But somewhere, the foundation cracked. It wasn't just one rock. It was the centuries of building on ground sacred to others, and then finding that ground heaving and unstable around you, writhing with the energy of other stories, other manifestos about destiny. He imagines Devin talking with Simon or with Jesus. Devin is more than deep enough to converse with Yeshua, Joshua, Jesus, that long ago firebrand. The priest wonders what Taylor and her mean girl band would make of this Devin, expounding on globalism and philosophy, on the tides of hope and despair. Devin, standing strong, tossing his round head a bit as he makes his points. Already they feel the need to prod him, aware in an animal way of something more below his deferential, stuttering exterior. Already they're aware that this fat boy is going to be grand when he's full grown. What would they do if he ever let them see him like this, unselfconscious, unconcerned with taking up space?

'I refuse to let this happen on my watch, Father. Things have to make sense. Like those three guys. Somehow, I know those three guys didn't just die. There has to be a connection.' He's grabbed the funeral guest book and opened it. He thumps it with one hand. '*This guy!*' His finger stabs a name. 'I figured out he's the one who wrote about them on Facebook. Why was he involved with all of them? Why won't he talk to me?'

Blindsided, the priest interrupts. 'You tried to talk to him?'

'I need to figure out if someone killed all those guys, and if it's linked to the marks on the wall, and why. Don't we owe it to them, and to Life, to be sure?' Devin is the one talking in capitals now. 'Don't we have to seek the Truth, seek Justice?'

***

Humans move one way through time. For Zabeh, it is a simple matter to find them in another when. For me, when is easier than where.

MISSY: IRONIC

Missy loves Alanis Morissette. She and Little Frankie used to pretend they were rockstar/detectives. They'd run around reading 'clues' they wrote and hid around the house for each other. When they'd figured out that day's mystery, one or the other of them would shout, 'Just in time! It's Show Time!'

Then they'd put on a CD and give a concert in the living room, shouting along with *Jagged Little Pill*, shaking their fierce little fists at the sofa full of imagined fans, tossing their imagined waist length hair. Frankie's hair was already very nearly that long then. Missy could never seem to grow her hair.

Nowadays, she keeps it sleek and short, a boy's crew cut lending her facial delicacy.

She's nodding her head in time with Alanis. The same CD has miraculously survived.

Missy sits in the big wing-chair in the corner of her mother's living room, her feet curled under her as she taps away on her laptop. She won't tell Hazel, but she likes to linger when her mother isn't home. She always asks if she can look at files, or whatever other excuse she thinks up. Her mother always says it's fine. Missy doesn't tell her how often she makes the task longer than it has to be.

Today, she seems to be working hard. Her slim brows are pulled tight in a frown of irritated concentration, her fingers flying. Every so often, she punctuates a thought with a sharp huff of breath, blurts out a phrase of song '…the free ride, but you've already paid…' tap

tap tap '…it figures.'

Spider, lying by the kitchen island, makes a decision. He gets up, paces over and lays his chin on her knee, wagging slightly and rolling his eyes.

She looks down. 'Oh, you,' she says. 'Push off, I'm working.'

He adds a tiny, panting whine. She sighs and pulls his ear slightly. 'Okay, then. Get off. Hang on there, big fella.' She unfolds, unconsciously elegant, and he admires her a moment before remembering to leap ahead and gambol meaningfully toward the yard door.

'Here you go, Spider,' she says, opening the door and following him through to the porch. 'One side now,' she says, pushing past him to open the screen door. 'Until you grow opposable thumbs, you need me. There you go.' She pats him as he gambols past her down into the yard.

She pads back inside, yawning and stretching her arms, and figures it is okay to make a pot of coffee. While it brews, she looks around anew at how easily the big dog seems to have been absorbed into her mother's household. It's not like Hazel is a super housekeeper, far from it. But the floors are free of hair, the cushions un-greyed by shedding, and she knows that Spider gets up on all the furniture, even if Hazel wouldn't admit it. Hazel makes as show of bitching at Spider, but she clearly spoils him when nobody's looking.

Missy figures he'll last all of fifteen minutes out there before he wuffs to get back in. She likes to tease her mother's dog, even though he makes her nervous in some way. It's the ferocity of his devotion, the way he seems to anticipate her thoughts sometimes. She's adopted her mother's habit of teasing Spider, but she wonders sometimes at the edge in Hazel's voice, the sense that she isn't entirely joking when she cracks wise about Spider's size, his heavy coat, his dog breath.

'He's a dog, Ma,' she had said once, 'And you picked him.'

'Huh,' Hazel had huffed, 'Shows you what you know.'

'I know, our animal relatives choose us, too, yadda yadda,' Missy had waved away the point, Hazel had frowned and lit a smoke, the moment had passed.

Missy cringes to herself a little at how easy it is to pretend disrespect for the beliefs she shares with her mother. Maybe that's why she makes a point of treating Spider with extra gentleness whenever she catches Hazel acting edgy toward the big dog, or when, like now, they're the only ones around.

Her thoughts are interrupted by a knock at the front door. To her surprise, Spider has not announced a visitor. If he's inside when people approach, he simply rises and stalks to a point in the hall where he can sit and glare fiercely at the door, silently large and poised for action. If he's outside, he usually makes some noise.

So, Missy's slightly uneasy, despite it being broad daylight.

Silly, she thinks, hesitating in front of the door. She opened doors for years before they got that dog. She opens the door.

'Can I help you?'

She squints at the tall young man on the doormat. He's a little lanky, his dark hair springing back from his peaked hairline and falling just the unfashionable side of short, not quite ponytail long. He's wearing jeans and sneakers, a grey zip front hoodie with a West Coast design down one sleeve.

'Uh, hi,' he says, meeting her gaze and then dropping his own. He lifts a hand, runs it through his hair, runs his tongue around his lips nervously. She pulls herself up and squints harder, ready to push, slam, lock.

'I.. uh…' he says, 'I'm a friend of your mom's.'

'Oh?'

'Yeah,' he nods. 'Kind of a relative, actually, you know, shirt tail…' He's talking slow, shifting his weight a bit, '… from back East, on the Rez?'

She looks harder. Big face, wide frame for all that he seems thin; eyebrows that peak up a little, lay a little heavy. She sees he wears silver rings, two of them on each hand.

'My name's, uh, Maengan.'

'Oh?'

'Yeah,' he says, 'Maengan Nolan. I knew your great gran Jane. She, uh, she adopted my dad, y'know?'

He's not pushing it, just letting her listen and observe him, and decide if she's comfortable with him being there.

Missy listens, observes. Spider has not said a thing, not run round from the back yard, not a whiff of a wuff from the alleged watch dog.

'So,' he continues after a few moments, 'I've been meaning to come visit. Moved into the neighbourhood a couple months back, and you know, ran into your mom couple times and she said to come by, so... uh... Is she home? I could come back ...'

Missy has her cell phone in her hand, so he can see that she's ready to speed dial if he's thinking of doing anything sketchy. But the phone is just a reflex now, something her mom taught her when she was younger. Today, in the quiet of the Saturday afternoon, with the smells of spring beginning to rise from the nearby yards and boulevard trees, she feels no danger. On the contrary, this polite, collected young man intrigues her.

'No, Mom's out for a little while, but you know, she won't be long.'

'I could come back—'

'It's a nice day, tell you what,' says Missy, 'Grab a seat out here, I've got coffee. Can I bring you a cup?'

'Sure, that would be great,' Maengan says, and he goes and sits on the chair further from escape, the chair where everyone passing on the street can see his face. She smiles, but not directly at him. Just enough so that he can see that she recognizes his politeness and respect for the responsibility of the properly raised man to demonstrate his good intentions.

'How do you like it?'

'Black, thanks.'

'Me too,' she smiles, and leaves him there. Inside, she grabs mugs and pot and listens, again, for any sign from Spider out back. Nothing. She slips the phone in her own hoodie pocket and rejoins her guest, pours for them both.

'Miigwech,' says Maengan.

'So,' says Missy, 'What brings you to town, Maengan?'

'Well,' he says, looking away, then down, then back again, 'actually, it was something Grandma Jane told me once, and I just never forgot it.'

'Sounds deep,' says Missy. She doesn't think it odd, then, that the only Grandma Jane she knows of is her mother's grandmother, dead long before her time, or his.

'Suppose so,' sighs Maengan. And then he laughs a bit, ruefully. 'She said, *go where the work is.* So, here I am.'

***

The first time I walk Spider, he actually tells me, *Take me to the Drag.*

What?

He looks at me. *I told you, I have work to do. You're part of it now.*

What does that mean?

He kind of laughs, not entirely unkindly. And he shows me.

What we do is we walk. We just make like ordinary people, one human, one dog, out for a stroll, but we are like the Bear Clan, walking the worst parts of town, on patrol.

'*We are Were-Clan,*' Spider would say, some sort of lame rhyming pun. But the thing is, there is something about a big black dog, ferociously snarling, to back off creeps. We don't stop the street trades, not at all. It would take more than one of anyone—bear, dog, zabeh, whatever—to do that. But we make it a little safer for the girls. They have a witness, and I, another woman, have the safety of this big black bastard on a breakaway leash. He can look incredibly intimidating. And he is prone to breaking his leash, see, and once, he leapt right on a guy, knocked him down, had him by the belt, shaking him and giving him the red-devil eye. The guy pissed himself in terror, too scared even to scream.

I laughed. God help me, I laughed at that. And it felt glorious and free, like the shadows around us were laughing too. And the girl got away.

That night, I slept better than I had in years.

***

Maengan drinks his coffee, makes conversation, and Missy finds herself warming to his obvious intelligence. He wants to know about the music program at MacEwan. He wonders if it has any connections with Ethnomusicology over at the U of A, wonders if its jazz-based curriculum has taken on any Indigenous influences.

'I don't know much about those things,' says Missy.

'Who do you listen to?'

'Old stuff, mainly, 80s and 90s pop,' Missy admits.

'Me too,' nods Maengan.

'U2?'

They both chuckle, rolling their eyes.

'How about Alanis Morissette?' says Missy.

'I prefer Alanis Obomsawin,' says Maengan, and talk turns to Indigenous film. They agree that Alanis should have an award named after her for all the films she's made.

'She's pretty much the Elder of Indigenous film,' says Missy.

'So's Gary Farmer, too, wouldn't you say?'

'Nope. Sorry,' says Missy, pouring more coffee. 'I just can't forgive him for that wig.'

'Wig?'

'In *Smoke Signals*,' says Missy, and Maengan laughs.

'Yeah. That was bad hair!' He bursts into creaky song, and she joins in—'*John Wayne's teeth! John Wayne's teeeeth! Are they plastic? Are they real?*'

They lapse into their best Evan Adams impressions—'Hey Victor!'—and how neither of them had managed to stay awake through *Atanarjuat*.

'Hey Victor,' says Missy, 'Don't tell the fam back on the Rez, eh?'

'Well, can I tell them you even seen Tagaq's *Nanook*?'

'Nah,' says Missy, 'before my time. But I seen *One Angry Inuk*.' She drops the cheesy movie imitation. 'What do you think of her work, Alethea Arnaquq-Baril?'

'Strong,' says Maengan, 'Sending messages people shouldn't still need.'

'Yeah. How about Connie Walker's work?'

Maengan sighs, shakes his head. 'I think it's a damn shame that it's necessary. That *Highway of Tears* thing?'

'No, that's Angela Sterritt.'

'Right, right, I mean the one about Alberta Williams. The radio podcast. Don't you wonder, is that cop telling the truth?'

They look at each other. Missy sighs, blowing out her lips the way her mother does. It's the questions at the heart of the podcast, unspoken: why did the retired cop reach out to the journalist? Why is he so sure Alberta's uncle killed her? Why couldn't he solve it? What's the missing piece there? Missy is about to tell him about her website, when Maengan shifts in his chair and straightens up, nodding toward the street.

Hazel parks her Jeep like she does everything, emphatically. She swings out the door, stops cold when she sees Maengan on the verandah.

'Hey Victor,' says Maengan, 'Is that your mother?'

HAZEL: CREEPS

I don't know how I managed not to bug out and run away when Missy was born. Not from her, from the City. I cried all the time then, or so it seemed. 'I just don't know how to raise a kid in the city,' was my refrain. Even after I'd made myself sick of it, I'd catch myself, out with Missy in her stroller, scanning for needles and junkies and hating that I was bringing her up here, not in the country.

In the country, I knew the hazards, and knew how to teach her to handle them. And they were clean hazards, straightforward.

I felt a whole lot better when Sandra first invited me to her dumpy little farm north of the city. It was so cute, eleven acres fenced for sheep, but overgrown now. Sandra just didn't have the time for that much livestock.

She did keep a flock of mixed chickens, like her own little affirmation of the beauties of miscegenation. Wyandots ran with Leghorns ran with Rhode Island Reds, and they all paid court to the little lords of the domain, two gorgeous black Bantam roosters.

'The Banty Brothers. That's Ralph,' said Sandra, introducing them. 'And that's Klein.'

'How can you tell them apart?' I asked, almost afraid of the answer.

Sandra laughed. 'Not much to choose between them, is there?'

Both roosters were shiny, high headed and quick moving, smaller than the smallest of their harem by quite a margin, but strutting along as if hydroplaning on cushioned soles, buoyed by pure testosterone.

So, until it all went wrong, Missy grew up with chicken tales and chicken lore, and inevitably, freshly killed chicken. It was a good place to keep her and Little Frankie grounded in the realities of food production, the circle of life stripped of any pretence.

By the time Missy became a woman, I'd taught her as much as I could about the circle of life among humans, too; how to discern respect, how to deal with creeps. I've sometimes wondered whether I could've toned it down. She's pretty harsh sometimes. Sharp. Judgmental. I tell myself it's better than so many other paths. Missy will never simper and play dumb, never shrink herself in search of approval and affection.

She doesn't have a lot of friends, but she doesn't seem to care. And the friends she does have are the kind that stick.

Little Frankie, now—Frankie was always somehow both more delicate and more deeply okay. Frankie's eyes were always shadowed; but she also knew how to crack wise, how to wheedle, how to outgun her sister—in so many ways much more sophisticated than Missy might ever be. They're a deadly combination, my girls, if I do say it myself. And mostly, it's getting easier not to worry.

But here's Missy now, all familiar and hanging out on my verandah, with—

'Maengan Nolan,' I drawl. 'Look what the dog dragged in.' I said it without thinking, but my hind mind is often faster than my thinking brain.

He laughs, colours up a bit, clears his throat.

'Hi Auntie. Sorry I didn't call. I—uh—' he shrugs, 'lost my cell. So, I was—'

'—in the neighbourhood, thought you'd drop in?' I quirk an eyebrow at him. No voice in my mind. This is interesting. I've gotten fairly used to the annoyance of Spider's thoughts in my mind, his commentary on things. It seems like any time I have an emotional reaction to *anything,* he uses that like a beacon or a cell tower relay, or something, and pings in a comment of some sort. I don't really know how it works, just that it does. And that it's odd that he's not picking up on my feelings at seeing Maengan here.

'So, Missy,' I say, pausing with a foot on the stairs, just leaning against the railing, 'You've met your … cousin?'

Missy shoots a look back and forth between us, sensing something. I dial it down, get a grip.

'Come on over here, Maengan,' I say, nodding at Missy.

After all, it's not his fault I've got the creeps. He's just sitting there being a respectful young man. He's taken the seat in the corner, so that she is not trapped, so that his face is to the street, visible, identifiable, open. He comes over, gives me a surprisingly strong hug, and offers to take my bags. Still no voice in my head. Hmm.

'Thanks,' I say out loud. Inside, I'm whistling. No response.

'Where's Spider?' I say to Missy. She's gathered up the coffee things to follow us inside. Maengan holds the door for her too.

'In the back,' she says. 'I'll go get him.'

'Spider?' says Maengan.

'Our dog,' she calls back, before I can answer.

***

The girls don't know about Maengan. I just never told them about him. Why not? I don't know. I guess he was just…a little too freaky.

They must have been, what, 15 and 12, maybe, when I went to Ottawa as a reporteur for an Indigenous health summit. Maengan was in town for some youth gathering, at the same hotel as my conference. Someone introduced us, because he's from my dad's reservation. I've never cared too much for all that *mitakuye oyasin* business, that was Big Frankie's thing; trying to claim all our Indigenous relatives retroactively, to seem more legit.

Dad left the Rez, never wanted to go back, never wanted that hard life for us. Why would I want to claim it now? Why would they want me there, even if I did go? I only look Nish in some lights, other times, the Slav shows through. And I'll tell you, growing up in that western backwater town where we did, it was work enough to stand up to the jerks from our little town who called us 'mongrel' for being part-Indigenous. Why would I want to go get called the same names by the other side?

We moved to Amiskwaciy, and like I said, it felt freer there, because so many people were so many kinds, who the hell cared? Well, Big Frankie sure did.

I dunno, maybe he figured he'd find some real good Indians, not like the derelicts the townsfolk sneered at or the non-derelicts who still hadn't a hope of being treated as equals in that town; and through association with them, he'd show those small-town bigots.

Big Frankie knew he was meant for better things. And he ran headlong toward those people who were making a career of shouting about their Indigenous Pride. 'Professional Indians,' Sandra and I would say, *sotto voce*, just loud enough to irritate Big Frankie, the way younger siblings do. But we weren't wrong.

The first time I saw Big Frankie blinking back tears and grinding his teeth about the shock of his new-found Indigenous Traditionalists picking at him for being half-Polish, I got the message. So, did I even try to tell him he would just never be what they wanted if they only respected half of his identity? Yeah, you try telling a big brother anything.

So, fuck'em all; I do me. Sure, I was at this conference, but I was never a Professional Indian, and I never even tried to be. I know I don't qualify.

That night at the conference, over a tedious dinner of pretentious food, I listened to this fat woman telling me about how we were actually all three of us—her, me, and this kid Maengan—related through Grandma Jane, and first marriages and second ones, and names that meant nothing, Senior and Junior this and that, blah blah blah. As if I should know all these people. And Maengan sat there and smiled, nervous. He was just some skinny kid, polite enough, but I really didn't have anything to say to a teenage boy just because we share some bloodlines.

So, it was just weird what happened later that night.

I was down in the bar, having a drink—you meet people at conferences, my girls were home safe, why shouldn't I? All the business done, people were getting on with the real enjoyment—change partners and dance.

This guy was one of those ones, though, that are too good look-ing, you know? All the women had their eye on him, and he was just enjoying it too much. And I couldn't see why I should give him the satisfaction of competing for him. Guys like that, they're usually lazy in bed, and not too interesting to talk to, because they don't need to try.

Anyhow, I was kind of tired of it, and so I made an excuse and stepped outside for a smoke.

The night was dark, so I didn't see him right away. Didn't see him at all, but I heard someone trying really hard not to cry out loud, and then as my eyes adjusted to the dark I saw him.

That skinny kid, hunched up in the shadows, on a bench in the hotel's sad little courtyard, below a broken lamp. He was so scared, like a wild animal. But also like a baby. And I talked to him low, walked over slow, like you do with hurting things. After a while, he let me take him inside and help him get cleaned up. We hardly spoke. There was little use in that.

'Police?'

'No. Please.'

Then he sat a little while and drank the tea I had found in the kitchenette cupboard (Sandra would have called that tea a miracle, or at least a Sign). And he told me as much as he was going to. No details about who attacked him, where, how, why.

Just this, in a voice of hollow wonder: 'It was like... suddenly a wind came, with a smell of—of pine and sweetgrass and ... and Grandma Jane was there. I knew it was her, from the pictures. She picked him up and threw him. And told me to go. And I went.'

He'd kept his eyes to himself while he told me. But then, he dart-ed a glance at me over the rim of the cup, took a big swallow. 'You believe me?'

I just nodded. It didn't matter to me what he needed to believe about how he escaped. All my bones were jellied by the thought that whatever happened to this kid could so easily happen to my girls. I just wanted to call them, to make sure they were okay. I wanted to fly home right then. But I just nodded. He needed me right now. I nodded, held his gaze, said nothing.

And then he borrowed my phone, called his family and went to his room. In the morning, he left with the rest of the youth group. Before he did, he came and found me in the restaurant.

'Miigwech, eh.' He clearly wanted both to say more, and never to have to.

I'm not much for the big scene either. 'Hey,' I said, 'no problem.'

And when he kept standing there, I got up and—like a fool—went to hug him. He just flinched away, got all hard-eyed.

So, I reached into my pocket, took out my card, gave it to him, as if that was what I had meant to do all along.

He held onto it a long moment, looking away at the daft corporate art on the wall. Other people were starting to look at us.

'Grandma Jane was a good woman,' I said.

He nodded, shook my hand, and left.

And now, here he is, on my porch, talking to my daughter.

I still don't know what to say. He's filled out a bit, but there's still something about him—maybe now more so—that makes my hair stand up a bit. I suddenly remember him, in the shadows, hurt, and I can see he remembers that too. We both get a little red.

Still, kid has guts.

'How's Grandma Jane... and everyone?'

I say it with what I hope is a neutral, but not over-friendly kind of smile. I don't want trouble. He's not looking at me, though, he's looking at a sketchy guy in hoodie and shades, slouching past.

As if on cue, Missy bounces back out the door.

'Mom! Spider got out.'

I sigh. Now what? Am I going to have to tell her and Maengan that I have no actual control over this thing that lives with me? *Where are you?* I think, looking up and down the block.

'Does he do that often?' Maengan asks.

'Does he, Mom?' adds Missy.

'He's new—,' she explains to Maengan, '—ish.'

As if on cue, Spider comes trotting out of a neighbour's yard, the one with the picket fence where both parents work all day, and pads to the foot of the stairs. He looks up at Maengan, head tipped to one side. Then he bounds up the stairs, growling.

Maengan puts down his cup, calm, casual, the way people do when they know how to deal with animals.

'Spider, sit,' I say, grabbing his ruff. *What is your problem?* I glare into his eyes.

'Guess he'd like me to go,' Maengan says, smiling at Missy.

She taps her phone there on the table. 'Text me, okay?'

I watch him walk deliberately away, shoulders squared. Spider sits beside me, muttering on under his breath.

***

It's not long after that that everything changes. I come home, expecting the dog.

'Who the Hell are you?!'

I keep a stick in the front hall and my left hand has it in an instant. He just lies there, blinking, on my sofa. Some drunk? Some druggie broke in?

And decided to take a nap? Look again, Hazel.

I look more carefully, notice his feet are bare, poking out from under my favourite throw. Dark hair, tanned skin. He goes to sit up and I realize, about the time he seems to, that he's not wearing anything under that throw.

'Hey!' I call again. 'Who are you? What are you doing here?'

I don't step any nearer, but I do let my voice modulate just a touch. This man is naked, ergo this man might just be a loony. Or whacked out on something.

He blinks a bit more, and doesn't seem to know where to look. Is he blushing?

'Hazel, I—'

'I don't know you. Do I know you?'

'Hazel. Oh, shit,' he says, running a hand through his hair, making it worse. He sighs, shifts himself into sitting, pulling the throw with him, hunching meekly, palms up and open on his knees. 'Oh, shit shit shit. I—'

'Look, what is going on here? How do you know my name?'

I don't threaten to call the cops. What are they going to say about a naked man in my home? They going to believe it's a B&E?

Not likely.

'I'm waiting,' I say, shifting the stick but trying to keep neutral. I'm frantically trying to place him. It's not like I don't keep track of the men. I'm not one of those too-drunk-to-remember sorts. I always learn their names, I'm generally sober, and I always know exactly what I'm getting into. Okay, maybe not exactly, but I would not forget a face like his. There's something there though, something oddly familiar, without being at all useful for jogging my memory.

'I'm waiting,' I say again. And it occurs to me to wonder where my big guard dog might be.

'Spider!' I call. 'Spider?'

'Here.' He says it low, in a tiny, sheepish voice. I almost miss it.

'What?' I stare at him a moment, then look around again. 'Spider?! Spider!' Now I'm getting mad. If he did something to my dog—'Look, fucker, if you did something to my dog—!'

'I'm here,' he says again, loud and clear. 'He. I. I'm him.' He's beginning to gabble, curling into the sofa.

'What the hell are you talking about?!'

I take a step into the room, stick starting to swing, and I can feel the rage beginning to swing, too, running up and down my spine chased by stone cold terror. Closer, I can see a white scar on his throat, like a splash of paler skin running down over his collar bone. His eyes, which look more frightened than I feel, are gold-brown.

'It's… it's me.' He holds up a hand. 'I'm so sorry, Hazel.' I stare at the hand. It's getting hairy, just that one hand. 'I did not mean for it to happen like this.'

I am not a fainting woman.

I just turn around and walk back out the door, lock it and lean against it, shaking. I've got nothing for this moment. Just staring blankly, still gripping my stick, holding it tight to my body as if its pressure is all that is keeping me solid. Can't even rummage my smokes out of my jacket pocket. This isn't real. Any second, I'm going to hear my dead gran's rusky voice laughing, and I'm going to wake up in my own bed, and none of this is happening.

A ludicrous bird sings in the big spruce. *Blue jay,* I think automatically. *Messenger.* This is definitely a dream. A car drives by, tinted windows, going too fast. *Dumb fuck,* I think. I smell the exhaust. Smell somebody firing up a barbecue nearby. You're not supposed to be able to smell in dreams. Or is it some other sense? Nothing makes sense.

The bird calls again.

Please, Grandma, I think, *say something. What did you send me?*

Hazel? His voice slinks into my mind. *It's me. Spider. Hazel. Please come back inside. Please?* He sounds, God help me, vulnerable.

I am so sorry. I was… and then I just… and I fell asl—

'Get the fuck out of my head!' I shout it out loud.

Big mistake. I'm standing on my verandah, in a perfectly blameless spring evening, shouting like a lunatic or a tweaking addict. Someone's going to see. Out of the corner of my eye, I see someone walking toward me—my luck, it's nosy Sandra. I take a deep breath, unlock the door, retreat inside as fast as I can, turn off the porch light. Anything not to have to try to explain this to her.

Spider is there, sitting on the floor. The throw is on the sofa. The naked man is gone.

Hazel, says Spider in my mind, *I am so sorry. Believe me, that is not the way I wanted you to find out.*

DEVIN: SQUASH BLOSSOMS

'Here's the thing,' says Devin. 'The family doesn't know what he was up to. They had no idea what he was involved with. As far as they were concerned, he was … you know… just a guy. Their d-dad,' he adds, ears colouring up again, and he tosses his head, just once.

'The husband, the go-to guy,' he starts pacing now. 'And they're saying there was something bigger in it, some kind of, you know,' he shoots the priest a surprisingly cynical look beneath his beetled brows, 'drugs, smuggling, international espionage. But Father—'

'Mmm?'

'What if they're just, you know, making stuff up? Grasping at straws.'

The priest says nothing, just breathes easy, sits calm, sips his tea and listens.

'People, people do, Father,' says Devin, his whole face red. He's blinking, pushing up his glasses, head tossing. 'I made stuff up, Father E. When—when Dad died. I imagined there was something in what he said, in his ranting about how people were out to get him. How he couldn't trust any of them, because they hated him for being, for being mixed. I remember…'

***

I consider Devin. Makwa watches over him. This is not easy, to be large among humans. Nest and trail, how strange. Among my elders, we honour all shapes. Why is 'Fat' a curse among these people? Or

is it a disguise?

***

Devin sits on Sandra's patio, blinking in the shade.

'Auntie, can I talk to you about, about Dad?'

'Oh,' says Sandra, and stops digging, squats back from the tomato box. 'Sure you can, my boy. Sure you can.'

She casually wipes her hand on her jeans. She looks over at the boy. He is clasping his hands between his knees, and the tops of his ears have gone red. He blinks, tosses his head a couple times, softly clears his throat.

'I've been thinking about him, Auntie, and... and how he went before he died.'

'Mmm.' Sandra angles her body toward him, sinks down to sit on the ground, cross-legged. Unbidden, a memory of Big Frankie flashes through her mind, Big Frankie huffing at her, '*Women don't cross their legs. You sit with your feet to one side.*' She nods at Devin, reaches over and plucks a leaf, examines it. She waits.

'The thing is, Auntie, he said people were out to get him. Said he couldn't trust them, because they hated him for being half...like being a half-breed is a race traitor. It's not true, is it, Auntie?'

Sandra sighs. 'Yes and no, Devin. It's one of those things that are both. True and a lie.'

'But he was so involved in the Indigenous community. And when he died, everyone came out to his funeral.'

Yes, they had, Sandra remembered, and how they had cried, drawn together around each other, though Frankie's actual family were somehow a bit apart.

'Here's the thing, Devin. Sometimes, people find it easier to claim somebody's love and worth after they're gone.'

'But why?'

Sandra lets the question lie. After a long silence, he picks it up, as if she's answered aloud.

'I suppose so, eh? I suppose he was a little—' he waves one hand, can't bring himself to criticize him, his own father. Sandra nods, smiles softly at him.

'Devin, he was very much *a little*. A little difficult. A little judg-mental. A little afraid. That's the thing, my boy. He was afraid he'd never be really accepted, and so he pushed back. Easier to be push-ing than to be pushed. Easier to be fierce and fearsome than to let on the truth, that you just want—all you want in life, is to belong to people.'

'But he did. Everything he did was about The People.'

He managed to say it like Big Frankie, verbally capitalized, trib-ally inflected, an Indigenous view of people, not a Communist one. Communism, background noise of her and Big Frankie's child-hood, distant history for Devin.

'Yes, Devin, that's true. But—and this is going to sound terrible, so you have to remember, I loved your father, truly—he turned his back on us, his own particular family, time and again. Criticized everything. He couldn't see himself as good enough. So, we were never good enough, either.'

The light stretches long fingers between them, warmth and im-personal comfort. Somewhere near, a bee sings for the joy of nectar.

'How could you take that?'

'I couldn't.' She says it frankly, as to a peer. 'At least, it took a long time, Devin, a long time to understand.'

Sandra has collected all the withered and damaged leaves within reach. She lets her hands rest for a moment.

'He saw us as mirrors of himself. And he was always working so hard to be good enough, that he saw us as evidence that no matter how hard he worked, he'd never escape the truth. We are not good enough for racial purists. We'll never be. He worked harder than anyone I ever met. And yet, even when the accolades were pouring in, he couldn't relax, couldn't enjoy it.'

Devin nods. He's rocking slightly, looking down at his shoes.

'He was always afraid that, one false move, and all the belonging would go away.'

When she says that, he snaps upright for a minute. Sandra sees it, remembers Big Frankie huffing at the kid, *Stand up straight for*

God's sake, look up. Sandra looks away, blinking tears, continues.

'The thing is, Devin, he couldn't see himself as good enough. Whatever happened when he was small, somehow, he got the notion that he was never okay just being who he was. So, anything that reminded him of that, he hit out at that. It was,' she takes a deep breath, 'it was hard to take.'

Devin is rocking more now.

'How did you turn out different, Auntie? How come you aren't like that?'

Sandra rises now, brushes off her jeans. She gestures to the boy, he gets up too. They proceed down the garden.

'This,' she says, her hands softly gesturing across the burgeoning ecology. Under a rhubarb leaf, a little red-black hen sits, beady eyes at half-mast. 'All this saved me. And never think I wasn't like him, sometimes. Still am. But I could see...You work in a garden, you come to understand. Life is willing, and Life doesn't care about the things we care about.'

She steps to the fountain, stoops and ladles water over her feet. 'Here. Cool off.'

He comes nearer, shyly presents a chubby foot, she splashes it. He sucks in breath, but quietly.

'Nice, eh?' she says. She reaches out to a vine crawling along beside the water.

'Pumpkins,' she says, 'pumpkins are all the evidence you need.' Her own are a riot of leaves, vining over the trellis Devin helped her build, climbing across the canoe. 'Look at these guys. They just want the sun, and they just go for it. They are one of the oldest plant companions we know, one of the Three Sisters.'

'Corn, Beans and Squash,' he intones, softly, singsong.

'I remember your mom teaching you about them. But Devin, the thing is, she never liked squash. And I think, it wasn't just the taste, or the texture, or whatever people usually say. It was also this—' she waves a hand—'Squash is a slut. Squash will not be ashamed. Squash will pollinate with anyone of their kind. Squash serves Life, not nation, not tribe. Just Life. Squash is fearless, it doesn't worry that the next generation might be a different colour, a different shape, taste different, grow outside boundaries. Squash is true to the sun, the season, and the soil. If I could have given her anything, I'd have given her that. But you can't...' Sandra's voice trails off.

'Is that why you gave her the squash blossom necklace?'

It was truly beautiful, heavy Navajo silver, the classic shapes. It had been the one present Sandra knew without doubt Big Frankie would approve of for his bride, and she had loved it. She'd worn the whole set with such joy, for so brief a season. It caught the last of the light, as they closed her coffin lid.

HAZEL: RULES OF ENGAGEMENT

There are rule books for dating. I've read some, thrown them across the room laughing. There are rule books for picking a career—as if those apply to Indigenous people, or any people who don't start out ensconced in the framework of the middle class. I've chucked a couple of those, too, along with the *Seven Habits* type of corporate spirituality spiels.

There are no rule books for coming to terms with having a were-wolf in your house. So I have nothing to throw but the stick, and that is just too meta... and too big.

We stare at each other for a long time, in silence. I think about all the stories that I've heard about shape-shifters. None of them are exactly good. Were-Dogs? Definitely never heard any good stories about those.

But there's the thing. I know that I didn't hear all the stories. I've known that for a long time, too. And I have, by now, shared a house for some time with what I thought was just (just?!) a psychic dog, and have been perfectly safe. I've felt kind of proud, if you want to know, of this evidence of my....I don't know...enoughness?...of this proof that I really don't need to pretend to be anyone other than me—mixed, modern and non-traditional—for the stories of my father's people to include me too. Not the come-to-a-bad-end stories, but the ones outsiders think of as Myth. I've been enjoying, if I admit it, the private sense of how cool I am, that I can converse with a being of another race, just like the real old-fashioned People of Power could. If I'm honest, I've been having *fun*.

So, looking at this were-dog—*my* were-dog—I make a decision, lean the stick back in its place.

'Look,' I say, 'this is all pretty freaky. But all in all? Now that I know, can I talk with you in your human form?'

I don't have any clothes.

'I noticed.' The shock is rebounding to giddiness.

No pockets in this suit, his dog-self laughs doggy-style, tongue out, panting.

'You're in luck. Wait a minute.' I lope past him, up the stairs, turn at the landing, call back, 'Ha! Stay.'

Back of the closet, in a bag, Joshua's gym clothes. The benefits of a busy lifestyle, you forget sometimes to finish the housework. I haul the bag out and shoot back downstairs before he gets the urge to follow me.

'Here,' I say, slightly breathless, holding out the bag.

He sniffs, backs off.

'Oh, come on.'

No, seriously. He wrinkles his nose. *WUFF!*

'Well, it's these or the blanket. I want to talk to human you.'

Fine…. the blanket then. Do you mind leaving the room, though?

I can feel a bubble of hysteria whelming up.

'I'm going out back for a smoke,' I say, and leave him to it, whatever this business of changing forms entails—nope, really cannot begin to think about that.

Instead, I think back to when it was weird enough that I had a dog… I'd just about gotten used to him, then Missy had to turn up, and I found myself telling her about the vision. Ridiculous. Not least because I had no idea then, what I'd gotten into. *My Grandma sent me a dog,* that I could say. *My Grandma sent me a Talking Dog,* nope. *My Grandma sent me a Shape-shifter?* Oh fucking no way I'm telling my girls.

***

I consider. Hazel could not see me, there in the arms of Shinguak. Humans cannot notice my kind in their cities. They cannot even see us in the Wild, where they are willing to speculate that something big, something different, something a little bit like them, might be hiding. We do not need to hide. Zabeh just walk Between, and very few Humans can see us. None has ever seen us in a city. Mostly because we don't go there. Also because their eyes don't work that way. So, I put on the form of her Grandmother, so that Hazel could see me. We had fun, Jane and I, to do that. Jane helped me, but I, Zabeh am here. I am here to help. Hazel called for Justice. So, call me Justice. I help Her. And Hazel. And Jim who calls himself Spider.

HAZEL: JIM

So, he wants me to call him 'Jim.'

And it seems simple, Hazel's just got another new man-friend. I can wear that. So long as he knows his place. Whatever that turns out to be. In this moment, I don't actually know.

So, I'm at the office, in case something here will make more sense than my current home situation.

I'm living with a werewolf.

Well, a were-dog. A shape-shifter. I am itching to talk to somebody who gets it. Why are so many of my family dead, when I could really use a chat? And why are the rest of them… Sandra? … I contemplate calling her. What would she say? How would that conversation go?

Big Frankie, now, he'd get into it with me on the proper nomenclature. I can almost hear him: 'Werewolf is a European concept. We have shape-shifters, of course, but we call them Rugaru.'

And then Sandra would jump in and point out that 'rugaru' is just the Michifization of the French 'loup garou,' which is, you know, werewolf.

And then Frank would protest that Michifization is not a word, and so on, and who would be able to tell me, what is the protocol—not in theory, not in legend, not in some pre-colonial fantasy of Pure Tradition—*what the fuck do I, here, now, a child of globalization, do with this man-dog shape-shifting thing that, for want of a better word, is my housemate?*

You'd think I'd just throw him out. It's bizarre to me that I can't do it. Why? Why did I say he could stay? Why did I leave him clearing out the back bedroom, that used to be the girls' room, tell him he could have it for his human self? I washed Joshua's clothes for him. Not the best fit, but good enough for now. He's covered.

***

And me? What am I going to do?

So, I'm sitting in my office, laying out solitaire, cards slapping on the table. I know, everyone plays virtually these days. I like physical cards. I like the feel of them in my hands. I like the sound. It connects me to the old people, you might say if you wanted to be deep about it. But it's not like these were my grandmother's cards. Cards don't last that long. This is just a deck I got at a gas station one time, somewhere in a small town, probably in Big Bend. I like to make sure I have a couple decks on hand, all the time. These ones are still a bit slippery, still a little new, but I lay out the pattern, start to play.

Coffee, cards, cigarettes.

Wouldn't it be handy if my Grandma turned up now, in a follow-up vision, to let me know what to do next, now that I'm stuck with her gift of Spider/Jim.

Why did I obey a vision? I really wonder. I've always been the cynical one, the leather jacket, the attitude. You want a person who would be expected as recipient of visions, try Sandra, or any of those women who style themselves Traditional and wear their rainbow skirts.

I can't stand those, to tell the actual truth. Big Frankie tried to convince me once that this was powerful and important, this wearing of a certain style of skirt.

'It's just fashion,' I'd retorted. 'Bad fashion, at that.'

Boy, he'd gotten pissed. I blew his spiritual calm right away with that.

'You can't say that!' He was fuming, literally stomping around the room. 'They were given in a vision! Women have to wear them, to properly respect the Mother Earth, and the Protocols.'

To my discredit, I think I actually rolled my eyes at him. I'm kind of sorry I did that now. Not because I think he was right, but because it made him so mad he wouldn't listen to my reasons.

And I have my reasons.

Those skirts look to me like nothing more than 1800s European puritanism, Victorian England with its obsession about sexual temptation, so bad that they covered the legs of furniture lest men be tempted by a well-turned table leg. A woman's ankle? Evil! Why then, when the Europeans had finally made a little progress against such a frankly disgusting, misogynist attitude, did Indigenous community, a century later, rush to adopt a vision that puts our women right into some kind of Pioneer Purdah?

'*You're avoiding the issue.*'

I start. Drop some cards.

'Who said that?' I actually look around, though I know nobody corporeal is there. There's a shimmer in the air, as if someone just moved, nearby. 'Gran?' I feel stupid, bent over, clawing at the fallen cards which static has stuck to the floor.

Silence. No more shimmer. No vision of an old woman laughing at me. My cigarette has burned down almost to the filter, a long ash hanging comically out over the ashtray. That's how I feel, like that ash is my world, and if I step out on it, it will crumble. But I never could stand stillness.

I need to make a move.

I rap the ashtray so the ridiculous ash falls, reach myself a fresh smoke, light it, inhale, think.

***

He arrived as a dog. People know I have a dog now. If the dog just runs away?

Then I'm left with Jim. Thing is, I don't know anything about how it really works for him. He tried to explain. Nearest I could make it was, he has some amount of choice over his shape, but not entirely. So, I'm not clear—could he manage to stay human at all times when other people are around? Alternately, could I keep up the pretence that he is just a dog?

I mean, he's been with me how many weeks now, and I only just today caught him in his human shape. He tells me he's been back and forth regularly when I'm out. Ridiculous how the mind works in overload.

'Naked?!' I'd blurted, as if I'm some prude whose biggest worry is that some strange man's ball sweat might be on my things. Actually though, that is pretty gross. I want to know who's sweating on my stuff.

But I think it's more than that. It's that he fooled me, he gained access to my premises under false premises. I knew I'd agreed to a mind-talking dog. I didn't know he was also human. I like to think I'm the one making the call, no matter how stupid it might be. My girls are like that too, and I suppose that's why they give me such a hard time. They always get on me about making sure I'm the one making the choices, as if it wasn't me who taught them to be that way. Nope, now they just see Mom, too weak to be without a man, too ruled by sex to make good choices, too prone to losers.

That's the thing. Missy met him as a dog, and the bastard made up to her. And she likes him. If I get rid of him, she'll hate me for that. But there's no way I can picture telling the girls the truth—well, if Frankie even gave me enough time these days to tell her anything—no, I can't see telling them that I got rid of the dog.

Later, I'll wonder why that seemed harder to do than to find a way to juggle it so that they didn't catch on that I'm now living with a shape-shifter. Were-dog? Whatever the correct term is for Jim's condition, I find myself thinking of it like I'm in a movie, and the title is *I'm Living With a Werewolf*.

***

The deck has me beat. I shuffle and deal again, thinking about my girls. Is it weird that I've never really worried about my Little Frankie? Even when she was tiny, she had that glow about her that seemed to say she was born on a fortunate day, at a fortunate hour, under a fortunate star. She was luminous, even as a baby, with something that—it sounds crazy to even think it—something that protected her from all the seedy, creepy, broken parts of life.

Missy now, she just ran head on into the world, like it was a wall of trouble and she was a born battering ram. Tore me for seven stitches getting out, and just kept on, headfirst at everything. Her, I worry about. She takes it all so personally. Like she's going to fix the world, or die trying. And that's the part that terrifies me.

Take this 'John TakeDown' site she set up. Why would she do that? Any fool would know it was going to generate a world of creepy commentary, stir up anger from every freak with an axe to grind. That wasn't even the worst of it. The worst was when Joshua—seems so long ago he was part of my life—Josh warned me that she needed to shut it down, quietly, quickly, because she was going to jeopardize 'an important ongoing investigation.' Seriously? He thought I would be the best person to tell her to stop?

'Who are you to talk, Mom?' she said, the last time I tried to talk sense to her. She knows the best defence is a good offence. 'What's all this Private Eye stuff about if it's not about being some kind of crusader?'

'Yeah, but for God's sake, Missy, I don't go around in a fucking cape daring people to take a shot!'

'Oh, don't you?' she'd shot back, and took off out of there. Me and my big mouth.

But, for a miracle, she actually took down the site. Josh and I together, we just asked her, and she took it down. And then I dumped him. Hahaha.

The deck has me beat again, I can tell already. Normally, I'd hang in there a few more turns of the card, but what's the use? I can see this lining up, so I crush the cards back into one thing, a pack, a deck, a unity.

Shuffle again, see what makes sense now. I turn my attention to the Nell August thing.

MISSY: EASY DOES IT

Maengan texts her the next day, to ask her out for coffee.

Figure I owe you one. What's good for you?

Tim's okay? There's one by my work.

She's nervous, walking out in her bike gear. It was that or the scrubs, and she was never one to wear them off site, even before the pandemic. She squashes the impulse to check her appearance. Missy knows what she looks like. Knows he's just looking for a friend to help connect him to the city, knows better than to make more of the ease between them than the obvious—they're distant cousins, and have similar backgrounds.

She spots him right away, locking a bike to the rack.

'Hey,' Maengan says, with a small, quick smile, 'What do you think? My new horse.'

'Not bad,' she says, and before their coffee's done, they've decided to go for a ride, see more of the valley. She's also given him the name of her contact in HR, and within a week, Maengan is working at the hospital's Pastoral Care Centre, and they're meeting up after his first shift to celebrate.

'It's on me. Whatever you want. Want a donut?' he says, waggling an eyebrow.

'No, thanks.'

They sit together in the slanted late day sun, drinking their black coffees.

'Got something for you,' says Missy, and hands him a small paper bag.

He opens it and pulls out a beaded lanyard.

'You made this?' His smile is purely innocent.

'Well, no,' Missy admits, crinkling her face ruefully. 'It's pure hospital gift shop. Sorry.'

'It's perfect,' grins Maengan, and he takes off his new ID, attaches it to the lanyard, and swings it gently. 'See how I catch the light?'

She catches the plastic card in its arc and peers closely at the image on it. 'Not too hideous,' she says. 'These things are usually just awful.'

'Let me see yours,' he says, and she instinctively drops his to cover her own tag.

'Oh come on, now, Ms. Jones,' he wheedles, 'it can't be that bad. You've seen mine.'

She smiles and hands it over. He sucks air in through his teeth assessingly, and turns the card this way and that. 'Nope,' he says, 'this does not do you justice.'

At a loss for how to respond, Missy picks up his tag again, frowns at it.

'A. Maengan Nolan,' she reads. 'A Maengan? Aren't you The Maengan?'

He laughs good naturedly.

'Come on, now,' she says, 'what's the 'A' for?'

'Promise you won't tell?'

'How bad could it be? Allan? Alfred? Abercrombie?'

He sighs. 'It's just too embarrassing.'

'Come on. Abner? Azreal? Aloysius? What could be worse than Aloysius?'

He's shaking his head, eyes squeezed shut. He opens them one at a time.

'Okay. Stop,' says Maengan. 'It's not Aloysius. Or Azreal, or Alfred…it's… Adolphus.'

She laughs. 'Seriously?'

He smiles lopsidedly. 'I'm afraid so.'

'So…' she says, 'you were born with it?'

'Yup. Named for my grandfather. And Maengan to give me a *Traditional Option*,' he says it in air quotes, shaking his head. He drains his coffee. 'You see why I had to leave home?'

'Yeah. That's a lot to live with: Adolphus Maengan. Wolf Wolf Nolan.'

'At your service.'

***

I consider Devin goes to water. I consider strange captive water. Strange smells. But he is like Zabeh? He knows water is where cells align, thoughts smooth.

DEVIN: MANATEE AND PANTHER

Devin thinks it over. Everybody tells him things about his mother, who she was, what she did. It's as if they don't recognize that he has his own sovereign experience of her. She was his gateway to the world, and he wonders if he himself will ever be that for somebody, a father, a physical means for another soul or souls to come to this place, this world.

Devin floats like a whale in the weedless shallows of the community rec centre pool, supported by water and exploring his whale nature. He likes to come here at this hour, when there are not so many people around. Then he doesn't feel self-conscious about them looking at his body.

People have such a need to judge each other, and he wonders why. Do whales do that, he wonders? Why would they? He supposes they could; that, for all we know, might be the material of their songs. He doesn't think so though. He thinks they have bigger issues to discuss in their songs, and that they occupy themselves with songs of praise, to keep the oceans flowing, with songs of news, to keep their clans informed, and with songs of doing, work-songs, shanties.

He essays a tiny hum himself, quietly so as not to carry far in the water. The lifeguard, yawning, is sitting on her stand, sipping a coffee and thinking her own thoughts. The only other people in the pool at the moment are two Muslim women, their swimming hijabs reminding him of seals. He decides that they could be seals, seal sisters bobbing in the middle pool, where it is just a comfortable depth for either exercises or just plain swimming, or bobbing and talking. Their voices drift and echo slightly in the otherwise empty pool, quietly quietly. He wonders whether they are mothers, and if so, do their children know them the way he feels, in some part of himself, he knows his mother? Not that he ever says so out loud. He understands that people mostly don't listen to him.

He doesn't command attention the way his mother did. Or so they say. They say she was so vibrant, so dynamic, you couldn't fail to notice her walking into a room. If you did, she'd soon find reason to change that, because she'd be involved in whatever brought people into that room. His mother was no bystander. He remembers himself tethered to her, and in her orbit, except when they went out with his father, when she would somehow create distance. And then after she died, his father would park him with Sandra, and Big Frankie would step away, pull all eyes toward him, not Devin.

Lying in the pool, he thinks about that. It used to hurt, once he was old enough to notice what his father was doing. But by then, he was so used to being pushed aside and bidden to be quiet that he just accepted it. Said nothing to Big Frankie, nothing to anyone else. He saw, though, how his own father's eyes went to slender, quick children. His own placid, chubby boy he would not sweep into his gaze; Devin, he'd pass over. Devin feels invisible, like he did then, a great floating whale of invisible, not what his father wanted as an heir, not what he felt he deserved. How could he have spawned this great lump, this soft thing? Devin the whale. But Devin is thinking now, and he dives under and surfaces, and quietly moves further from the hijabis. He doesn't want to attract their attention either.

This is his body, and he examines how it feels, buoyed by water. He is surprised to find he sinks a little too easily. Not so buoyant after all, he is unexpectedly low-lying. He doesn't know why, but the water wants to envelop him, and so he stays in the shallows. Perhaps, he thinks, he is manatee rather than whale, born for the shallows, slow moving and soft. He likes this idea, and adjusts his breathing.

Now he is a manatee, floating in the grassy shallows, the green and warmish water embracing him. He is one, but he is many. He imagines others of his kind. Endangered by their own slowness, gentleness, some might say stupidity. There is that, though—Devin knows he is not stupid. Perhaps others don't see it, perhaps they are too easily led, and too easily believed his father, but there is some stubborn core in him that refuses to see himself as stupid. He drops his face into the water, lets the tears wash and stop. That word, *stupid,* has pulled him out of his manatee reverie, and he forces his mind back to the image of Floridian waters. Here, he is in the green and singing waves, here he is at peace. The world is full of motor boats, but he is among his kind.

He imagines the seal sisters are really more manatees, murmuring together about their children and their migratory routes. He imagines that they love this shore as ardently as he does, this peaceful time and place, these shallow, quiet waters. He waves an arm, languidly, and his wristband catches his eye, proof that, for a very reasonable sum indeed, he can slip away to Florida whenever he chooses, escape from the hard-edged northern city, from the daily humiliations aimed at the stout, from the ache of missing his mother. Here, he can float, at one with himself and the world, and knowing that, as there is never just one manatee, he too must surely have compatriots.

He shifts to contemplating the priest in that light. The priest is no manatee. In the Florida of Devin's mind, the priest must be a panther, even more rare, morose and continuously seething, his long tail twitching. Devin supposes that a manatee and a panther might be good friends and allies, both misunderstood by the world of vacationers and sports fishermen, seekers of human greed and need all around them. He smiles, imagining the panther and the manatee.

***

I consider Devin floating in captive water. Heart light but I am lonely for water. Here, in when there are no humans, I slide into this where of water. O water. Nibi, I sing so small, gi zha ge go. Love to you, nibi.

Nibi holds me, I dance in nibi, we sing shapes of sparkle in dark quiet, small. No humans. No other eyes. Nibi, I sing, gi miigwech way ne me go. Heart light golden in water. Water light my home. I consider Devin. Wise human. Wise.

MISSY: BIKE PATHS

Missy stretches out into it, the sun on her back as she swoops along. She's hit her stride and pedals with ease. Ahead of her, Maengan rides as easily, his hair caught in a simple pony tail, flowing along his long back. It's become their weekend habit, too, riding the trails. He looks back now, unsure, and eases up. 'Which way?' he calls over his shoulder, waving her past. Missy bombs by with a grin, bearing right. The trail turns sharp through an open gate, end of pavement, becoming a broad dusty swath plunging down to run the river's edge. To their right the green water flows, appearing calm to a casual glance, its turbulent speed revealed in the slight rolling further out. Somewhere a dog barks, splashing in the shallows, chasing a stick or a duck. Missy and Maengan flow on like water, past the golf course above them.

They ride hard all the way down to the bridge, where Missy pulls up.

Gliding up beside her, Maengan peers at the railing. There's a shinier swath fairly recently rebuilt.

'That's where he went over.'

'Who?'

'Guy who killed himself. I don't know how I feel about that.'

'About what?'

'He was one of them I put on the website. He was known to be a bad trick. Known to be mean. And you know, mean people so seldom commit suicide.'

Maengan scoffs. 'You think not?'

'Well,' says Missy, 'the way I see it, if you're mean, you've already decided what to do with your pain. You force it on others. Seems to me it would take a lot for someone like that to stop, once they'd made a habit of it.'

'Huh,' says Maengan. 'How bad was this guy?'

'I...' Missy shrugs, 'I don't really...' she colours up a bit. 'Bad enough.'

'Bad enough for what? Do you really know?' Now Maengan is looking at her, his bush-black eyes intent. 'How can you really know what he was like, Miranda?'

'Look. People ... people tell you things. I worked Emergency, you know. And some of those girls from the streets come in with all sorts of hideous injuries. The way people abuse hookers. Like they abuse cats. And then the girls don't want to come in, you know, because who's going to treat them any better in a hospital? Mostly they take care of themselves, or their pimps do. You know, fix them enough for them to get better enough to get back on the streets.'

They look out over the river, green water muddied by the turbulence stirring up the bottom.

'So, this one time, this girl came in.' Missy feels cold suddenly, remembering. 'She was so thin. Not just crack-thin, but hungry too. And covered in scars. Old breaks badly set. She'd been... she'd been torn up... down there... wouldn't talk about it to anyone. But I sat with her, on my break. Not supposed to do that, but I couldn't not. Brought her a cookie, you know? Just a lousy cafeteria cookie. She was so hungry...'

Missy stares off over the treetops out across the river. On the south bank there is forest dark enough to make you forget you're in a city, forest that smells clean and sharp and healthy.

Suddenly, she turns to Maengan.

'Let's cross over.'

From above, the place where the car went over the rails looks no more significant, just another repair, just another place. And the traffic beside them roars along without notice, as they ride along the separated path, and at the end, descend again into parkland. The sun continues shining. The river continues running.

Maengan rides behind, his dark eyes thoughtful on Missy. She looks like what she is, a fit, strong, capable woman. Her short hair has been whipped stiff by the wind, but it looks as rough at the hospital, crushed under her cap, rumpled by inattention. Her hair confirms for him how she keeps all her focus on her patients, in fierce solicitude, as if by will alone she can close the wounds, burn away the fevers, right every wrong. This is her relaxing, pounding along the forest path, taking the constant shifts of terrain in stride, riding like a wild creature running. He pushes a little harder, but it's nothing to her. She kicks it up another notch and he grins, loping behind.

HAZEL: TIMING

Nell August. Pffff....

The thing is, I'm stuck there too. The family gave me money and I've followed every lead I could find, and there is stone cold nothing. It's been too long now and I feel like a fraud going on with it. But I feel worse about that meeting to come, where I have to tell Delphine August that there is nothing to be done, I can't figure out who killed her girl.

She'll get mad.

She'll lump me in with the police. She'll accuse me of racism, say it's because I'm half-White after all, and I don't really care about The People. She'll cry. That'll be the worst, worse than any threats of retaliatory medicine she or any of her relatives might also try using—they're that kind of people—to scare me onward.

Not that they could. They've got nothing there, though I don't let on. The thing is, once you've faced down your own internal visions of Hell, the childhood fears that the old-style Catholics are so good at feeding and elaborating—Once you've broken Church law and lived to tell?

There's not much, spiritually speaking, that can really scare you then.

Think about it. Rome. The Eternal City. The city that once held the power to declare all our people here damned—or worse, without souls. They divided the world with a line and laid out that Doctrine of Discovery—that still stands unrepealed, because they know that repealing it would still break every institution we call civilization wide open.

I've got a queen in the wrong place, and nowhere to move her. Pull the deck together, shuffle, deal again. Lay it out careful, still thinking about Rome, and the great cathedrals.

How powerful was Rome then? How powerful was faith? Somehow, the powers could press whole towns and regions into generations of service to build cathedrals that still stand.

For better or worse, whatever their relationship to Heavenly power, those fuckers had power on the Earth, and they hold it still. I can't ever, I suppose, explain to my girls how much it cost me to find the courage to defy the Church.

Even though their dad had left me, left us, and had no intention of coming back, I went through a personal hell getting to grips with the fact that I'd have to be the one to file for divorce, because George never would.

It would suit him better to let the marriage stand, and be okay with the Church in public, but keep on fucking that teenage fool he found... He wanted to have his cake and Edith, too. Ha! I snort as I see two queens, black on red, turn up their bland faces to me. ·

Edith, can you imagine it, is the actual fucking name of the fucking embryo he left me for. She called herself *Édith, like Piaf*, and played the ingenue, with the little wispy voice and sucked in chest and everything. It was creepy. But he fell for it. If I'm honest, he encouraged her to act like that. Okay, Édith the Embryo was eighteen—legal—but you have to wonder how long he'd had his eye (and God knows what else) on her, before she turned up on his arm that day...

A space opens up, and I slip the black queen into it. Now a king turns up, King of Hearts with his fat lips and dagger, and I flick him down on the black queen. Queen of Diamonds sits exposed.

Actually, in the long run I'm glad ... because Frankie ...when Little Frankie started to become a young woman, when she went from caramel colt to nymph, could I have trusted George around her? He never, to my knowledge, bothered Missy, she was always such a tomboy thing, but Little Frankie?

My blood still chills a bit at that thought. It's unfair, of course. Just because he married me the second I turned eighteen, and Édith still looks like she's twelve? A man draws a line at his own blood, right?

Bah. I'm too fucking cynical by half.

In this world, you have to be really young, or really crazy, not to be a little cynical. Well, I was young once. Probably crazy, too. George seemed like a real life fairy tale.

What? Who, me? Looking for a fairy tale? Was I ever that naive?

No, the truth is, I gave a shit that my parents—both still alive then—would be pleased that I was marrying in the Church. And I gave a shit that I was pretty sure I was pregnant. And I gave a shit that George looked at me like I was beautiful. Fuck. What an idiot I was.

But not too stupid to learn from it.

My girls can say what they want about the bad choices in men I've made since their dad, but what matters is, I went into every relationship with my eyes open, no more stupid expectations.

And Josh? Josh just seemed like… well, the last of what feels like an entirely other reality. I can't stress too strongly the point that my reality now includes that I'm living with a werewolf.

Josh was all about timing.

I light another smoke, considering; get up and move across to the one window that opens.

Not avoiding the issue, I think, to nobody at all. *Something here I need to understand.*

I sigh, looking out on the dinky view. This isn't going to help the Augusts.

But they're exactly in line with why I'm cynical.

It was clear as soon as I met the Augusts. Their daughter, poor dead Nell, was the sum total of all their shitty decisions as parents, as much as she was a victim of whoever actually killed her.

She was a hooker. She lived a high risk lifestyle.

Her family wept and called her their baby, but they'd probably lost touch with her in her teens when she ran from the dysfunctional cradle, carrying all her belongings in a black garbage bag or a cheap backpack, but towing the heavier inter-generational load. That one she never put down.

She had that face, the crack face, so very taut-skinned, so thin all over but with a wiry energy crackling through her, present even in her pictures, the ones they had of her and the official ones. The one thing that I never told the Augusts was that I'd seen her before.

I'd been walking home early one evening and I cut through the Community League park. I remember the light, that time of day when you really notice how short the days are getting. I remember there was a man and a woman, sitting at one of those picnic tables (why are picnic tables in parks always that weird raw-hot-dog brown?) totally absorbed in whatever they were talking about, leaned in across the planks. Her feet were wound around each other, his jiggling, like he wanted to reach out to her with them. He was wearing a striped knit sweater, and his hair fell softly across his handsome profile. He reached up, not to his own hair, but to brush hers back, and then dropped his hand softly down over hers. He took her hands, and the sun literally lit up her face just then, and that dazed look in her face, that dazzled blinking, all I could think was 'Thunderstruck.' There's that song, right? Not the AC/DC one (which I also love), but that girl singer, Ashley Z, who first gave up auto-tune and made it fashionable again to record without effects.

'*Love is like lightning, and I'm thunderstruck,*' I remember, I saw that woman in the park, saw her face and I thought, *that is what that line means.* No, I'm not romantic regarding my own self, but if you had been there, you'd have seen this, too.

It was like a spell fell over them both, with the evening light and all, and they stopped talking, just looked at each other—*nobody and nothing else in the world.*

I stopped. I didn't want to go closer.

Then he got up, gently let her go as they both untangled from the clunky table and when she stepped toward him he took her hand again and smiled, so soft. She had this look like she'd been hypnotized, not even looking back at him, she didn't need to, she was in his sway.

And he was no less bound, gazing at her, leaning down to kiss the top of her head, laughing, incredulous at the discovery that she existed.

Why do fools fall in love? That ancient 60s tune broke in on my thoughts—funny how you can remember songs that were in your head when you saw things that stick with you. Why is that?

Anyway, I was mesmerized, I have to admit. Not because the sight of them filled me with longing to find such a love myself... Nope. It was just the light, and the way time seemed to slow down. But that doesn't last. I could imagine all sorts of less than magical moments that might follow this one golden one.

As if to underscore that thought, another woman came around the corner of the Community League building just then. She was thin, walking fast, dressed a little too lightly for the early autumn air. Her handbag swung out and clipped the other woman, who skittered clumsily aside calling, 'Sorry'.

But Nell clearly had other troubles. She was in a hurry, her two-tone hair flagging out behind her in a skinny wave. As she drew near, the same beam of rosy sun that I'd taken for love magic caught her face now, and cruelly highlighted the acne scars, the too-tight feverish complexion, the cords of her thin neck with its choker tattoo. *Thunderstruck.*

Unlike the couple, Nell saw me. Her eyes flicked up, flicked down, then to the side and hard past me. *Leave me alone,* those eyes said. She was used to being judged, didn't want me to notice her. Those eyes, though. They were an unnaturally opaque greenish colour—colour contacts over Cree black eyes, I later learned. Like the hair, designed in a desperate attempt to recast her darkness into something more exotic, a tan on a blonde beach boy's dream. Those eyes, and her haunted face stayed with me. I lost sight of the lovers, but Nell, in that brief moment, hit me so hard. *Thunderstruck.*

It shook me so much when the Augusts brought her case file to me and I realized, skimming while they talked and sobbed, that I had seen her on what was probably the last evening of her life. So sue me.

After that, I wanted a beer. And I went to the little booze shop, and Josh walked in and made some lame overture. I wasn't thunderstruck, just distracted.

MISSY: ART PARK

At the park they dismount and walk their bikes slowly down from the parking lot and along the gravel path leading from one installation to another. The art park is empty, though cars hum by in the midday lull. Down the hill, the arch of the new bridge shines white against the sky.

'What do you think of that?' asks Maengan pointing his chin out toward the bridge.

'I like it.'

'Me too.'

'It's got harmony.'

'How about this?' They survey the art park.

'It's a lot to take in. This, for instance,' says Missy, and they circle the two concrete turtles, each with its central shell covered in tile mosaic. 'I mean, this is pretty bog-standard literal, but nicely done,' she gestures to the one that shows a medicine wheel, the four cardinal directions, the four sacred colours, within each quadrant traditional symbols—bison, Métis flag, feathers, eagle, bear paws.

'Bog-standard?' asks Maengan.

'Something Mom picked up from an old—' Missy looks away. 'Someone we knew said it. It's Brit slang. Like run-of-the-mill, you know? This one's more interesting,' she says of its companion, which is mostly shades of blue, and seems to depict a Round Dance, but also features a strange tree on which sits an outsize redheaded woodpecker. 'It feels more specific, know what I mean?'

'Yeah. Say, how's your mom?'

Missy shrugs.

'How's that dog?'

Missy shoots him a frown, then forces another shrug. *Why should he care?*

'Dog-like, I guess. Friendly, hairy... why do you ask? Does it bother you that he didn't like you?'

He flushes a little.

'Well, no. I mean... he just seems like a lot of dog, if he were inclined to be hard to handle.'

'Pfff,' snorts Missy. 'Nice of you to care, but you've met my mom, right? If that dog bites her? Trust me, she'll have started it. And she'll end it.'

He stares at her.

'I'm kidding,' she says without conviction. 'They get along great. And anyway, Mom knows animals. She grew up on a farm.' She frowns again. 'So—'

'Okay,' blurts Maengan, flinging up his hands in mock surrender, 'I confess. I, Wolf Wolf Nolan, pride myself on getting along with dogs. And it bugged me when your mom's dog didn't fall for my obvious charms.'

She smiles back.

'Probably he doesn't speak Ojibwe, didn't know you're one of his kind.'

Maengan nods, then moves on. They don't speak, just gaze on the various works. At last they come to a ruddy brown stone plinth etched with images of fossils. On top, a big-eared canid—fox? coyote?—curls, ears up in perpetual bronze alert. At the foot of the plinth, as if resting in the shade, lies a bronze rabbit, boldly relaxed behind the predator's back, in an attitude of fat sleepiness.

'I like this one best,' says Maengan. 'You know, if I had to pick– which we don't,' he adds, smiling. 'This is all really well done.'

'Yeah,' agrees Missy. 'But do you think it will make a difference? I mean, a real difference to the people who are still struggling? Who are still living in the pain? On the streets? So, a homeless Nechi comes along here, how's he or she supposed to feel? Will they feel proud of 'our people'? Or will they just get mad because on some level this is bullshit.'

'Well—' says Maengan, but she's on a roll.

'No, it is, Maengan. Bullshit. Middle class people can invest in art like this, so that they can show off to their middle class friends and say, *See, we honour Indigenous culture here. Look at us, we are a city who is proud of our Indigenous people.* But that '*our*' is the thing. Indigenous is still an object, still possessed. These artists, they're the ones who've been able to stick it out through bullshit university programs and learn to talk academic artsy crapola language—I mean have you read artists' statements? They're full of absolute bafflegab, navel-gazing crap. So these artists, how close do they live to 'the people' anymore? Or are they all just sipping lattés and sucking back free wine at openings, dressed in Indigenous chic, happy to be fawned over by the rich bitches who still—still!—prey on the most vulnerable among us.'

'Yeah, but Miranda,' says Maengan, 'that's expecting a lot of artists, don't you think?'

'What do you mean?'

'I mean,' says Maengan slowly, as he eases down to sit in the grass, 'art isn't responsible for fixing everything. But it plays its part. You think about how it got this way—think about all the images of us that went along with colonial violence—'

'And still do!'

'And still do, and you see how these artists are taking on that piece. They're changing the image. Changing the way we are seen. That matters.'

'It doesn't feed people.'

'Doesn't it? You ever meet any of these artists? Most of them have families. And if they make any money, they share it. They take care of their own. And that's more than a lot of us are still able to do. They work their way through a university system that's hostile to them, and they make it stick. They have to fight stereotypes and bullshit all the way along. You going to begrudge them a latté? Or a glass of wine?'

'No! I'm not.' Missy huffs, 'And don't make me into the bad guy here!' She stands a moment more, hands on hips, glaring down at him. Then she strides over to the bikes, wrenches hers upright, leaps aboard and she's gone.

'Hey!' calls Maengan. 'Hey! Come on, Miranda! What gives?'

He watches astonished as her back view disappears at a ferocious pace. Sighing, he picks a leaf of grass, runs it thoughtfully between his fingers for a while, gazing again at the bronze rabbit. *She looks insolent,* he thinks. Like she doesn't care that people are still starving, still addicts, still trapped in their terrible lives. The rabbit feeds herself, dares what she dares, and rests in the shadow of the predator, leaning cozily up against the enormity of time.

Maengan leans back on his hands, stretches his spine, wonders what to do about Missy. His heart is beating awfully fast. Is he supposed to chase her now? He figures that might be the worst thing he could do. So he just sits, lets what's left of the afternoon's sun share what warmth it will. In a few minutes, he slides up to standing and, hands in pockets, strolls slowly and thoughtfully around the park again peering intently at each piece of art as if they might contain the secret of making up with a firebrand when you've set her off. He knows one thing for sure, and that is that he's going to make that effort. Once his heart has settled, he climbs aboard his own bike and heads out, taking the path that heads west, not following Missy. All these paths cross the river, over and over, like a braid. There are so many ways to get from one side to the other. He might as well enjoy the view, he figures, and soon he's loping along at a good pace, content to explore more of the valley while there is light.

***

Missy rides it out, leaves her anger on the trails, lets it fly away behind her until there is nothing but the shirring of the chain, reminding her of her six months in Korea, the cicadas in Seoul shirring gently through the evenings. She stops, looking back over the river valley. This is a good city too. But Seoul was a kind of freedom for her. If only she'd found someone there, not got lonely and come home.

Lonesome now, she calls Little Frankie. 'Hey, want to meet me at the Italians?'

'Sure. I'm not up to much that can't wait. How soon?'

'I'm on my way up there now. About ten or fifteen?'

'Not possible. Give me half an hour.'

'Okay, see you then.'

She rides slower, up through the ugliness of the Quarters, where the rebranding developments lie uneasily over the old ugliness of Boyle Street, which festers up like a pustule underneath.

She thinks about how Seoul, ten times bigger, seemed in a way smaller. The scale of things was tighter, the neighbourhoods thrown together with their higgledy streets and roofs, down around Itae-won-dong. Itaewon, of course, was too near the American base not to have its own ugly stories. She hadn't thought about that then, hadn't wanted to. She'd wanted to know the light, the bright, the bustle of Seoul, not the underbelly. But still she had gone to Itae-won-dong, not for the knock-off shopping, but for some kind of thrumming that went through her when she walked there, the edg-iness that made her feel sharper. *She must be her mother's daughter after all.*

She wishes she could tell Hazel and Frankie about Seoul, but that is the fate of the traveller. The best stories belong only to the ones who were there. She supposes she could take up writing, be-come as good as old Alan Booth, whose tales of Japanese backroads Maengan had lent her. She'd read them smiling at their strong sense of lives lived. Booth didn't go into the underbelly, either. He just accepted people and wrote about them. He didn't pretend to any kind of goodness himself, he was just as he was, in life and in his stories—a prodigious drinker, a would-be womanizer, a lover of old ladies and workmen, and a singer of ballads.

Missy rides on, reckoning.

That's what's missing here. Where are the ballads? Where are the songs that tell of what people did, the great deeds and small, the little songs for little ceremonies and ways?

'It's the folk songs,' she says to Frankie. They've got drinks and lucked into a table on the sidewalk, a little apart from the rest. 'The folk songs are what got destroyed all across the land.'

'Exactly. That makes so much sense, when you think about it,' says Frankie, her long limbs flowing over the chair, her long hair flowing like buckwheat honey, her eyes deceptively dreamy. 'But how is that possible? Do you think the old people didn't have folk songs? Or what?'

'Everywhere has them.'

'Everywhere I've heard of. We had to have had them back in the old times.'

'So that's a horrific marker, if you think about it, of the devastation here, that this land's folk songs are gone. Replaced. *Four Strong Winds,* Stomping Tom, all that …' Missy waves a hand as if to brush away Canadian folk music. *If she weren't so hot-headed, if Maengan were here, he'd love this conversation.*

'There are the ceremonial songs, but people hid those.' Frankie looks away across the street, across the park, the trees top-lit with late sun now, the shade below warm and full of families.

Missy follows her gaze.

Under the trees, a pair of obvious street people, their earthly goods in a mishmash of suitcases and plastic bags. The woman is finger-combing her long dark hair. She's just washed it in the spray park; either unaware, unconcerned, or too itchy to care about the disapproving stares of the families with children. You do what you have to do.

'I guess,' says Missy, 'when things are that bad, you drop down to what you absolutely can't let die. The ceremonial songs, the basic ones. All the…' she waves a hand, 'fluffy stuff, all the stuff that's for fun and play and just singing casually, that stuff disappears.'

'And you lose the dimensionality of living cultures,' says Frankie, then winks, 'Unless our Indigenous ancestors never had fluffy songs; maybe we were traditionally one-dimensional and humourless?'

'No,' says Missy wryly, 'The People are known for our humour, right?'

'We take our humour entirely seriously,' nods Frankie. 'But you make me think. Where are those songs? Songs for weddings, songs for dating?'

'Well, what about 49ers? There's dating songs in those.'

'But they're modern, new, made-up for the new culture of pow-wow. Post-colonial, which is old-time now. Not new like UpTop and …' now Frankie waves her own hand gently, encompassing all the things they both know as their current social moment.

'But still, pow-wow is new in longtime terms. All the real good old folk songs of the land—'

'If there were any—'

'Had to have been. But they got hidden away.' Frankie has lemon gelato, and licks it slowly from the spoon. Missy averts her eyes. Frankie is devastatingly beautiful at the best of times, and Missy can't stand looking at her displays of over-the-top sensuality.

'Frank,' she says, flicking her eyes to the spoon. In that eye-flick, years of conversations about a woman's rights and responsibilities, about how to be, about self-defence and pride and beauty and rules and risks.

'Pfft,' says Frankie. 'I don't care if I do entice them. It's not like they're my responsibility. Isn't that the new dogma, Missy? Your hard-on is your own problem, not mine?'

Missy shakes her head. 'Oh, Frank.'

Frankie, of course, was never entirely oblivious. The object of her siren posing appears. Guido, out from behind the espresso counter, drifts toward them, wiping the empty table nearest them.

'Buona sera, ladies,' he croons, his dishcloth caressing the table-top. His eyes flicker here and there, lighting on Frankie like butter-flies drawn to the salt on her skin. He looks like he wants to sip her from head to toe.

'Hi,' says Frankie, giving him a bambi glance.

'How is your gelato? Satisfactory?' he says, caught in Frankie's orbit, not even trying to include Missy.

'It's cool and fresh, and going down smooth,' says Frankie, and they laugh together, softly, like she's said the cleverest thing.

'Let me know if you need more,' says Guido, and he stops any pretence of working, just stands gazing down at Frankie. 'It is such a beautiful evening, isn't it?'

'Mmm.'

He runs a hand through his hair, gets hold of himself. 'Let me know if you need anything,' he says, remembering to smile at both of them, then retreats, attempting to saunter.

'Why do you do that?'

'What? He's cute,' says Frankie.

'Seriously? Guido?'

'Seriously, why not Guido?'

Oh Frankie.

'But seriously,' says Frankie, 'what is up, Miss?'

Directly asked, Missy finds she's a bit loathe to explain. Her own actions now seem ridiculous, disproportionate. She heaves a sigh.

'I had a bit of a tantrum, Frank.'

'Oh?'

'Social Justice Warrior moment.'

'Oh.'

'Yeah. Typical Miranda, right? Got all bent out of shape about the politics of things—'

'Who'd you blow up at? Not—?'

Miranda looks away.

'Shit. This Maengan guy?' Frankie shakes her head, her hair incidentally finding some left-over glow from the sunset far behind them beyond this shady sidewalk. 'Why?'

'It's beyond me, really,' says Miranda, moodily swirling her half-empty cup.

'Yeah. But what happened?'

'Well, you know, we were riding down in the valley—'

'So I gathered,' says Frankie, nodding at Miranda's shorts and tank, the bike cooling its heels nearby. 'Did he try to take advantage of you in the eerie, unpeopled wilderness?'

'Frank, stop it.'

'Sorry. Carry on.' Frankie looks at her levelly, listening.

'We stopped at the Art Park, you know?'

Frankie nods, straightened and alert.

'And I don't know, I just got to thinking, you know, about the way the art industry, all the cultural industries, lie to us all, make us do things we don't want to do just to get a career going.'

Frankie nods. She knows. They've been over this ground before, too.

'I know, I know,' says Missy, 'I really do. You have to be tough to follow that path. To choose to be an artist. And as soon as I started talking, I knew I was sounding like a pompous, judgmental ass. Worse, I knew I was sounding jealous. Like I went into nursing because I wasn't tough enough to make it as an artist. Like I did it for the money, and I'm jealous of what I gave up.'

Frankie says nothing, gazing noncommittally at the trees with their crowns of flame.

'And I know—you know I know—that I gave up arts because I knew I didn't have anything to say in that way. I don't regret it. Except—Maengan was looking at me, and I felt like I had to explain everything, all that, all over again. And I just didn't want to.'

She sighs again. 'So childish of me, eh?'

Frankie still says nothing.

'I should've said something. 'Cause, see, he doesn't know what I'm thinking. He doesn't know me. He just hears this loudmouth know-it-all, tearing people down. And he's sitting there in the grass, and he's looking at me. And suddenly, it's like—it's like—it's like we used to look at Mom, you know? When she'd get all mad about the world and rant at everything?'

'Oh yeah,' says Frankie, 'I remember.'

'It was like that. But like I was Mom, and I couldn't stop myself. I just got so mad. Like he was mocking me. And then I took off.'

'Gee, Sis, that's rough.' Frankie gives her a totally serious look. 'That was the worst thing, with Mom, wasn't it? She just couldn't get that we weren't making fun of her.'

'We were just scared. Scared that… scared that her anger meant the bad things in the world were bigger than her, more than she could deal with—'

'And if she couldn't deal with it, how could we?'

'We were just trying to keep from freaking out. And so there I was, and I looked at him, and I thought—no, I didn't even think, you know, I just left—but I guess—'

'You thought you were freaking him out, and you didn't know how to stop.'

'Yeah.'

They sit in silence for a minute, both of them watching the trees. A slight breeze is trying to convince itself to lift in the syrupy warmth. Finally, Missy speaks.

'I lose more boyfriends that way.'

And they laugh.

'Not that he's a boyfriend,' she adds, quickly.

'Why not? He's not really our cousin, is he?'

'Fourth half-cousin on one side, by adoption. He explained it to me in detail.'

'You like him?'

'I … he's easy to be around. Interesting.'

Frankie is looking at her with her flirting face again, Frankie the social diva, a slow grin bubbling on her face. 'Oh yeah?'

'Yeah,' says Missy, raking a hand through her hair, which has dried into sweaty spikes. 'But it's not like—' Her hand, in descent, knocks the spoon, tips her cup of gelato. It lands on its side, rolls out of reach.

She is annoyed again. It's so easy for Frankie, they just fall at her feet. For Missy, things are different. She is intense, and that fire scares men off. She tells herself she doesn't care. She's not her mother, desperate for a man. She will wait for a person who can take her as she is.

She is the sort of person who gets up and steps over to where the cup has rolled out of sight, looks around until she sees it has landed in the gutter, and picks it up. She frowns at its bent shape—how did that happen?—but says nothing, just pushes it into the recycler.

***

Di di di di. I consider gelato. Gel-a-to. It is poison, small poison. Like those twigs you have to eat and re-eat until you get the good out from the poison that protects it. No. Not like that, I consider. Outside round. The small poison is first, but also last, of gel-a-to. The good is first, too. I consider how they cool their throats on it, how their tongues light up to it. Ge-la-to.

I am a sister, too. I want to taste. It is easy to call the cup. I taste. It is surprise. Where does this grow? Ge-la-to oh oh oh ri oh…I will consider it more.

***

'Hey,' says Frankie, 'wanna come over? I found something I wanna show you.'

Saturday afternoon is fading out, and nothing to do but clean her apartment, and it's clean enough. Not like anyone ever visits.

'Sure,' she says.

'Not gonna ask what it is?' chirps Frankie in her ear.

'Nah.'

'Good. I wouldn't tell you anyway. It's a soup-rise!'

Missy has to smile at that, hearing Frankie pronouncing surprise the way they used to spell it as little girls.

***

Frankie's place is like her, easy to look at. It's just an ordinary apartment, but she's made it her own, and it smells of elusive coolness. The simple furniture is well-arranged, and the colours all blues and greens and plums, all designed to harmonize with Frankie herself, so that she moves like a tawny puma through her lair. She trails a hand across the scarred dark bookcase on the west wall, the one that was Big Frankie's.

'Ah, here it is.' She turns, triumphant.

'Remember when we saw this PBS special? I found it on DVD.'

They like DVD. Missy likes VHS even better, the grainy sense of thick time overlaying images.

Frankie spins the case her way, she catches it. 'Native America!' cries Frankie.

'No way? With Robbie Robertson narrating?'

'The very one,' grins Frankie.

'Got popcorn?'

'You get it started, I'll set this up and make some ice tea.'

As the hot air popper whines, they lean against the counter in Frankie's galley kitchen, one on either side, Frankie by the stove.

'Remember that feeling, that… I don't know… kind of amazed guilt? Mom and Dad weren't just making shit up to make us feel better? That there really were ancient cities here, as big or bigger than any contemporaneous cities anywhere in the world?'

'Yeah.' Missy nods. She sneaks a look under her lashes. Frankie looks away, her face a bit red. She doesn't like to be seen being nostalgic. Who would?

'Hey,' says Missy, 'can we watch that city episode? That's my favourite—Cities of the Sky.'

'Mine too,' says Frankie, as the kettle adds a shriek, and the popcorn maker winds it up. Missy turns it off, passes it to Frankie, who fills the pot while Missy rummages in the fridge for flax oil and hemp seeds, pours them on, stirs by hand. Then nutritional yeast, spirulina, smoked salt, all neatly lined up along the counter top. She shakes the bowl, adds a bit more seasoning.

Frankie nudges her aside, reaches into the fridge and pulls out two old-fashioned glass pint mugs full of ice, each with a mint leaf improbably frozen in the exact middle. These go on a teal-blue tray, découpage over wood. It once belonged to Big Frankie, but looks like something Little Frankie would have made for herself anyway.

Missy divides the popcorn into smaller bowls, doing her best to leave behind the unpopped kernels in the big bowl, the bowl that had also been Big Frankie's.

Frankie pours the hot tea into the steins, and the ice pops and hisses as she carries the tray into the living room.

***

Settling, they lose themselves in the history and mysteries of Cahokia, Teotihuacan, the Inca realm and all the fallen cities of Turtle Island.

'This was the thing,' says Frankie, as a Choctaw man talks about his pride in descending from mound building people, 'this video, you know, made me decide what to study.'

'I always wanted to ask,' says Missy. She looks over at the wall above the bookcase that was Big Frankie's, where there's a map, one of Aaron Carapella's Indigenous maps of former nations, tribes, confederacies. Her sister has framed it neatly and simply, the frame painted plummy blue.

'Hey,' says Missy, 'nice frame. Getting too good for p'nubs?'

Frankie smiles at the word for thumb tack—*p'nub*—one their mother passed along from a poet named Wabegizhig—the Clear Sky. They've never known whether p'nub was a real Anishinaabek word, or just an invention.

'Look closer,' says Frankie, 'still got the holes.' The corners of the map, sure enough, bear the scars of being tacked to the wall.

They turn back to the show, quiet for a while, contentedly munching their popcorn, sipping cool mint tea.

HAZEL: BOOTS AND JOBS

It's been another day of trying to figure out what happened to Nell August.

Another useless day. I walk down the street, and find the skin between my shoulder blades crawling. Every sound, every motion caught in the corner of my eye, sets my nerves humming anew. It's the smells more than anything that overwhelm me. I'm out of smokes. I know I have more at home, so I figure I can wait. Still, days like these, I remember why I smoke.

How can people live in this level of reek without something to cut the smell?

But then I suppose it's the den thing; to every badger, their sett smells of home and safety. I've come to equate home and safety with a tobacco-dulled damp tang of gasoline, diesel overtones, the chalky alkalinity of concrete wet and dry, a thousand kinds of domestic exhaust, and the warm solicitude of bakeries, restaurants, grocery stores.

But sometimes, like now, there is just too much of it, and no tobacco to filter it out.

I click along, listening to my own boot heels—*human is the form that wears shoes.*

I remember, as soon as the thought comes, that that is only a regional truth.

I remember the theatre workshop I took because it was an optional add-on to the arts-option political theatre class I'd had to take back when. The visiting African political theatre specialist chided us all for using shoes as character shorthand. We'd thought we were clever, with our pile of shoes, which we'd put on as movement masks, to differentiate between hero and antagonist, powerful and weak, rich and poor.

'What would you use in the communities I know? There, nobody has shoes.' His handsome black face had shone with disdain and vision. 'You would come in and present yourself as a worker for justice, as a teller of truth, and not recognize the privilege you flaunt with your different shoes scenarios?"

I had left that workshop frustrated.

No point approaching the African. He wouldn't know why I was different from anyone else there. He wouldn't see beyond my surface, not so different from the other well-fed upper-middle-class kids who still thought Africa was all charity-cases and corrupt cannibal kings. In those days, Africa was in turmoil, sure. But if I'd said, 'I get it,' he'd assume that I was one of those fawning groupie-girls who were only on campus for kicks until they got their Mrs. degree. No, I gave him a level glare and stalked out, clicking my good boot heels, thinking 'Fuck you.'

In Amiskwaciy, everyone has some sort of shoes. It's too fucking cold not to. No shoes? You're dead. And I had seen people who had fuck all else; but however crappy, they had shoes.

He must have heard my self-righteous internal rant. He followed the click of my boots to the student bar, bought me a drink, and we lasted all of the weekend. I have always known, good footwear makes the difference. I at least taught my girls this, to hunt good shoes, quality, well-made and unobtrusive. We're still friends, online, Minkah and me.

He's back in Ghana, married, a bunch of kids, assistant dean at his old university in Accra.

He's about the only one who, when I told him I was doing work as a Private Investigator, didn't say it sounded flaky.

I've kept him posted, via email (so old-fashioned), since he helped me solve my first case.

Fact is, I hadn't set out to become a P.I.

I'd been doing transcription, medical and court, two separate things. And then one day, I noticed something in some notes I was transcribing for a doctor, and it rang a bell. The doctor was talking about a person in the court documents I was transcribing.

I had to think through the ethics, so I emailed Minkah. He called me back right away, and we crunched through the issues involved, and he helped me make the obvious decision. I just had to figure out what FOIPP—Freedom of Information and Protection of Privacy—rules applied, and then Minkah helped me create a path for getting the information where it needed to go. It cracked the case, and an Indigenous family who'd otherwise have been screwed found justice.

I was hooked.

I kept my transcriptionist jobs, and as far as most people know, that's what Hazel LeSage does. But, discreetly, word spread, and since then, I've become a resource, mostly for Indigenous folks in Amiskwaciy, despite me never setting out to be a Professional Indian. Like I said, I'm only half-qualified for that. But it turns out that being able to accurately unscramble doctor's hand writing, decipher various kinds of shorthand, and pay attention to what I read, are all pretty good qualifications for being a Private Investigator.

No, I don't have a license. That's something Minkah's been on me about—when am I going to get a proper license?

'And this is an African telling you this, Hazel,' he said, last time we talked. 'Think about it. We are the ones with the history of unlicensed just about everything.'

He laughed, his handsome face crinkling up. The years had been good to Minkah, and he could make jokes about the African corruption jokes that used to make him so angry, back when he was here.

I don't have an answer for him, except to say that he's not here now, and that's no kind of an answer to give a good friend; but the truth is, I don't see how it would help me help the kind of people I help, when they need to figure out what happened when things go wrong. So, I don't have a P.I. license.

I do have a werewolf. And at least now, I have a werewolf with a job.

And also, he's not asking me to take him for walks. What was that about, anyway? Now, apart from our 'missions' when he gets his dog on and we prowl the drag, scaring away creeps, he just puts on his coat—Josh's old coat until he got his first paycheque and picked out his own at the Value Village—and goes for his own damn walk.

It's funny how you get used to things, though. I tell myself that hey, after all, this is what we Indigenous Folk are meant to believe, that shape-shifting is just a normal thing that happens. It's in all our old legends. But what would all the Traditional people in town say if I told them? It's the first time I can think of a good reason to be relieved Big Frankie is gone. His former crowd, the academics and urban neo-traditionalists, do not tempt me at all to go and ask them, *What do I do with a legend come to life, living in my house, mooching off me?*

It's like anything else, you look at the practical things, and solve them. The talking dog has a job, but he wants to live as a man, too. So, get the man a job.

'Spider—'

'Jim.'

'Jim,' I say, over coffee one day, 'you're not a bad cook, and the place has never looked better, but don't you think it's better if you … get a job?'

There. I'd said it. It's out there.

'I mean, I can see a few obstacles…'

He nods. 'Uh huh. ID. CV. References?'

'Well, do you… have those things?'

He blows a little air out his lips. Taps his slim fingers on the table.

'It shouldn't be a hard question,' I say, trying to be neutral, trying not to crack wise about how he ought at least to buy his own dog food. He doesn't eat it anyway, just keeps a canister in the kitchen, and nobody's ever looked to see if the level changes. If the girls are coming over, he'll put out a bowl. I say nothing, though. For once, it's obvious to me that I should just wait quietly and listen.

'I—' he sighs deeply. 'Hazel… I do have those things. Not here. But I do.'

'Where?'

'Back… back home.'

'Which is?'

He frowns. 'East.'

'Look, what's the big secret? I mean, I know your *big* secret. You're a shape-shifter. What's more secret than that?'

He looks at me, his yellowish eyes sad. 'I wish I could tell you,' he says, 'but… look, it's not that simple. Now that I'm here, there are things… things it's better if you don't know.'

'Well, you're living in my house. Don't you think that gives me some right to know a few basics? Where you're from, why you're here, what's your profession apart from Canine Crusader?'

He frowns, shakes his head, looks kind of foggy and lost for a moment.

'I used to… well…' he looks really uncomfortable, itchy in the sport shirt that's a little too loose.

'Can I just ask you to trust me, for now?'

'Trust you?'

'I'm here because I was sent here. I was told that you would come get me, and that you are the person who will help me… do what I have to do.'

'Look,' I say, 'I've been patient—'

'I'll get a job and pay rent.'

'It's not about the money. I shouldn't even have to explain that to you.'

We'd talked some about this, Jim and I. As soon as I found him human, we started comparing notes. Sort of. And then we'd sort of stopped, by tacit agreement, trying to unravel it further. Or someone would arrive at the door, or a phone call, or … anyhow, turns out we neither of us know how to talk about the weirder aspects of all this.

***

He runs a thin hand through his hair. 'I'm sorry. Sometimes, I don't even believe I'm really here. I ... should just leave.'

'*No.*' I'm surprised how fast and adamant my voice is, how it echoes.

We stare at each other. I don't have any explanation, but looking at him sitting at my table, I just know, in that same stupid fatalistic way, that if I couldn't get rid of him before, I sure can't now.

He clears his throat. 'I do have money, by the way. I got my sister to transfer some.'

He has a sister?

'You have a sister?! Is she...'

'A werewolf? Not that I know of,' he gives a thin smile. 'You don't want to cross her at her moon-time, mind you. But no, far as I know, she's... okay.'

Suddenly, I remember one of the cousins, screwing up the punchline of a stupid kid joke. And I tell him about it.

'It's supposed to be, '*I used to be a coyote, but I'm all right noooooowww!*' but she said, '*I used to be a coyote, but now I'm okaaayyyy!*'

We both start laughing, and if it sounds a bit hysterical, well, what do you expect? Why wouldn't a werewolf have family back home, just like anyone else in this globalized world?

***

Within a week, he's got a job, over at the local Rec Centre, as a personal trainer. Seriously?

'Seriously?' I look him up and down. I mean, he's not like the usual personal trainer type—not like Josh, for instance, all conspicuous muscles. I suppose he does have a sinuous strength, a wiriness... I give my head a shake.

'Your eyes were stuck,' he quips. And winks at me. He's changed, somehow. Smoothed out, more at ease. I guess I can understand that. After all, he has a job now, a legitimate cover story, and aside from flaming visions of blood and fangs in the night, I can almost pretend he's just a guy who lives with me. So of course, he feels more at ease now that he's got a job.

But I'm not sure I like this new attitude, this cocky energy. It's way too familiar. I liked him better humble and confused. So bite me. I needed some kind of upper hand, didn't I? Wouldn't you want some leverage if you had a shape-shifter in your house? And now, well, I see that I've made a tactical error. He has his own money, like a wife squeezing out from her husband's thumb in the olden women's lib days… I stop myself. I'm not some oppressor.

Okay, I used to keep him on a collar and a chain, but still… his choice.

Nope. That just sounds kinky, now. There is nothing I can say.

'Congratulations.' I keep my voice neutral.

'You can come for a session with me sometime,' he says, quirking an eyebrow at my midsection, 'Special rate.'

'Go to hell,' I reply, 'Special rate.'

The memory makes me smile as I click along, though I might kick anyone who accused me of looking forward to seeing my were-wolf when I got home.

MISSY: LEGENDS

After the episode, Missy turns to Frankie.

'So, all those stories turn out to be true. The ones that tell about how we used to have really sophisticated societies, 'til somehow we went wrong. Something happened, we had to migrate, and that's how we came north?'

'Yeah. Also how the Aztecs went south. I keep wondering if it might be something like a big earthquake, down in the Gulf of Mexico, that sent tidal waves up the Mississippi, wiped out the shoreline societies.'

'There's no evidence for that, though, right?'

'So far, I don't know if anyone's looking.'

'*Chalice and the Blade*, eh?' Missy nods at the shelf, at an old red-jacketed book, a gift from Sandra which they both read at some point. 'Nobody will find what nobody thinks to look for.'

'And they won't look for the evidence, because they can't get their heads around pre-Columbian Indigenous folks as sophisticated urban scientist types, studying the sky.'

''Cause that would mean admitting the whole 'Noble Savage' thing was rank propaganda.'

They sigh, somehow contented. Familiar conversations, cradling them down through the years, first heard from the older generation, now somehow still the framework for their own investigations of the world.

In Frankie's case, she's well into her Masters' studies, presenting papers on pre-Industrial Indigenous societies, looking into linguistic connections that revealed little known aspects of life in old Turtle Island.

As for Missy? Frankie slides a look at her sister, who is frowning at the screen. *Nothing*, she supposes, *like knowing you had something that was taken from you.* If we'd really never been anything but ignorant savages, colonial history wouldn't be so unjust. And Missy is the queen of burning against injustice.

Missy turns to her now.

'Hey Frank,' she says, 'you know, all these stories, they've turned out to be true, right?'

Frankie nods. 'More and more evidence says so. And I certainly hope so, for the sake of my career.' She says 'cah-reah' and touches her fingertips to her décolletage, like an ancient movie star.

***

I consider Missy and Frankie are dreaming awake, dreaming through this thing they watch. Fillem. Move ye. Dock you men tary. Kind of a Between. Humans. Their own eyes can't see me, but they can make these tools that show them things they cannot see. How do they know what is real?

***

'Well,' says Missy, 'Do you suppose that means other old stories are true, too?'

'Which ones you thinking of?'

'Well… shape-shifters, for example.'

Frankie considers. 'How would that work?'

'Well,' says Missy, 'you know our DNA is really close to other animals—like 98% match with chimps, for instance. And then there's corn—' Missy nods at the screen, where Robbie narrates on into another episode. 'Origin stories about corn, when you look at them, talk about how Corn Mother—'

'Gave her body,' finishes Frankie.

They've both talked with Sandra, in the garden, and listened to her speculations about the relationship between people and corn, which grew up along with humans for thousands of years and cannot reproduce without human intervention.

***

They are my fillem. They are my move ye. I consider when these girls watch and talk, could they see me? Sweetness of gel-ah-toe. Sadness. They more need to see him. I consider Maengan is safe with them. I reach and pull his heart strings.

***

A slight breeze interrupts them, tinkling the ceramic mobile Frankie hangs by her kitchen window. They exchange glances, each thinking the other must have opened the window.

'Anyhow,' says Missy, 'maybe shape-shifters are just born with, I don't know, an extra gene, one that allows them to switch the arrangement of the rest of their genome, like switching channels on a radio.'

'Tune into Chimpanzee,' says Frankie in a fake announcer voice. 'Only, of course,' she adds in her natural voice, 'nobody goes into chimp around here, because chimps aren't endemic.'

'Yeah,' says Missy, 'exactly. The ones who live here with us, who share this environment and are made up literally of the same building blocks of food, and water from the same watersheds, same minerals, same environmental stressors, those are the ones we have enough in common with so we can switch into them.'

'Makes sense,' says Frankie. 'People turn into bears, or ravens, or—'

'Wolves and dogs' says Missy. 'Think of the stories we used to hear. Mostly shape-shifters are canine, right? Makes sense, because we've been symbiotic with dog-kind for longer than with any other animal.'

'And that's worldwide,' says Frankie. 'Makes you wonder about the known history of dog domestication. Is it the case that we and dogs took up together in one place only, and then the practice spread, with the single-origin theory migration of humans?'

'Or is it,' says Missy, 'that where you get humans, you get dogs? Like Sandra and that other book, did she ever offer it to you? She was all into it a while ago—*Mycelium Running*—about how Western science was suddenly catching on to the significance of mushrooms, of fungi as communication networks.'

She puts down her bowl, brushes bits of husk off her chest.

'Hey,' says Frankie, 'don't get that on my couch.'

'I'll clean it up, don't worry,' says Missy, and returns to her theme, ostentatiously picking husks off the couch as she talks, flicking them into the bowl.

'So anyway, look at it. Where you get humans, you get dogs, right?'

'Umhm.' Frankie is slower to finish her popcorn.

'You also get werewolves.'

'Werewolves?'

'Yeah. There's werewolves in stories all around the world. What if they're still around?'

Frankie considers. 'I suppose it's possible. But where? And what would they be doing? And,' she continues, warming to her theme, 'Are they Indigenous werewolves? European style? Or Métis? Or even more mixed now, globalized like us. What do they call werewolves in Jai Hind? In Zhong Guo? in Africa? How do they understand shape-shifting, scientifically?'

'What a weird thing that would be to study, eh?,' says Missy, the epidemiologist in training.

'Fortunately,' Frankie replies, unfolding from her spot and stretching up like a cat, 'I have my work laid out for me, or I might be tempted to switch fields of inquiry. But it's certainly intriguing in an oddball way. Pee break,' she adds, unselfconscious, and glides away.

Missy sits frowning. *What would werewolves be doing here, indeed? What would bring them to her city? Would they prey on the most vulnerable?*

She scoffs to herself. It's not something to say aloud, except to

Frankie. Anyone who took her seriously—and who would?—would only suppose she was making excuses for the human predators they knew were taking a toll on the abandoned and outcast. In her mind, she sees the skinny street girls, like underfed yearling rabbits, cornered, not by psychotic humans, but by literal wolves, all hair and teeth. But didn't everyone know wolves hunt for food, not for power? The attacks on those girls who she sees in Emergency are about sex and power, and only a human would hunt like that. Then again, a werewolf is a human invention. She needs Frankie to hurry up. She needs to pee. And she feels another kind of pressure, in her mind.

She thinks about some of the wounds she's seen on the girls who come into Emergency. She can't get over Maengan's reaction when she told him about it.

'Like they've been savaged by wolves,' she'd said, unlocking her bike, full of the need to ride hard.

And he'd said, as if he knew anything about it, 'Wolves would never do that.'

'How would you know?' she'd snapped.

'Because I—'

'You *what*?! You're an actual wolf, Maengan? Is that what you're telling me?!'

He'd flinched away from her, spun around, walked away. She'd stood gaping.

Smart, Miranda.

She really needs to pee. *Tell your sister about it.*

'Frankie,' she says, when they've both had their break, 'it was just so weird! If you'd seen his face! I mean, it was awful. I felt like I'd hit him, you know?' Frankie nods, eyes wide, and it's like they're kids again for a moment, helplessly looking at their almighty mother, bruised and shaken. Frankie sighs.

'So what happened?'

'Well, I just stood there. And then, a few minutes later, he came back.'

She had just stood there, stunned. He'd passed her one of the

Tim Horton's cups in his hands.

'It's decaf,' he'd said, with a lop-sided smile.

She'd taken her cue.

'Good thinking,' she'd said. 'Sorry.'

'It's okay,' he'd said. 'Long day. Hard work. I get it.' And they'd sat on the curb and drank their coffees, and then they'd gone for a ride. And she'd thought she'd let it go, but she sees now, telling Frankie about it, that she's still bothered by it.

'Well,' says Frankie, 'look at it this way. He came back.'

'And I yelled at him again, and left him in the Art Park.'

'Yeah,' says Frankie,' I see how that's not the best. But... maybe you had a gut feeling, you know?'

'What? Like I instinctively knew he really is a werewolf?'

'No,' says Frankie, 'although that would be fun, wouldn't it? It's more likely that you had an instinct that you just needed your own space to deal with seeing someone so damaged, and you don't know him well enough to be sure you can trust him with your vulnerabilities. But maybe he was trying to show he liked you enough to get there with you. Maybe he's like us. Maybe he meant exactly what he said—he gets it.'

Frankie sees her sister's distress, and flips her long hair, slips into a joking tone. 'Or maybe he just likes his ladies crrrrusty!'

***

Leaving Frankie's place, Missy feels conflicted still. Should she call Maengan? What would she say to him? She takes out her phone, and just as she looks at it, it rings.

'Hey,' she says, sheepish and tentative.

'Hey,' he replies. 'How you doing?' He's cautious, too.

'Um, okay.' Deep breath. 'Listen, about the Art Park... sorry, I know I was rude, and I probably wasn't fair, and I'm, well, I'm sorry, I just—'

'It's okay,' he breaks in.

'No, no it's not, really—'

'Listen, are we going to argue about that, too? If so, you want to at least hang up and walk with me and do it in person?'

She looks around, and he waves in the dark, leaned against the wall of the 7-11 on the corner. He straightens up, walks along to meet her.

'Feel like a stroll along Whyte?'

She nods, suddenly struck shy. She's not used to this. He doesn't seem angry, no radiating remnants of upset. She clears her throat, but can't think of what to say.

They walk in silence, over the railway tracks, then stop at the light. The public toilet is doing a brisk business, and the sidewalks are lively. 'So…' she tries.

He raises his hand, puts it just briefly on her shoulder.

'Look, Miranda,' he says, giving her a straight look, 'I mean it, no worries. I get it. You care about things. That's a thing I really like about you.'

He drops his hand, looks away. The light changes.

***

They walk on, through what passes for darkness in late spring, not talking, but more at ease, past the Wee Book Inn with its windows bright and old-fashioned looking, the various boutiques closed for the night, the dessert places, bistros and bars doing a brisk trade as people make the most of the short, mortal season of warmth. The balmed air stinks slightly of exhaust and warm pavements exhaling.

'Hey,' says Maengan, as they come up on the old St. John's Hospital. 'You hungry? I could sure go for some sushi.'

''Kay,' says Missy, and they turn in at Tokyo, the noodle shop sharing ground floor commercial space with a pottery studio, a hair salon and an all-night Indian Buffet. Around and above them, the old brick building seems to sigh contentedly, retired from its long history of life-and-death into noodle vending premises.

They get a seat by the window. Missy makes a point of pulling out her chair, not waiting to see if he'll feel he ought to do it for her.

'Love these chairs, eh?' says Maengan, pulling back his own. They look IKEA-light, blond wood and black metal, but they're made of iron and bottom-heavy. 'So,' Maengan says, once they've ordered, 'tell me your Sushi Origin story.'

She tilts her head. He grins.

'Okay, then,' he says, 'I'll go first. I'd just come down off the Rez, was in Ottawa for a youth conference, and we went out to the By-ward Market—ever been?'

'Nuh-uh.'

'It's like Strathcona Farmers Market, all artisanal cheese and bricks, but even cheesier. They've even got horse and carriage guys clopping around. You've been to Ottawa, right?'

'One time, with Mom and Dad, but I was tiny. I have no idea what it's like, don't remember anything except that it was frickin' cold. I just wanted to stay in the hotel, and they dragged me all over to look at sights.'

'Yeah, it's cold in winter, eh? Way colder than here. You know, we have the coldest capital in the world, except—'

'Ulan Baatar.' She stops short. Most people she knows glaze over when she starts on geography. Even if he started it, he didn't do it so she could show off her knowledge. She shouldn't have cut him off. She's ready to be exasperated and shut herself down. But Maengan just smiles.

'Don't you love that name?'

She smiles back. It's a complicated thing, this joy in geography, and the sad understanding that most of their contemporaries don't know, and don't want to know, about Ulan Baatar.

It's after ten when they leave.

'Where to now?' says Maengan. 'You up for a stop at the Wee Book Inn?'

They stroll back down the avenue, the night air swirling around them like a friendly dog, brushing their bare limbs. She steals a glance at him. He's not like other guys, Maengan. There's no sense of tension crawling in her belly, wondering whether he's going to make some kind of move. He's just there, easy and calm, a warm presence. He's still relatively new in town, but he acts like he's always gone for sushi here, always hung out in the Wee Book Inn.

She catches sight of them in a window. She's walking with this tall, seriously good looking, head turning guy, and he's not even looking at their reflections, or at the heads turning. She wonders what he's thinking.

'Hey,' he says, as they wait for a light, 'do you think I could rock a man-bun?'

She stares, open-mouthed. And he laughs, that easy, light-hearted laugh. She feels her heart skip. 'Seriously,' he says, rolling his ponytail up as high on his head as he can and giving her a probing look.

She's saved from answering by the busker on the opposite corner, who chooses that moment to kick into a Beatles cover, loud and slightly out of tune, but provoking a passing gaggle of college boys to join in.

Maengan drops his hair. 'Why is it, Missy,' he says, 'that people are still playing the Beatles? Still singing along? Do they learn that stuff in the womb, or what?'

'Maybe it's genetic by now,' says Missy. 'The Beatles gene.'

'Dominant, or recessive?'

'God, definitely recessive, if I get a choice.'

'What? You don't like the Beatles?'

'Mah. John Lennon was a wife-beater.' She doesn't have time to fear she's done it again, too serious Miranda.

'And he sang like one, too,' says Maengan. 'I never liked his tone. But you have to grant that Paul was okay, right?'

'Hmm. Okay,' she says, feeling a bubble of glee, 'but what about George?'

'Spiritual George?' says Maengan, and he says it like it's a title, adds in a singsong, 'Spiritual George, the mystical little Beatle.'

It's something Frankie would do, and Missy, astonished, hoots out loud.

'But Ringo?' says Maengan, 'I always feel like if any of them were a Secret NDN, it would be Ringo.'

'Not Spiritual George?'

'Nope,' he says categorically, 'Ringo for sure. I mean, look at his name. Ringo is bad enough, but add the Starr? Got to be. It's practically a Secret NDN shout-out.'

'Oh my God,' says Missy, 'is that why Kinny Starr is Kinny Starr? Is she his secret daughter?'

They reach the Wee Book Inn and enter laughing.

***

Maengan can show them all he is. It is a balancing. Heart lights together. See how I help.

HAZEL : THE REAL WORK

Now, I'm nearly home. I can see my salmon house through the gaps in the fruit bushes this end of the street. I click my heels hard on the sidewalk again, to give myself a rhythm by which to think. *Click.* Just for this moment, forget about what happened. *Click.* Think about the Augusts. *Click.* Maybe call Minkah. *Click.* No, no way am I dragging him into this. *Click.* Not Sandra. *Click.* Who would believe this? *Click. Click.* Nothing.

I click my heels firmly. It's not working. I cannot shake the memory, the horrifying thing. I have to find Spider and find out whether—find out *what* happened. I'm sweating, and it's not that warm, and I'm not being chased, but I can't help walking faster. I just have to know.

At home, it's almost anticlimactic to open the door and see him curled up on the sofa, brushy tail tucked over his nose, eyes half-open like some sleepy hungover party guest.

'Jim.' I say it on a puff of breath. He doesn't move.

'*Dog.*' Now it comes out as a growl, and he sits up suddenly. His eyes lock on to mine. And he looks—what? sad? desolate? almost unrecognizable in his anguish.

Close the door, he says in my head. *Just close the door, Hazel.* He sounds weary, ancient.

I close the door, but I don't go nearer. I stand, tall as I can, my boots digging into the floor, rooted. I force myself to bring my hands from behind my back, drop them at my side. The silence hangs between us now. My heart is a hammer. I don't know what to say, come to it.

You knew, he says, *but you didn't know. You couldn't.*

He blinks, and his eyes look bottomless, all the canine power of abject sorrow concentrated now in his gaze bent on me.

'You—'

Yes.

'No.'

Yes. It's real and it's true and it happened.

I find I'm shaking and one hand has crept back to the door handle.

No, he says. *Please, stay.*

I shake my head.

He gets up and I shrink back, thunk, against the door. But he slinks around the corner, out of sight. I close my eyes, squeeze shut my ears, nose, everything.

Hazel. Now I hear another voice in my head.

Grandma?

Hazel.

I smell smudge, and I hear her voice.

Listen, my girl. You asked for this, and now you have to see it through.

I can't.

You can.

I just can't. But the smudge smell grows stronger, and I gulp a little, suck a little in. It flows, cool and green and real, down into my lungs. I can do this.

Yes, you can.

I open my eyes.

Spider has gone human, and Jim's sitting on the floor, burning smudge. His long bare feet seem to gleam against the bare wood, his hands resting on his knees, and his head bent.

'I—' I clear my throat, try again. 'I—'

'You're angry.' He says it quiet and clear.

'You're goddamn right I'm angry!'

Suddenly the rage and fear come roaring out of me, and I stomp across the floor. But he sits still, looking up at me, the smoke wafting between us like a talisman. I draw up short and stand there, heaving like a romance heroine's bosom.

'Sit?' he offers, without any overtone of irony at all.

I pace, instead, away from him, around the room, *like a caged animal*. Damn, even my inner dialogue is in on this.

'Please?' he asks again, his human voice slightly raspy. 'Come and sit. We'll talk it out.'

'Just like that?'

'Just like that,' he sighs. 'Or the best we can, anyway.'

And slowly, because there is nothing else to do, I stop pacing and circle back to him. I sit down. He combs the smoke over his head again. I do the same for myself.

'You want to know what happened.'

'I was there.'

'You were there. But you want to know if what you saw, what you heard, was real—' he reaches a hand toward me, a hand shackled in silver rings. 'Know this, Hazel,' he says, softly, 'know that I'm really, really sorry. It's brutal. It's the hardest thing.' He locks eyes with me, and I see into him, see that it really is true. He is weeping.

'But then,' I say, 'why?' *Why did he do that? What exactly did he do?*

'I don't know why—'

'You know!'

'No! I don't! I didn't—'

He gives himself a shake, takes a few deep breaths.

'Look, Hazel. You knew I was a shape-shifter when you took me in. You went with me all those times before. You *laughed* when I scared that sicko behind the Hungarian deli. What did you think I could've done different?!'

'Why were you there at all?'

'I had to go there.'

'Why?!'

He looks around, blows out his breath. Looks down at his hands.

The sage bundle flares, exhales more smoke. I know why. Narrative imperative.

Like when you see a gun on stage or onscreen, sooner or later, it will be used. You have a werewolf. What do you think he'll do to a human, if it comes down to it? I nod. I knew he might kill, and I'd thought I was okay with it.

'But I had no idea about the worst part.'

'What's the worst part?' He asks. And I hear my grandma chuckle, a sad little noise.

'The worst part?' I shake my head. But he sees me. He knows. I might as well admit it.

'The worst part is, I'm glad that man is dead. He deserved to die. You can't suffer a monster like that to live.'

THE THING

It happens like this.

It is a dark and calm night. We are patrolling, Spider and I, the shabbier side of 95th, along a broken alley. We've narrowly missed being clipped by the school teacher in his red car. 'Fucker!' I hiss. I know him, I know he's drunk—sorry, *impaired*, which is what good white middle class drivers are, when the poor are drunk.

Never mind him, grunts Spider.

He's standing stock still, head up, ears flagged full out. A truck has pulled into the parking pad behind a garage, half a block down. A girl is getting in, her skirt hitching up as she hops up on the running board, then reels her trailing leg up into the cab. I can't hear their conversation, but I know Spider can.

Shit, he says, *Action time.* He wheels about, pulling hard, a bad dog on a sudden scent. I curse mildly, partly out of fear, partly out of annoyance that he's yanked my arm half out the socket. *Come on, come on!* he urges. *Blondie's Roadhouse Motel.*

Cold sweat instantly cloaks me and I break into a run.

'I can't run all the way there!' I gasp. *The car*, he snaps in my mind. As we turn onto our block, Spider suddenly swings wide, bolts between my legs from behind, trips me onto him, and before I can catch my breath to curse him, has made the 300 yards to the car and shaken me off. *Go! Go! Go!*

I fumble with locks, climb in, open the passenger door and he flows in beside me.

How do you know? I ask, as we bomb along just over the limit. I'm thankful, suddenly, for the times he's made me practice driving routes to the various hotels and motels in our end of town, and the endless walks, keeping track of roadwork and other potential obstacles on our general routes.

Smell it on him, he says. *And don't you remember? He's been grooming that girl.*

I do remember now, seeing that truck at least twice, and that particular skinny-legged street girl getting in. Both times, they stayed in the alley. After, she climbed down, adjusted herself, and just walked away. He sat there idling, watching her depart, then drove away. Funny, I remembered now that he wasn't a great driver. The truck seemed too big for him.

'Where?'

Blondie's Roadhouse Motel. I don't ask how he knows.

I don't have a super car, and I am not a daring driver, but we make good time to Blondie's. Its parking lot is crammed with big pick-ups, the big red one parked among them. Before I can open the door, Spider has clawed and shouldered his way out. I'll notice later that he's ripped the paneling. That'll cost.

But now, I pull down my toque and I follow my dog. He is that darker shadow slicing his way across the darkness of the lot, coming to rest against a ground floor door, round the back, farthest from the lamp posts, farthest from the CCTV cameras. We are not the only things lurking in the dark.

I am twenty feet away when his shadow ripples, drops, rises back up into human form.

Time has slowed down, slowed to a crawl, and I swim uselessly against the gelid stream, inexorably swept toward him.

How the fuck is this happening?! I want to scream, but I can't. There's a scraggy clump of cedar next to the window, and I drift in the tractor beam of horror until I fetch up against the branches, feel them scratching me, holding me still.

Jim knocks on the door. He is naked.

I can somehow see both door and window, but I don't want to

look.

I can hear the TV inside, some inane cop procedural droning with its canned music toward its formulaic inevitability, a little too loud for seduction.

Spider knocks harder. What the fuck will he say to the man?

But it is the girl who opens the door, and she just steps back, completely shocked to see a naked man at the door. She stares at him wild-eyed, then snaps her head around to the man on the bed. He has stripped down, I see, to an improbable white undershirt. His shoes, still on, gleam dimly of polish. He had pulled the blanket over his naked groin, but has now dropped it in astonishment, and is staring, dink out, at this incredible sight.

'Sorry, man,' says Spider, pushing in, shoving the door closed with his backside, leaning against it in feigned relief. He scrabbles with his hands, knocking a corner of curtain open, flailing to cover his own privacy, and the girl recovers first, throws him something. The man's shirt, it turns out.

How am I seeing this? No way is this the view from the crack in the curtains. I shake my head. Vision blurs, but it settles, clearing like some caricature old TV screen.

What is this? Am I seeing through your eyes?!

Shh. Just stay quiet.

'I, uh,' Jim wheezes, 'I got in over my head. Crazy chick. Crazy! Took my wallet, my clothes.' He has one hand up, touching the collar hanging loose around his neck. 'She uh, she likes… you know… stuff… but Jesus! She flipped!'

The man in the bed has become urbane now, visibly puffing himself back up after the first shock and fright. He has assessed the situation. This stranger, not a threat, is a man humiliated by a woman. A potential ally and under his power, standing there naked in nothing but a dog collar. The man in the bed is clearly high.

'My shirt,' purrs the man, reaching out for it. With an all-boys-together grin, he directs the girl, 'Doll, get the man a towel.' The girl leaps to obey, brings back a motel bath sheet, holds it out at arm's length. She doesn't quite avert her eyes as he switches coverings, but her own are frightened, not lusty.

✳✳✳

Her thoughts are clear as words. *This could go any number of ways. Will these men hurt her? Will the stranger leave?* She is measuring his arousal, because that is the measure of her odds of leaving this room either twice as rich, or leaving with nothing but bruises and maybe a couple broken teeth, the men having her utterly at their mercy.

I can see she is no fool, and I know she has been with this man on the bed before.

The stranger, she thinks, *he is clearly kinky and God alone knows what he's on. The bigger danger, though, is the man in the bed, who has affected to take out a cigarette, even though there is a big no-smoking sign over the bathroom door.*

And me? I am frozen into place against the scruffy cedar, as if paralyzed. They cannot see me there in the dark. I don't understand how I can see them.

The TV cop music turns ominous. As if it is his own personal sound track, the man in the bed smiles.

'Well, stranger, what's your name?'

'Bill,' says Spider.

The man says, 'Bill, I'm Dave. This here is Doll.'

I get a better look at Doll. She has the underfed look of a runner, or a user, and her dark brown hair is softened with cheap pinkish highlights at the end. *'Every woman should dye her hair,'* I suddenly, improbably hear the voice of Ted the Hairdresser from the old TV show *What Not to Wear.* Doll must have seen that episode, too. She wears a short skirt and knee-high boots, both in cheap, slickish material; but her blouse is feminine and shaped by darts and vents into something that makes the most of her slight figure. It's not even open too far, just enough to show a flash of silver, a Playboy Bunny pendant basking against her dingy skin.

She looks nearly normal, nearly like some high-spirited teen. And she might be anywhere from fifteen to forty, really, face stretched tight over good bone structure, her lips full and faintly shimmering. She looks like so many young brown girls, and she looks like I should know her.

'Now look, Bill,' says Dave, 'Doll and I were having a private evening here.'

'I, uh,' says Bill/Jim with a carefully calculated stall, 'I just don't know what to do. I don't want to go to the cops...' he tugs at his collar, shakes his head slightly in embarrassment, 'I don't want to—'

'No, no, no worries,' says Dave, having made his decision. This could have its advantages. 'You're clearly a man of the world, Bill; and you're among friends here. Isn't he among friends, Doll?'

Doll hesitates, looking back and forth, eyes a little too wide.

'Come on, Bill, you look like you could use a drink,' says Dave, and waves Bill over to a seat beyond my line of sight. All I can see is Doll and Dave now.

On the dresser beside Doll sits a briefcase, buffed like Dave's shoes. Man of means. There is a bottle of Canadian beside it, two glasses already used. Cheap booze.

'Get the man a drink, Doll,' says Dave. She steps into the bathroom, brings a third glass. He takes the glass, waves her back into the bathroom. 'And Doll, freshen up a bit,' he adds. She takes the hint and closes the door, but I hope she is pressed up against it listening.

Dave pitches his voice below the TV, I can't hear.

'What you got in mind?' says Bill/Jim, letting the creepy intrigue trickling up into his tone. Him, I can hear.

Dave lets his fingers trail across his own throat, lets one eyebrow quirk. Now I hear him, too 'And enough cash for you to get sorted, get your stuff back. Like nothing ever happened.'

Bill must have nodded. Dave nods too, smiles as Doll reemerges. She gets ice from the mini-fridge, makes them all stiff drinks, passes glasses around, then stands for a minute, knees slightly trembling, between the two men. Calculating her chances.

I see through a red haze rising.

He grabs the girl by both arms. She squeals.

Shh, he murmurs, *close your eyes. Do it, Doll.*

I am aware that my own eyes are already squeezed tight, but I can still see through Spider's view. I hear rustling as Dave rises from the bed.

The girl is shuddering, struggling slightly against Spider, making little noises like a kitten, like a blind baby.

I promise you, it is okay. Play along.

Out loud Jim says, 'Take it easy, Doll, we're all friends here. Right, Dave?'

Dave stands beside the bed, sweating in his undershirt and brown shoes. He's getting a bit excited, his face flushing. He rubs his nose.

'You like a little blow? Coke,' he corrects, with a nervous chuckle, stepping carefully around the end of the bed. 'Or I've got blitz, meth, what's your candy?'

Jim steps back a half step, Doll moving with him. She looks at Dave, her little chest heaving. She tries a little flick of her ombré ends.

'Yeah, a little blow,' she lisps, 'and another little blow…'

Dave chuckles. 'Whatever floats your boat. Me, I'm plenty high enough for whatever.'

Jim lets go of Doll and she steps away, while he slides over to where Dave has laid out a couple of lines on his briefcase lid.

Dave, all gentleman, rolls up a bill and hands it to Doll. As she bends her dark ombré mane over the line, he presses against her from behind. When she's done, he steps back, turns her by the shoulders, presses her down to her knees. She giggles as he bends over her, with a groan, to suck up his own line. Then Dave waves a hand to indicate another little leather case sitting on the gross little bedside table.

Time is too slow. Trees shake. I shake.

Jim steps over, as if this is a perfectly ordinary situation, and opens a little brown leather case, no bigger than a shaving kit. Inside, I can see braided leather coiled up, and something long and gleaming, a flexible serrated blade.

Shaking in the trees.

Doll has slid Dave's shorts back off him. Jim turns and sees Dave's eyes have a wide, glazed heat in them, his voice husky when he says, 'Hold on there, Doll. Hey, Jim, you want to prime the pump first? Get on over here.'

Doll is not kneeling, I see, she's crouched in a squat, her long legs shaking.

Dave leans across the bed, picks up the brown case, puts it down on the near side of the bed. 'Go on, buddy,' says Dave. 'Or do you need a little more inspiration?'

I see Dave reach into the brown bag, pull out the braided leather, a long thong with metal glinting in the loose fringed end. He wraps the thong once around his hand, chuckling.

The red haze surges hard into my eyes, blinding me. The last thing I see is Doll's glazed face up close, as Dave suddenly grabs her, pulls her in.

To Her! RAGE! RED FIRE! Claws! Fangs! Screaming. Blood. Something flying, falling hard, wet red destruction, a body ripped into pieces.

Through red haze, I see Spider whirling, all hair and teeth, wind and hair and blood everywhere. I see nothing. Hearts hammering. My heart, theirs, a tidal roar of anger. 'Justice!'

The door flies open, a figure wrapped in bloody cloth reels out. The girl, alive.

'*Go!*' I hear the voice.

'Hey!' She cries, and I startle for a moment. 'Who—?'

Is she talking to me? But no, she's looking around, completely saucer-eyed with terror, and I hear it again

—GO!—

She flinches as from a physical blow, then she's legging it away, sprinting barefoot, high heels clutched in one bloodied hand. Light flicks the ombré tips of her hair as she crosses from shadow into light, back to shadow and she's gone.

I blink.

Red. Heat. Pain. Rage. Racing heart.

I blink.

Inarticulate roaring, sobbing, ragged breath heaving.

I blink, frozen in place.

I blink, and slump against the trembling cedars.

Hazel? Spider's voice is ragged, faint, indistinct.

I move.

Hazel. Wait. He pants like a dog. *Don't open the door. Wait.*

I stand there in the dark, shaking and stunned. I don't know what to do. Sounds filter through from inside. Water running, something moving carefully.

Hazel. Get the car.

I—but—are you—? Is he—?

Hazel. Do it. Go get the car. Please. I'm okay. Please.

I walk to the car, my mind whirling, stomach churning.

I don't remember how we get home, but I remember all our windows are open; both of us sucking in the wind, breathing hard and deep, our eyes streaming. The reek of blood, and something indefinably worse, flows over us.

***

I shake. With Giizhikag, as they go away. These Giizhikag, these Giizhikens, these little ones, say nothing. Their puny arms try to cradle me, pull me into nest. But it smells, the thing left over, the body of man, above their cool green. It reeks. It is not delicious. I shake.

How could this thing dare to try to hurt Her? I shake. Giizhikens say nothing. I see Her, she got in the te-ruk with that bad man. She. I leaf back through to where and when. I see Her, one when before. She is looking for something. No. Shaking. She is waiting for him. Her heart is dark. Her screams Mother. She holds poison in her mind's eye. This man is centre of the web. He is poison bringer. She set the trap, Giizhikens. I consider this to the trees. They shake. But they say nothing.

AFTERMATH

I am living with a werewolf, and he just brutally murdered a man. And I saw it happen. Except I didn't see it happen. Not exactly. I saw *something* happen.

I can't even make my mind think about it, really.

So, I just walk, alone. And when I get tired, I come home.

Sometimes, he's there. Today, he's not. Then when he comes in, he looks as grey and tired as I feel.

Still, we don't talk. I can tell he wants to. I can tell there's more. But I can't make myself feel ready to find out what that more is.

All I know is, I am somehow involved in a murder. What will I tell my girls? That's all I can think about. My girls. I could tell them there was another girl there, and she reminded me of them. Except she didn't. She was slight, and vaguely pretty, and young, but she was old as the hills. Old like nothing I ever wanted to touch them.

Chills chase up and down my spine. And we circle each other, Spider/Jim and I, in some macabre and wordless dance. It feels worse than the worst of my teenage years, that miasma of paralytic fear that drove me to notice and return George's attentions, instead of going out to carve a place in the modern world, like my parents hoped I would.

I think of them, semi-paralyzed by racism, classism, language barriers, and I guess they also figured they had no ground to stand on from which to push me toward something other than a fresh-out-of high school marriage to a controlling asshole.

George gave my life a centre and a purpose, and he didn't seem to care that I went along with him because it kept me from confronting the terror of the future.

I grew up in the Cold War, when the threat of nuclear annihilation made a lot of things that society used to value seem awfully empty. Who cares about your position in the strata of society when, at any minute, someone could push the button? It was all over the media.

People talk about the media now, but the media then was also pervasive, maybe more so, because there wasn't any sense you could talk back to it. It was concentrated, uni-directional, and it was coming at you.

The serious media, the news media, was all about the nuclear threat.

And the pop media, that was all about nuclear annihilation, too.

Duran Duran said, *We'll be the band to dance to when they drop the bomb.* Prince sang and shrieked and wailed about going crazy in the face of the Elevator of Doom, set to bring us all down by the year 2000.

Then there was the end of the Cold War, but before we could catch our breath, we got the Gulf War.

By then, I had my girls, and was coming out of the fog of their pre-school years. Those years, they absorb you. I lost track of George, even though he was still coming home. I didn't listen to Big Frankie when he started dropping hints about maybe I should think what I might do for myself. What the fuck did he know? He was busy being a new-Trad phony Indian rockstar activist, and dumping his kid with Sandra. Pathetic Sandra, no husband, no kids, happy to putt around the farm and take care of Devin.

Sandra. Fucking Earth Mother Sandra, saying nothing, just looking so smug and superior. And when George dropped the bombshell of leaving me for Edith the Embryo?

What fucking bullshit did Earth Mother Sandra offer? That I should find some gratitude for what I did have, instead of fixating on what I'd lost. *Fuck off, Sandra.* Funny how all that runs through my mind, and all I can think is, *it's nothing compared to this. I live with a werewolf. He killed a man.*

***

I look at Jim.

He goes to work, saying nothing. Comes home, says nothing. He's taken to fixing up all sorts of little things around the house. I cannot even comment on that.

I don't know what anything means. So, I avoid him, too. And when his projects are in my way, I step around them, step around him. He doesn't even look at me. He is very careful, very polite about it, about keeping his gaze to himself. I return the favour.

One or the other of us is going to have to break the impasse, but I don't know how right now.

***

Ri ri ri roo roo roo. I consider smaller than the little song of mosquitoes in spruce branches. This when, this where bleeds green with sorrow. Heart lights, heart lights, come heart lights. I consider so small.

***

I see him slumped on the sofa now, the lamp light on his salt and pepper hair, just staring at nothing. And I feel my heart thundering. My eyes are too tight. I don't know where to start, but I have to say something.

'You! You did *something*. In the first place. You tracked me down and invaded my life—'

'No. Hazel, that was all you! You took me home. I couldn't do anything about it. I was a dog!'

'You were never just a dog!'

'You have to believe me!'

'I've seen what you are!'

'No, really,' he says, and he sits up, feet planted on the floor. 'I'm serious, Hazel. Listen to me.'

I've spent nine days running, nine days doing everything I can to ignore and avoid him, to try to shut it out. I know that he won't try to stop me if I run again. But he's been silently fixing my house. He's burned smudge for us, he's waited the whole time, just waited. I have to stop running. I look back at him. One step takes me into the room with him.

You have to think back, Hazel.

'Why are you doing this to me?'

'I'm not doing anything to you. *You* called *me.*'

'I saw a vision. My grandmother—'

'*Your* grandmother talks to you from the spirit world, and you think *I'm* controlling you? You think you don't have a choice? It's your gift, and your path. Why can't you understand, I don't know any more than you do! I came because... because I was called.' He sighs.

I hate to hear it, but I know he's right. It's been tailing me, dogging me all around town all week, little toenails of thought following me wherever I go, however much I walk.

Click.

You called him.

Click.

You heard your grandmother's voice.

Click.

You're the one who recognized him.

Click.

You started this.

'Why do you think I agreed to come with you?' He says, breaking in on my thoughts.

I look at him, and I see the moment again, there in the Humane Society, see his dog face and my own hair rising. *He knew me, like I knew him.*

'Think, Hazel. Why couldn't I just escape from that cage anytime I wanted to? Why did I have to wait for you?'

'I don't know,' I whisper.

***

I don't know anything. I used to know Josh, who smelled of Old Spice aftershave, who cradled me close. I'd breathe into the hollow of his neck, and he smelled the same, always. When did that suddenly become unbearable? Why did I throw him away, based on a vision?

Surely he'd deserved better. But I threw him out without a backwards glance, because I knew, even before I met Spider, that something was just too wrong to go on as I had been.

***

I grew up through cynical 80s, the desperate 90s, into the new millennium and its talk of an Indigenous renaissance. I'd given up on believing in any of *that* crap when Big Frankie died. I couldn't stand Sandra, her fucking Earth Mother act, as if she had a goddamn inside line to the answers—as if it hadn't all gone bad for her too, when George took the farm, when Big Frankie died.

Then the Twin Towers thing, and the whole Western World spiralling into madness. And Rigvedi's religious reforms, after the devastation of Mumbai. And the East tumbling into riots, and the deals with the new Emperor; and how here, we literally changed the shape of the land to solve a crisis. Nobody had seen it coming, everyone had said the Fox Creek Fracking earthquakes were no big deal. But we got to grips with it when we found out how explosively wrong we were, and it wasn't Yellowstone that blew out to let off the pressure, but some unmapped faultlines up in the Birch Hill kimberlite fields. We called the world to help us, and we built Up-Top. We could do all that, change so much, but not stop the women disappearing, and the girls.

Maybe I was just tired of trying to think of good reasons to stay sane in a crazy world.

I remember the night before the vision. My fists on the bark of the old pine. The night full of acrid stink. My eyes streaming. Screaming at the wind. I think maybe that's the night I went crazy.

Suddenly, I'm just crying again.

'I get it, Jim. It's me. I don't get it, but somehow, I brought you here. You're here because I asked for you. And now we're killers. That sick bastard deserved to die. If it wasn't your decision, if it was mine that made … *That*… happen, fine! I'm guilty. But fuck it. I can't let the bastards of the world just keep grinding us down to nothing.'

I'm crying. He's looking at me, sitting there with his feet planted, his hands resting ready on his thighs, neck long, eyes quiet. I cry, and he just watches me. I can't stand this. 'So tell me,' I snarl, 'Was he the only one?'

'The only—?'

'How many have you killed?'

'Hazel, I didn't—' he stops himself.

'Didn't what? Didn't keep count? Didn't know how to stop? Didn't think somebody would ask? That *I* would ask?'

'Spider,' I say, catching hold of myself, pulling it together. This is all too ridiculous. I'm not here for ridiculous. If I am crazy, I am crazy. But I will not let life just happen to me.

'Spider. I am talking to *you*. Not Jim. I want the other you. Right now.'

He makes a little noise in his throat. I see something flicker in his eyes. I stalk over to him.

'I want you to bite me.'

He leans back, as if he can escape into the sofa.

'Hazel! No!'

'Yes,' I say, leaning in over him, letting the rage bubble, 'I want you to bite me.'

He shakes his head, and shifts as far away as he can. I step in, closer. He starts to rise, but I'm in his way. He shakes his head again. 'Hazel, please, think—'

'Think it over? You were going to say that?' I feel my blood running like ice-water now, but I'm steady. 'I've been thinking it over for too long. Now,' I say, leaning down over him. 'You will do this for me.'

'That's not how it works.'

'Bullshit.'

'And I don't want to.'

'You will.'

'Don't—'

'I didn't ask if you wanted to, Dog!' I say, and I lunge at him, pinning him down, shoving my arm into his face. He struggles, jaws clamped shut. 'Bite me!'

He twists away—'NO!'

'Bite me!' He pushes, flails, grunts as my knee connects. 'Bite. Me.' He actually curls into a ball, and it stops me.

Oh my god! What am I doing?

He's curled in a ball on the sofa, rocking and creeling to himself, whining like a dog. He looks up, heaving and red eyed, as I back away. I turn, I run.

I hear him gasping behind me, 'You can't make me.'

I hate him.

MISSY: CRACKS

Missy and Maengan arrive to find Frankie already outside, sitting on the shabby fringe of grass outside her building. Somehow, with Frankie on it, the grass seems to glow with joy, perhaps reflecting her ridiculous beauty. Missy keeps side-eyeing Maengan, waiting to see his jaw drop, that slack look men get when Frankie notices them. He didn't do it before, he still doesn't.

'Hi.' Maengan speaks first, surprising her.

Frankie flows to her feet, unselfconsciously dusts her butt for stray bits of grass, and grins at them both. 'Hi yourself,' she says, and offers one golden hand. Maengan shakes it, and Frankie turns to Missy, gives her a quick hug. 'Whoo!' she whispers in Missy's ear. Missy feels her face getting hot, but Frankie, ebullient, doesn't notice.

'So, Maengan Nolan,' she says, 'Missy tells me you are from Dad's Rez? Some kind of shirt tail relative?' She glances at the sky blue shirt tucked tidily into his chino shorts, flicks an eyebrow up, and they laugh together. Missy feels her jaw go tight.

They walk now, down to the Avenue and along it, westering toward the crowds of summer people, the three of them abreast, Maengan between them. When the crowds get thick, Missy forges ahead. She doesn't want to see Maengan liking Frankie, doesn't want to get more angry at Frankie for her unselfconscious beauty, her warmth, the way everyone loves her.

'Slow down,' says Maengan behind her, and she feels his fingers catch her bare elbow. He holds on to her, eases himself up beside her, on the outside, leaving Frankie to come up on her right, and now Missy is in the middle.

In the middle, Missy feels an irreal shimmer to the summer air. A crow swoops down, just ahead of them, and plucks something tasty from the garbage barrel outside the convenience store. He perches in an elm branch, laughing as they pass. *Ha ha ha.*

Missy's not sure what's so funny, but she finds herself smiling, and clamps down on the giddy flutter.

DEVIN: SLUGS

Sandra's listening to Rodney Crowell croon about *Stars on the Water* when she hears the gate.

It's Devin, sure enough, and she lifts a slight wave to him.

'Come in, come in, I've got lemonade,' she says and lip-points to the table, unconsciously in time with the loping southern beat of the music. The same song she's loved all his life.

Devin gets a glass, drinks deeply. 'You always have a glass ready for me, Auntie. How do you know?'

Sandra just smiles. She works a while, and Devin moves in to work alongside, weeding, inspecting leaves, removing any dead and damaged ones, plucking slugs and dumping them into an empty cat food can.

'Auntie,' he says, when his can is full, 'remember that movie you loved, *Seven Years in Tibet?*'

'Mmhmm?'

'There's that scene?'

'The one with the worms, when they are building the movie theatre.'

'What do you think about that? The monks saying that those worms were once their mother, so they had to pray to them and move them by hand?'

'Well,' says Sandra, 'In a certain sense, doesn't it make sense? Energy and matter, DNA moves through the world, takes all sort of different forms. I think it's like that. We are in these bodies, we feed them with the bodies of other forms of life, we are literally made of everything else.'

'You are what you eat.' Devin nods, still not moving. 'So what about these guys, Auntie?'

She looks at him. She remembers how she felt when the German gardener just silently killed them. She never would have dared to ask about it.

'Well, you see, slugs are honourable people, in their own right. But they are in my garden. I make a choice to take responsibility for this piece of the world. I decide who lives here, to a certain extent. I can't control it all, because I don't know the relationships between all the beings, don't have the full picture. So, I wouldn't kill all slugs, because they obviously belong. I will kill them if they are in my garden, though.'

'Why not just move them, like the monks with the worms? Or like they move bears in parks?'

'Because they'll come back. And bring their relatives, and eat everything that I have pledged to protect. So, they die.'

She stretches, easing her back. And she gets up, goes to the garage. 'Hold on a sec.' She ducks in, re-emerges with a curved bottle, half-full of liquid.

'Now, if there were only a few of them, I might move them out into the alley and let them make their way. But there are too many this year for the balance I have taken responsibility of maintaining. So they die.'

She nods toward the larger can sitting on the brickwork beside the garden bed. 'Put them in there.' He reluctantly tips the can.

'It might not be a prayer like the monks but,' she says, smiling at the boy, 'they die happy.' She pours the liquid, dark red and fragrant into the can, swiftly overtopping the slugs, who slowly writhe in the wine. 'And then I tip them out, and whoever eats them gets a marinated treat.'

'Auntie,' says Devin, who's begun to pace now. She frowns. He's surely too old now to be freaked out by the killing of slugs. They've had variations of this conversation before.

'Auntie,' he starts again. 'What about people, then? Humans? Is it ever right to kill them?'

***

Sandra I consider among your squashes and strawberries. Softness, sadness, harmony. You make nests. You nest for Devin. He sees things. He counts.

***

Sandra blinks. He's pacing in earnest, tossing his head slightly, the way he does when he's intently thinking about something serious.

Sandra gets up, dusts off her jeans and ambles over to the table in the shade. 'I need a break. You?' She pours a lemonade, tops up his glass. He comes over, picks up the glass, but doesn't sit. Glass in hand, he looks around the garden. She waits. His gaze goes to the slug can, to the fruit bushes, the vegetables, the flowers.

'Do you think,' he says earnestly, turning his soft eyes on her, 'there are people who forfeit their right to life?'

'Such as?' she says.

'Well,' he says, sitting down now, 'what about, for example, those men who kill the street girls? I mean, they're like predators, you know? Do you think they deserve the death penalty?"

'Oh,' she says slowly. 'I see. Let's think about this.'

'I do,' he says, tossing his head a bit. He reaches over, plucks a mint leaf, rolls it around his fingers. 'Those girls. So many people look at them like they are slugs. So, are the killers just gardening?'

'Are they?'

He tosses his head, nibbles the leaf, keeps rolling it. The scent of crushed mint drifts faintly around them. Sandra sips her lemonade slowly.

'No. I don't think so. No. They're more like... like they think they're wolves, or what they imagine wolves are like. You know, they're thinning out the herd, preying on the weak ones at the edges.' He looks at her.

'But that only works if—' she says.

'It only works if you believe we are each other's natural prey.'

'And all around the world,' she says, nodding again, 'all around the world, we agree that it's not just business as usual to kill each other. It matters to us. It's significant. Oh,' she says, 'we make rules around it. In some places and times, it's okay to kill—war, famine, the old ways where the old ones are taken out to the ice, for the sake of the larger community—'

She picks a mint leaf herself, eyes on a bee foraging among the goldenrod. 'But those girls—and boys, too—those people are not culls. They're sad, they're hurting, broken, vulnerable, but not culls.'

Devin gulps some lemonade, tosses his head, pushes up his glasses. 'They are like lettuce. And the ones who kill them, they're like … like the slugs… so, Auntie… is it justified, do you think, to kill them?'

Sandra feels a sudden chill at the absolute stillness in him now, at the way he has stilled and focused, all of his attention on this question.

She feels suddenly very afraid, suddenly aware that she can't afford to not know the answer he's looking for. She looks around her garden. She doesn't want to breathe because she doesn't know what to say. The moment stretches, aching.

Then Devin sighs. 'See—' he says, and she can't help it, she flinches. *Is he going to tell her something she doesn't want to hear?* He is staring at her and she makes herself look back, meet his still gaze. 'What?' she barely whispers.

'Auntie, I think I've discovered something.' His eyes flicker. He's seen her fear. And in the dappled shade, he reaches out and touches her hand, lightly, as if to say, *have no fear, it's not me.* 'I think somebody is killing men who prey on the street girls.'

He tells her all he's found, and it is moving toward evening when Sandra walks him out.

'You'll call Hazel, Devin?'

He nods.

***

It's the priest who makes the phone call, the next morning. He figures that there's not much to lose doing that. After all, this woman is some kind of relative to Devin, in addition to being a Private Investigator. He feels odd, though, like he's slipped through some sort of fourth wall, and now he's on the inside of the television world, the only place he's ever thought of PIs as existing. But he's holding a card with her name and number on it, and Devin says she's real, so he punches in the numbers.

'Hazel LeSage,' she answers, her voice low-pitched, matter-of-fact.

Just like a TV show, thinks the priest.

'Hello.' He's stuck for a moment after that. He's not used to being stuck for words, and that annoys him. Perhaps it makes his voice a shade waspish. 'I'm told you're a private investigator.'

'And you would be?' there's an answering combativeness now in her tone, an edge below the dark brown of her natural timbre.

'This is Efren Mannfredsson,' he answers, swiftly deciding against the Father. 'I was given your name and number by Devin Buck.'

He goes by his mother's name, and Hazel feels an unexpected pang, today—her brother's child, but who would know?

'Devin? Really,' she says, and there's another tone in her voice now. 'Devin said to call me?'

'Yes. He…' the priest thinks fast, about all the things that people think about priests who are friends with teenage boys. 'He believes you may be able to help with a bit of a mystery.'

'Well, now,' she says. 'Tell me more.'

'Would it be alright to meet?'

'Of course.'

'Perhaps in Little Italy?'

'Where do you have in mind Mr. Mannfredsson? Spinelli's?'

He'd been thinking of one of the more quiet places where only the old men roost, thinking Spinelli's was too bright, too busy, too open. But then he thinks again; maybe bright and busy and open is just the thing.

'Spinelli's sounds good. What time might you be available?'

'I could meet you this afternoon, around 2:30, if you'd like.'

He hadn't expected such a fast turnaround, but he's not about to turn it down. 'Okay.'

'How will I recognize you?' she asks.

Fair enough.

'I'm tall. White. Middle aged. Pony tail.' He stifles a chuckle. 'Bit of a cliché walking, really. I'll have a—' he clears his throat, decides against his favourite buckskin, 'black jacket, and a blue notebook, turquoise blue.'

'Okay. I'll spot you. Two-thirty then.'

When he arrives, the big part of the lunch crowd has gone, and the afternoon idlers have the café about half full. He recognizes most of them, and most of them nod to him.

'Father,' they say in greeting, and he nods back.

'Afternoon, Jakob. Jane. Mrs. Spinelli.'

In the corner, he spies a couple of writers, hands waving, doubtless discussing *the book that will change everything*, or at least get them nominated for a city book prize. This place is popular with a certain segment of the arts crowd, and also the city-building social justice types. He spies a local journalist, waves with one eyebrow quirking, enough to keep him at bay. No reason to get the local press involved. That would be all he'd need.

The priest orders a tall Americano, and a spinach twist; flaky, oily, but substantial enough to steady him. Not that he needs steadying. He's no wilting flower.

He's been sitting for a couple minutes when he sees her. It has to be her. There is something in the way she cuts a quick glance around the place that tells him she's likely good at her job. He watches as she makes her way through the tables. He's deliberately chosen a table tucked down in the corner, where the room can be seen, but one doesn't draw too much attention. She walks right over, offers a hand.

'Father Mannfredsson, I presume?' There's a slight challenge in her tone.

She's got a certain resemblance to Devin, but it's hard to pin down. So's she, looks-wise. She could be any number of ethnicities, could pass unnoticed in a lot of places. Like his sisters. He, himself, always calls himself 'White,' because it's easier. Not because he's ashamed, but because it's a long story, about a man he left behind; a man born out of war, son of a Swedish-American boy in Manila, a Filipina nurse. Genetics—his sisters unmistakably Asian, himself a raw-boned, blue eyed guy whose genes are hidden behind his height, his eyes, the slight tilt of Virginian vowels… he lets most people think he's just another American White Guy.

HAZEL: OMISSIONS

Around here, some call Father Efren the second coming of the legendary James Holland. Mannfredsson once put up signs in the local playground, 'No Shooting Up, No Shitting, No Sex for Sale: Kids Play Here,' then patrolled swinging a mag-lite like a bat.

I get a coffee, and since he's eating, I add a croissant. I figure that makes us even. *Crumbs on both of us.*

'Crumbs on both of us,' says the priest when I take a bite, and the pastry shreds. He quirks an eyebrow and brushes phyllo off his t-shirt. Guy's wearing a t-shirt, black jacket, jeans, hiking boots. As if he's not a Catholic priest. But, despite myself, I'm a tiny bit charmed. That bugs me.

'No flies on you, though,' I retort.

'You knew who I was?'

'Hey, Father, it's still the Google age.' He nods, conceding the point. *Can he possibly not realize everyone knows who he is, around here?*

'I see you don't have a website, though,' he says in reply.

'Nope.'

'Cards get you enough business, eh?'

My card does not actually say 'Private Investigator.'

'People come to me with questions.'

'Me too.'

'Okay,' I say. 'We've done the bonding minute. We've got things in common. Look at us, both eating pastry. Both of us sought out by people in crisis, with questions. So? What's your question?'

He bridles at this. I'm not surprised.

'Well, look, Ms. LeSage, I appreciate you coming all the way out here to meet me. I don't have time to waste, either. Devin says you may be able to help.'

'How do you know Devin, by the way?'

There it is. The underlying suspicion that every priest expects. *How do you know a teenage boy? Why do you speak of him as if you are friends? Are you a predator?*

My skin itches, looking at the priest. *If you had hackles*, drawls a dark voice in my mind, and I dart a glance around. Of course Spider's not here in this place. That would be ridiculous.

You're right, says the voice.

Shut up, I growl, half out loud.

The priest frowns, and I turn it into a throat clearing.

'Sorry,' I say, gulping a bit of coffee, 'pastry went the wrong way.'

He gives me a half smile, eyes calculating. He's knows exactly what I've been thinking. Well, he knows part of it. The part that is me.

'Listen,' I say, 'you know I've got to ask, how do you know Devin?'

He sucks in breath in that way that smokers do when they're wishing they had a cigarette, exhales.

'Devin took a job last summer, helping maintain the grounds. Old Robbie is getting a bit long in the tooth for some of the heavy lifting and Devin wanted a job.'

He pins me with his glinting eyes.

'He's a good kid. Smart. He comes by with questions, and we talk. And no, I've never molested him.'

The priest's eyes are hard, rock hard, and clear as ice. Eyes like huskies' eyes, when they take offence. And then he smiles.

'I'd mind more if you hadn't thought to ask. These days? The history of the Church in that regard? Only a fool, or someone without the guts to give a damn wouldn't wonder about a priest hanging out with a teenage boy. You don't know me—'

I nod. 'But I do know Devin. And you do, too. He's got a lot going on under that gormless exterior. Always has had.'

'Yeah,' he says, 'that's Devin.'

The priest's eyes thaw a little bit more, and we just look at each other a few beats, reading what we see. He breaks first, a grin flicking across his face. He's actually quite handsome, in a worn-out sort of way. I can't stop the answering grin.

'So, Father—'

'You aren't part of the Church, are you?'

'Nope.' He has no need to know that wasn't always true.

'You can call me Efren.'

'Thanks. But I don't mind Father,' I say, looking around. Nobody much is looking back at us, but there are some old guys not too many tables away, and some of those old guys have sharp ears. They might not pay too much attention to a woman asking a priest for advice, not the same way as if I call him Efren. Still...

'Listen, Father,' I say, 'it's feeling a bit crowded in here. Want to take a walk?'

'I do my best thinking walking,' he says, the eyes definitely tending to summer now.

We finish up our coffees. He slides his finger round his plate, licks up the crumbs. Me, I'm more for thumb pincer action.

Outside, the priest takes a moment to light a smoke. He owns this neighbourhood, people nod and wave, he waves back. I light my own cigarette.

'Where to?'

We cross the street into Giovanni Caboto.

'Did you know this place before they redid it?' he asks idly.

'Yeah,' I say, taking in the families at the playground. There's a mom sitting on a bench, while the kids shriek and slide. A dad finishes retying a shoe, lifts one of the horde up onto the monkey bars. He slopes over to the mom, peels off his t-shirt with a grin, and turns to leap onto the jungle gym, showing off. She tucks his shirt into her bag of kid stuff, adjusts the baby on her lap, watches him with a half-smile. *Was I ever that innocent?*

I shake my head. Right, back to us.

'So, Father,' I say, 'what is this mystery?'

He walks strongly, this priest, explaining it as he goes. We cover ground, all the way down and around Santa Maria Goretti, the wind picking up in our faces as we turn west.

'So, where was this thing,' I ask, 'that made Devin start investigating?'

He takes a bit of a deep breath. 'Over here.' We're near his church now. We turn down an alley, and he stops, pulls out his cigarettes, makes a long job of shaking one loose. 'Look over there,' he says quietly, 'At the wall.'

I frown, stepping a bit closer.

There on the wall, three lightning bolts have been scratched into the brick. Not painted, this is no graffiti tag. They're carved, deep, sharp, angry.

My spine crawls. Three marks like lightning. Three dead men. Did I help kill one of them?

Forgive me, Father, for I have sinned.

***

Her

When you're ten, you don't know you're in a story; most people don't anyway. But She knew, you see. She knew it had to be a story, because stories end. And all you have to do is wait for it to end. And if you can't wait, you look harder, you look for the place where you can turn the story, the place where you can make it end. She has time. She lies quietly, like a Rabbit in Her lair, and gazes at the art on the hospital walls until She sees me looking out at Her.

There is no fear. Golden Hearts! That is where I consider Her. We sing, ri ri, small, while She leaves Her body to rest.

Gather,

I gather sage on the wind
I gather cedar, gather pine
I gather sweetgrass, and wild willow tang
And all the healer's flowers...

Every when Rabbit's body needs sleep, She finds me. We sing.
Golden Heart. Seasons.

ABELIGAMUJ

Nell needs to get to the city to see her kid in the hospital, so she needs this ride. She doesn't want any trouble. She is not what he seems to think she is. He can't see. He can't see anything but his own hungers, his own calculation that this might be fun.

For a while, they ride together down the road, through the pit of the night, into that part of the northern summer when the dawn is coming, but everything seems just a bit other than real.

He looks at her, calculating. Her hair stands on end as he deliberately drags his big hand down her arm, circles her wrist, shakes her just a little.

'So skinny,' he says. 'You this skinny all over?'

There is a rabbit on the road.

He's laughing about how he'll have to swerve to hit it.

He turns the wheel.

The rabbit turns.

Nell rises stunned from the ditch in the dawn, watching the broken car burn. Then she starts walking south. There will be someone else coming. She needs to see her daughter.

HAZEL: CLUES

I dance hard. Been told that about myself, and once I got over being embarrassed about being seen, I had to admit it's true. I dance hard. So I dance. As hard as I can. Locked in, safe from prying eyes, music loud enough to carry me, not so loud as to attract attention. I've never understood why people can't take in music unless it's rattling their bones. Not that I don't like a good loud immersion from time to time, but I can swim in the sound at low volume, too, especially if I know the song. And I've known these songs for so long now, I could dance them without the soundtrack at all. But I keep it on low, just for the kick of the drums.

After I'm good and sweaty, huffing for breath, I fill my mug, drain it, and fill again. Sink into the grotty armchair and read the files again. I can see why Devin hasn't gone to the police with all this. They'd laugh him off, at best; more likely, put him under surveillance, looking for enough evidence to connect him to something bad enough to get him off the streets. No, a big brown kid bringing in his file of suspicions would be lucky to even be given a hearing.

But my spine squirms. *Why me?* Everybody knows I'm not seeing Joshua anymore.

I find my heart is thudding not just from the dancing. *He can't possibly know?*

I read it through. There's nothing here that points at me, but Devin has that almost autistic, slightly creepy kind of prescient extra sense thing going on. What if he's given me this to see what I'll do? What if he's trying to get me to tip my hand, admit that I live with a shape-shifter, that we're vigilantes, that I am an accessory to a murder, and it is one of these guys. Dave. John David Lancaster. Blondie's Roadhouse Motel.

I find I don't know what comes next. Do I get up, find Spider, show this to him? Do I pretend I'm just the logical choice for Devin because I'm the nearest PI, and related, to boot. I mean, how many PIs are there in this town? Let alone PIs with the background to listen, to give a rat's ass about this?

And there it is. He's stuck with me, and I don't know how to help him.

Of course you know what happens next. In the too-quiet, suddenly stuffy afternoon, comes a tapping at my door. Almost a scratching. I don't want to get up, don't want to acknowledge it, but I felt him approaching. He knows I know it's him, knows that if I don't answer the door, it's because I'm trying to hide from him. And we're trying to move past that. I get up and open the door.

'Hi,' he says, brushing back his hair with one hand. I feel confused, suddenly, taking in his human self. The breadth of his shoulders, the way his neck curves up so emphatic and strong, his hands, his stereotypically springy hair. He doesn't look exactly like he should look, if this were some Gothic romance novel. But this is Amiskwaciy. This is not some draughty European castle, this is Latitude 53, like the avant garde art gallery. This is a city of slightly provincial pretensions, a city trying to reclaim a history it never lived in the first place. At least never openly. This is a métis city, a globalized mutt. And Spider/Jim? He is the most métissaged person I've ever met, looking at me with his odd coloured eyes, and I've been standing there for a century, just looking back at him.

'Hazel, what's going on? Tell me.'

'Okay, I will. But first, tell me something.'

He steps inside, closes the door. 'What?'

'Before, you said you didn't know why you were sent here.'

'I didn't.' He frowns. 'But I've been trying to put it together.'

'You had to know something. You were watching for that girl, weren't you?'

He sags into a chair, his head in his hands, then sits up straight. 'Yes. I didn't know until I saw her. I thought it was some kind of crazy dream. And I still don't know how… but I do know she is why I'm here.'

'Who is she?'

'If the dream is true?'

He's had a dream, too? This is news. I don't know what to make of it.

'I dreamed… someone I loved came to me, told me I had to go, had to use my curse to help you. Told me it was the only way I could save her.'

'The one you love?'

'No. Her daughter.' He looks over at me, face anguished. 'My daughter.'

RABBIT: 'VALENTIMES'

Happy Valentime's Day, she scrawled in crayon, making sure the letters stay inside the heart she's drawn with wavy lines, its edges imitating the scalloping on the store bought valentine she picked up from the edge of the school yard, where someone dropped it. Rabbit couldn't read well enough to figure out whose name was scribbled in the 'to' but she did know that, if she brought this card to the authorities, it would cause some sort of fuss. Rabbit didn't like fuss, it always made her stomach clench. So, she'd tucked the card in her hoodie pocket, saying nothing. In art class, she palmed a selection of stubs from the plastic crayon tub, just the short pieces nobody ever wanted, and slid them into her hoodie pocket too. The paper was her own, given out by the teacher. Rabbit carefully made her official Valentimes card small enough that she had paper left over. Later, at home, she tore the bottom off the school work card, and used the stubby crayons to make her own card. She saw how they spelled the day, but she corrected that—everyone said 'Valentime's' and so it was only right to make the word look like it sounded. It fit better.

Once the card was done, Rabbit looked around for a snack. Nothing much to see in the cupboards, but she found a little something stashed in under the cushions of their ratty love-seat. This was correct, too, as Valentimes is about love. Rabbit curled up on the love-seat, ate her snack and abided. Mommy would be home, and tired, and Rabbit would give her the card, and her tired eyes would light up a little. Rabbit drifted off to sleep, thinking of this.

She woke when her mother came in. The smell came first, the sweet hideous smell of her. Then her beloved self opened the apartment door, and Rabbit could see right away that she was hurt. She carried herself tightly, moved too carefully. Rabbit, eyes barely slit open, watched her mother for a moment; her faded, too-tight face in the dimmed light. Her mother was looking at Rabbit, and Rabbit saw a look of such pain on her mother's face, not the pain of the bruises she cradled, but some deeper thing that made Rabbit's stomach want to crawl right up into her heart.

'Mommy,' whispered Rabbit, fishing out the card, 'I love you.'

She uncurled while her mother stood frozen, uncurled, slipped quickly over, and pushed the little card into her mother's dangling hand. Her mother looked at the card, and for one moment, her ravaged face went soft with a wondering light. Then she began to cry. Rabbit took her hand, led her to the love-seat, and curled down beside her, resting quiet, not crowding her, not crushing her bruised bits, her own hand hot in her mother's trembling hand.

'Happy Valentimes Day,' she whispered, and, as her mother's breathing smoothed out into sleep, she softly sang the song her mother taught her, the oldest song she knew...

I gather sage on the wind
I gather cedar, gather pine
I gather sweetgrass, and wild willow tang
And all the healer's flowers....

When her mother is peaceful, Rabbit rises, goes to the sliding door, pushes it open and eases out onto the balcony. Her mother is so proud of having a balcony. Rabbit loves this place, how her mother has made it into a little garden. And she steps out into the shabby little garden, and looks up at the moon, wordlessly humming.

Dreaming now, Rabbit's mother remembers mornings, her mother in the kitchen in her underwear, cooking an omelette for her family, and how she'd say, to the greasy air of the room in general, 'Never forget that White people don't want us. Unless we're all dead.'

One day, Nell started talking back. She couldn't stand it anymore, the hopelessly smudged walls and floors, the sagging ceiling, windows looking out on a horizon, beyond which—

'There's no place in that world for us. You can't trust anyone out there.'

'I go to school, Ma,' she started, 'and—'

'And now you know better than me?' Her mother's rage came swift as a pot boiling over, her sad belly wobbling. 'I been out there, and I can tell you—'and as her mother raised a scarred arm to begin her usual rant, the story they've heard in variations down through the years, Nell snapped.

'Not interested.'

Her mother's breath whooshed out like she'd been gut-punched. Her face went slack. Nell couldn't stop.

'Not interested,' she repeats, feeling the power she didn't know she had. Then her mother turns away, tears running down her face.

How could Nell explain what she really meant, that she meant no disrespect to her mother? That she hurt for her mother, ached for her endless martyrdom, and just didn't want to be any part of that anymore, didn't want a life where her existence could only be one more burden on a back bent to breaking.

She felt the power of something out there, beyond the horizon, and some answering thing inside herself, like poplar buds straining to break open.

That was the day she decided she would go, and began to make her plans, in secret.

Her mother could sense something fearful had changed in Nell, and glared at her under her brows, but said nothing when her man was around, keeping it private, personal, safer.

But then, Nell went too far. She gathered her courage and her newfound sense of truth, and tried to share it with her mother.

Her mother, in sweatpants that day, and a long-sleeved sweat-shirt, moving carefully, nursing a fat lip.

'Mom, victim is a state of mind.'

'I'm not a victim, here, girl.' Her mother's rasping voice, shards of pain, endless echoes of it.

'Well, I'm not going to live like this anymore.'

'So, you're better than me, then?'

'No, Mom. I want more. And I—' she began to say *'want it for you, too,'* but her mother cut her off, shaking her arms at Nell, as if her scars are bangles ringing beneath the cloth.

'You! You don't know what I do for you! You don't know when you got it good. And you don't know what it's like out there. You think I'd ever send you to school if it wasn't the law? They'd put us in jail if I didn't, and you going to tell me how *important* education is?'

'If you want to change things, yes!'

'How you gonna change the facts? They hate us!'

'They don't even have to, Ma! You hate us enough for all of them!'

Their voices weren't yet loud, but they cut through the shabby walls. Nell's words cut.

'You're a martyr. You're paranoid.'

'Doesn't mean they're not against me.'

'I'm not you. I want to live! *Noli illegitimi carborundum,*' she'd hissed.

Her mother spit back, 'The fuck you say?'

And Nell stomped out, determined to prove her mother wrong, to take action on her brilliant insight—*don't let the bastards grind you down.* Nell shouted it out in Latin, loudly this time, this phrase that proved there was a whole world of people who knew better.

'Noli illegitimi carborundum!'

And he'd been waiting, her stepfather, needing some way that he could tell himself he was loyal to her mother. He heard her defy her mother's wisdom.

And so, he'd ground her down.

And even when she thought she'd escaped, even when she found James, and the unlikely marvel of love bloomed between them, even then, he followed her.

When James vanished back to the east, abruptly, with no chance to argue, she withdrew into her little apartment, made herself live smaller; ate less, worried as her belly rounded. She understood, she needed to eat now, and eat well.

One day a man appeared, who offered her work—'Smart girl like you, you can figure out how to help the department, right?'

And she needed the money, because she was going to have to provide for her family, and she took the job. She didn't trust him, even though he smelled like Old Spice, but she needed the work, and it wasn't so hard, at first.

HAZEL: UNKNOWN CHILD

'So, let me get this straight. You came here to hunt for a daughter you didn't know you had?'

'Yes.'

'Well, why didn't you tell me?'

'I… well, at first it wasn't really clear to me. Nothing made sense. I woke up and I was a dog.'

'You mean you didn't know you could shape-shift?'

He rakes his hand through his hair.

'No. Or not really.' He's stressed, shifting in the chair. 'I knew *something* happened to me. But when it did, I had no awareness of it. I had no memory after, either. Just sometimes,' he looked at his hands, 'sometimes I'd be cut or bruised, and so tired.

'And people started looking at me strange. Everyone started getting nervous, me too. Things were happening that didn't make sense. I knew something was wrong. So, I pulled a geographic.'

'Pulled a—?'

'Geographic. It's therapist talk for what addicts do. We run away from things, like the place is to blame for our problems.'

And I realize I've shoved the file under a book on the table by the ratty chair. I cannot look that way. I just want to run.

'Look, Spider.'

'Call me Jim.'

'Jim,' I rasp, 'I have to go. I—you have to leave. I'm just going out.'

'I'm going with you.'

'No, Jim. This is not something—' I can't believe I can't think of anything that I can legitimately say he shouldn't come to.

'It's a Women's Circle.' I blurt. He turns slow and looks at me with his left eyebrow nearly on the ceiling. *Shit.* He knows I don't do that sort of thing.

'I—they—look, remember—ah—' I'm babbling now. Why a Women's Circle? *Think, Hazel!* 'It's—a new client! She—she will only talk to me there—'

'Hazel,' he says, but I grab my jacket and keys and back into the hall, and he follows. But now he's too close. I summon some indignation. He's always crowding me.

'Don't crowd me.'

'Haze, don't lie. This has nothing to do with some Women's Circle. You're obviously lying. You're all flushed and sweaty,' he says. He knows I'm not comfortable with him doing this, describing me out loud for anyone to hear. 'You look good all sweaty, you know.'

'Shut up.' But he's following me. And then the door is shut and locked behind us, the file is safe from his prying eyes. I don't think he even noticed it. Bastard notices everything, mind you. But it's just another file in an office thick with paper clutter. I'm thinking furiously, going down the stairs, what kind of detective work do you do at a Talking Circle? I'm not Sandra, but I've just used her kind of excuse. Realistically, what ceremonial thing, however badly enacted, however hokey, gets a PI in a lather? I've got the length of a stairwell to think of an answer for that, because he'll corner me at the bottom. I have to have an answer that will make him back off and let me go. I need to think and I can't think right now; not with him right there.

As we reach bottom, I've got it. I turn on him, there in the little back vestibule.

'Jim,' I say, and now it's me who reaches out and touches him, locking eyes. 'Spider. I need you.'

He looks surprised for a moment.

'I need you,' I say, backing him into the corner, my arms sliding up and around his neck. I look deep into his eyes, inches away. 'I need you to bite me.'

I'm laughing out loud running for the Jeep—the look on his face—but I don't kid myself. He is a werewolf and he can track me. I shut up as I start up and turn the radio on loud. I push buttons 'til it hits that automatic seek feature—I love older cars—and shuffles itself randomly through the stations, creating sonic incoherence to cover my thoughts. That's a little trick I'd accidentally happened on one day, though I'm not convinced it works all on its own. I drive for half an hour before I feel I can safely stop.

I'm somewhere in Millwoods and I find a spice market to go into. This is what I need. Walking the aisles, I go slow, breathing in the far away worlds captured here. Worlds of cumin and cardamom, worlds of ginger and turmeric, masalas that have nothing to do with the mix of human and dog, human and wolf. Hindu culture has its myriad gods and demons, but none of them know me, and I wander unknown and safe here.

***

O consider. Find heart lights. Consider this is for strength. Nest of others who shine.

HAZEL: MOTHERS AND DAUGHTERS

Fat old ladies and mothers with tiny kids wander at their own speeds, on their own missions, involved in stories whose roots I cannot begin to divine. An old lady catches my eye, gives me a little nod, and I think, 'Lady, you have no idea,' but then I look around. I've wandered into the 'Puja' section.

'Durga puja,' says the woman, waving one hand toward a display of metal disks. I smile noncommittally and make to move on, but a younger woman has appeared around the end of the aisle and glides over to us, her hair gleaming and perfect.

'Durga puja,' the old woman says again, waving her hand between me and the discs.

'Yes, Mommy-ji,' says the woman, putting a gentle hand on her elbow. To me she says, 'She thinks you're a Durga worshipper. Or maybe she's recommending Durga to you.' She shoots the old woman a look like daggers.

'No no,' I interject, 'don't apologize.' I smile at them both. My mother lost her mind once, and I've never forgotten the kindness of strangers who understood how delicate that journey is.

'Tell me more about Durga?' I say, looking from one to the other to include them both. The mother smiles, tilts her head, takes a deep breath.

'Durga,' blurts the daughter, 'is the Mother Goddess. Her name means 'The Invincible One.'

I smile at them both, not sure what to say but wanting to keep talking. 'Sounds like a mother, alright. Invincible.'

'Yes,' says the daughter, relieved. The mother smiles at us both, reaches a hand toward an image. 'This is Durga on her Tiger,' explains the daughter swiftly. 'She is the Goddess of Victory, and she conquers demons.' The mother shakes her head, coughs. The daughter still looks a little embarrassed, but now she's relaxing. Then her mother speaks, peering at me.

'Do you have Indian descent?' she asks. And the daughter blushes.

I'm colouring a bit too.

'Well, not like you mean. Indigenous, we say now.'

'Oh,' the daughter says.

'Oh,' echoes the mother. 'You are the other kind of Indian. I remember, when I came here it was so confusing. I would hear people talk about Indians, but they weren't talking about us, they were talking about people from here. Are you Cree?'

What I am is gobsmacked, my jaw slack. Red-faced, I don't know where to look. I'd assumed she didn't speak much English, and here she has a classically bright voice, lilting, correct. She is grinning at me. The daughter looks exasperated.

'It's okay,' says the mother, 'I was toying with you. You see, I took you for one of us, but one who is perhaps Anglo-Indian, perhaps from a family that has forgotten our culture.' She shoots a look at her daughter. 'But you are Cree?'

'Anishinaabe,' I correct. 'That's—'

'Ah, yes, from the East,' nods the mother, 'Ontario, if I am correct?"

'Mommy-ji is a retired professor of anthropology,' says the daughter.

'Yes,' says the mother, 'and as such, I wish you would not call me Mommy-ji. As our new friend here might say, one must respect one's elders.' And she turns to me again, eyes gleaming behind her glasses. 'Tell me, new friend, what brings you to this store?'

'Just… ' I fish for an excuse. I can't say, *I'm using the smell of spices to hide from my werewolf.* 'Er… I um… actually, I was just driving around. Day off, you know? And I thought hey, buy some tea, some masala...' I trail off. There's a glint in her eye, like she's entirely not buying it. 'Truth is,' I sigh, 'I had a fight with a ... friend—' I shrug, 'and... just went for a drive, you know?'

'Ah,' says the daughter, 'a friend. A man?'

'Come on,' says the mother, 'we are all women together here, in Durga's aisle, we can surely relate to each other about these things. Every woman knows how it is with men.'

They really have no idea, I think. But it's soothing here in their presence, and light glints off the metal disks, and I find myself letting them convince me I have time to go for tea in the little place just over in the strip mall, and we walk together in the balmy evening, and I think I am not going to think about this too much.

We sit awhile, talking names.

Diya, the mother, explains that her name means 'Lamp,' and thus she supposes it is fitting that she became a scholar. 'I gave my daughter the name Shanaya,' she explains, 'meaning 'eminent, first ray of the sun,' hoping she would become a doctor, or some other eminent creature.'

'Oh, Mother,' says Shanaya. 'It also means, *born on a Saturday*, and you can't take that away from me.'

'True,' says the mother, 'at least that, you will always be able to say you got right.' They both laugh.

'I'm a lawyer,' adds Shanaya, 'which is useful, if not eminent, right Mommy-ji?'

'A horrid profession,' winks the professor.

'We have the name Shania, too,' I say, mostly to avoid the subject of what I do. 'You've heard of Shania Twain?'

'Of course,' says Diya, '*Man, I feel like a woman*,' she lilts, shimmying a little in her seat.

'It means '*on my way*,' supposedly,' I say, 'but you know, some people say it's not really an Anishinaabe name at all.'

Shanaya has her phone out. 'Yes, yes,' she says, 'it's in her Wikipedia page. '*Her biographer says there is no such name in Ojibwa nor in Cree.*'

She says it *Ah-jib-wah*, reading it from the page, and I almost correct her, but I don't want to break the mood here.

Diya says, 'Yes, she had an Ojibwe (she says it right, and winks at me) step-father, was adopted.' I look at her. 'I remember, you see, some years ago, there was a young Anishinaabe scholar, Catherine Sewell, who devised a course on Contemporary Indigenous Music. One of my students was in her class, and came to me quite in a flap. This professor Sewell had given them an assignment to do a biographical essay on an Indigenous musician, and had thumped her desk and declared, *'And no, you cannot do Shania Twain. She is NOT Indigenous, so don't even ask.'* It was a tiny tempest in a tea pot. Of course, sadly, Ms. Sewell died very soon after that. I never did get to meet her.' Diya sighs.

Shanaya takes charge. 'Ah, Hazel, Mother will talk all afternoon now, she is heading into Academic Stories Land. Perhaps you need to be getting back to your friend?'

'Or your job?" says Diya. 'May we be so nosy as to ask what you do?'

'I'm a transcriptionist, medical and legal; and also—'

Here it is. Do I tell them? It's not like I'm embarrassed, not at all. It's just not something I generally tell people who haven't already heard of my other work. But there is something about these two ladies, their lack of connection to all the things that I'm currently running from, that makes me feel daring enough to tell them all my jobs.

'Promise,' I say 'you won't make any TV-related jokes?'

They both raise their eyebrows, identical arches, identical expression. I clear my throat.

'I'm also, for a very few people, very privately, a Private Investigator.'

***

Driving again, I shake my head. That was weird. That's the sort of flaky synchronicity thing that should happen to Sandra. Still, it was timely and entertaining. And I have Shanaya's card tucked in my wallet, with Diya's number and email on the back.

'Email,' I hear her lilting voice, 'I guess I am kicking it old-school, what?'

I'm still smiling as I swoop down the hill toward the Walterdale Bridge, its clean white arch like a breath of fresh air. The spring air feels good through the open window, and I wonder when people will get back to Accidental Beach—an engineered site now, but still named for that first reckless summer when they were building Tawatinaw Bridge. The pilings shifted the flow of the river, so the old sandbar that used to be home only to gulls and geese became an unlicensed, unplanned, anarchically beloved magnet for all sorts of people. Guess that's one thing we got right, as a city, that city planners added in the building of Accidental Beach, when we did all the other terraforming. It has an official name, too, but nobody uses that.

***

I turn right after the bridge, right by Telus Field, down into the shady flats, find a spot to park, and take to the paved trails down along the river. They're well used, and a comfortable stream of roller-bladers, cyclists and walkers large and small ease past me. I like this time of year, the fullness of it, and this feeling of being part of the humming, muscular throb of this city. I go right on liking it for a whole five minutes more.

Then I spy the police tape. People doubling back, the stream diverted. My skin prickles with alarm. This could be anything. This could mean anything. But in my marrow, I fear.

***

I fumble out my phone. There's a text from Missy, *call me?* I call her, heart thumping.

'Hey,' she says, and I can tell I'm over-reacting.

'Everything okay?'

'Of course, Ma,' she says. 'But… um… actually, do you have some time to get together?'

She's out and about, she says, and suggests we meet over at the little teahouse down in Riverdale. From here, it's a fifteen minute walk, and nobody drives in Riverdale. On foot, I can slide down to the river bank bottom trail, around past the yellow tape, maybe see, if I wanted to, what was going on. Or I could stay quiet, slip by like a ghost, and they'd never even know I was there. On foot, I am free.

So, I just step out and walk.

I swing east, along the multi-use trail, well used under the sun that's tending toward supper time. At some point, I head south. I get into the rhythm, let it all flow by me, thinking about how little is actually known about Nell August's demise. So typical. So brutal. So unlikely that I'll figure out who did that to her, despite Joshy's touching declaration of his faith in me. How disloyal of me, calling him Joshy in my head like that, the way Missy did, the little sing-song lisp she used to use—a Frankie move, that—meant to ridicule him, keep him at a distance. My tough girl. Not going to get attached to another one of Mom's Men. But then he wore her down.

I remember the day I found out. She dropped by unannounced, not unusual for Missy.

What she had to say, though, floored me. She told me she'd run into Josh at her work, he'd been accompanying a prisoner to Emergency, and took the time to look her up, over in the women's ward.

'Caused a bit of a flap,' she grinned, 'the police looking for me. And then, of course, when he asked if I had a break coming up and could go for coffee with him, you should've seen the faces.' My own could probably have given them a run for their money.

'And?' I finally managed.

'And Mom,' she said, cautiously, 'I think… ' she ruffles her hand through her hair. 'Mom, I didn't know what to think. I mean, why would he do that?'

I was at a loss myself. 'I guess… I guess he …'

'Mom,' she said, taking a deep breath, 'he said he thinks you two could really have a future, and he sensed I didn't trust him. And he said that was fine. Normal really, to be expected, and—'

I was starting to get pissed. 'Mighty White of him—'

'No, Mom,' she said, 'not like that.' She sighed. 'I mean, it *was* weird, yeah?'

'Yeah. Finding you at work? Interrogating you?'

'Mom—'

'Who the hell does he think he is? We've only been—'

'Mom!'

'A few weeks and he thinks he has the right—!'

'Mom! Stop.' She reached out and put a hand on my shoulder. That stopped me.

'Mom. I'm trying to tell you. I didn't mind. It was… kind of nice… once I got over the shock. And look,' she said, 'he even said to me that he knew, he knew it was kind of a bit much, and he'd thought maybe he shouldn't do it, maybe it was crossing a boundary, but he was there for work, see, and they had to do some sort of test on his prisoner, so he thought, nothing ventured—'

'—nothing gained.'

I finished for her. Typical Joshua. How many times in our short time together had I already heard him say that old cliché? How many times did I secretly marvel at how he made it seem fresh somehow? Not that I'd tell Missy that. I'm too gob-smacked, like the Brit boyfriend used to say, a saying the girls picked up and used to shout around the house—*gob-smacked, gob-smacked*—until the day it became more than an expression…

Missy, I was astonished to realize, was trying to tell me that maybe, just maybe, she approved of Joshua.

And by the time I dumped him, she'd stopped calling him 'Joshy' to me. She'd ask him about his work, when she saw us. And she listened to him when he explained why she should take down John Takedown.

I shake my head. My tough girl. She was so defiant when she told me about getting in trouble for that. I was so proud of her I didn't even know what to say. Proud, and terrified. I'd already seen some of the worst people do to each other, no way I wanted her messing with some of those people. So I told her it was for the best, leave police work to the police. They have guns, they have armour, they have back up.

Of course, she took out her anger on me. I get it. It was far from the first time one of my kids had turned their frustration on me when they didn't know what else to do with it. The world, my old dad used to say, is not easy on Indians. (As we were called then, in the larger world. As some of the old timers still call ourselves, having appropriated the label, or 'cause we love our dads.)

***

Tonight, though, she says she's doing okay, just wanted to see me. I hold my eyebrows down and we sit together for a while, sipping ice tea in the Little Brick, enjoying the smells of the new City Farm, and of someone barbecuing down by Riverdale Hall—a miracle that it's still standing, centre of so much change. It's not as old as this little house-turned-café, but it holds a lot of local history. I'm thinking idly of dancing there, back around the century's turn, when Missy lets it slip out casually that she's been going around with Maengan Nolan.

I think of him, hunched and bleeding in the shadows. Shake my head.

'He's really nice, Ma,' she says. 'He's got a good job. He gets along with Frankie, too.'

I remember, then, a long ago time, George and I and Sandra, so young and naive. That's what I'm frowning about, not particularly about Maengan Nolan, but it's enough to set Missy off.

She gets that shut-down look, finishes her tea in a hurry, pays with her digital thing before I can say anything, and like that, she's gone. I just watch her go, her back view on her bike. When did it happen that all I usually saw of my oldest was her indignant backview?

Thinking about all that, I walk back, past the Jeep, keep on walking, down through the legislature grounds; all the groomed green, a gardener puttering in one of the many flower beds. I'm going to have to go home soon, I think, and just deal with this. But I waste some time, take my time looping back to the Jeep.

It's getting dark by the time I return, and I open the door to find, wonder of wonders, the smell of dinner. Spider/Jim is nowhere to be seen, and there's a note on the table.

'Huh,' I say, reading. He's taken himself for a walk. Funny guy.

As I'm reading, I hear a knock at the door. It's him, of course. He slips in quickly.

'Hey,' he says. 'So, did you find the food?'

'Don't tell me you cook?'

'I wish.' he said. 'No, I don't. And I'm afraid you've officially got a boyfriend. Don't be mad, please—'

'What?!'

'I met Sandra.'

'Oh.'

'She was just passing, she said, and wondered what I was doing here.'

'I thought I told you to lay low.'

'I was trying to.'

I sigh. Wave it off. After all, I know how Sandra is. Good thing she's not interested in investigating, she'd probably put me out of business, the way she can find out stuff.

'So, what did she give us? Any good?' I know it is. Sandra is an amazing cook, even if her gifts always come as a Trojan horse for her nosiness.

He nods with a shrug when I ask if he wants some, so I nuke up two bowls full, and we sit down, the length of the table between us. We devour Sandra's pilaf. I had no idea I was this hungry.

'Look who's wolfing it down,' he cracks, as I go for thirds. 'Too soon?'

My turn to nod and shrug. The food is keeping that bubble of hysteria down; there's that.

But it's been a long day, and like I say, I'm no good at being stuck. Somewhere today, I've made a choice. Doesn't matter if I don't understand it. I'm in this, stuck with a partner in crime.

I give him a smile back.

'So… you play cards?'

***

After a few games, he leaves me to the deck and my own thoughts.

The thing is, Nell August wasn't just a hooker. She was a survivor. She'd put her stepfather in jail for a while, for what he did to her and to the rest of her siblings. She'd been banished from the family, of course, the way truth-tellers too often are. She'd gone through all that, and found herself a place to stay, and had been going to upgrading. She'd looked like she was going somewhere. And then it had just stopped.

She'd fallen back off the map, fallen back down into the dark that waits for the poor, for the ignorant, for the ones who don't belong. She'd started on drugs, and she'd never been able to stop. She'd become a wraith before she died, and stalked the streets like a bad omen. Those kind of people seem to curse all the new downtown developments. Pour your millions into the gentrification, they will not be silenced; they will ooze along out of the cracks in your facade, and you will have to ignore them so hard, they'll blind you.

They will be like the unstable ground under your high-rise.

You were told, weren't you? There were coal mines all through the river banks of Amiskwaciy, once.

What you weren't told is that those tunnels are not abandoned, not utterly. They became a repository for the crimes you don't want to even admit are possible, never mind the category of crimes you want paved over and forgotten.

There are holes in the earth that demand sacrifice to make them right, or the ley lines that keep the earth healthy become clogged with arterial roads and sick smelling air, and people are magnetized like red blood cells and congest in the cities; too many people, too few souls to go around.

The earth needs some soothing, and some of them remain to be soothers; but some of them don't want to be soothed, and they themselves become black and cruel, and they lack the means to be other than what they are, simple and insane.

The world belongs to those who will write it and right it and wright it, and all these weird imagistic thoughts are blurring together, but I'm beginning to sense a pattern in Nell's life. Tracing it feels like digging over unstable riverbank; any thing I poke at could drop me into the shafts of forgotten histories and buried tragedies.

***

The first time I call Shanaya, I'm nervous, but right away, the warm candour in her voice sets me at ease. Before I know it, we're laughing about meeting in the Durga puja aisle, about life and mothers and culture, and arranging to meet for lunch.

At lunch, that first time, I try so hard to imagine telling her why I need a lawyer. And I can't.

So, we make a date to go to a movie. And we laugh and talk and that turns into another lunch, another coffee, a regular habit. In a few weeks, I feel like I've known her for years.

I don't tell Jim about her, but I walk with him when I can. Somehow, we both know not to tell anyone who we're looking for—which you might think would hamper a search. And it does. We know she exists. We know her given name.

'Abeligamuj, Nell named her,' Jim says. 'She wrote to my sister and told her that. You know what it means?'

I nod, make no comment. It's a Mi'gmaw word, not common as a name, but kind of cute.

And there can't be too many girls running around with a Mi'gmaw name, right? But we can't find that name. It could be she changed it, Anglicized it. And it could be because she's a ward of the state. Jim is not sure, because she should be 16, old enough to be on her own, but that's still young enough to be in Care.

***

When I consider, She and her song are in my heart-light. I am in this where for Her. I hold this to my self. I do not tell my nest. She and her song tell me, consider go where and when humans. She is holy. She needs. I have. I go.

RABBIT: FOOD COURT

Rabbit is a food court baby. When she was little, her mom would drop her off in the food court, sometimes with a few coins, sometimes empty handed, tell her to wait at a certain table 'til Mom came back. Rabbit was scared, at first. She didn't know how to get the food, but she was so hungry. The first time, her mother came back, saw Rabbit sitting there clutching the coins in her grubby little hand, and got this horrible hard look on her face. The one where she's not going to cry. She grabbed Rabbit a little too hard, and pulled her over to the place with the fries, took the few coins from Rabbit, and bought some fries. Rabbit watched, hungry and scared.

Next time, she lisped, 'I can do it,' to her mom, and pushed the coins across the counter. The lady there, her dark eyes sad and kind, took Rabbit's money, gave her change with her fries.

'You want gravy, honey?' said the fry lady. Rabbit shrugged. She didn't know about gravy. The woman put some in a side dish, pushed it to her, her dark eyes shining unbearably sad. 'On the house, honey.'

The fry lady watched out for her, then, watched Rabbit coming in, sometimes with her thin, bedraggled mom, more and more often alone. When Rabbit sat down without coming to her counter, the fry lady would find some excuse to slip out to her with a little dish of fries, gravy, ketchup. One time, she offered Rabbit a hot dog, but Rabbit ate it listlessly. The fry lady tried her instead with a little salad from her own lunch, slipped surreptitiously into a paper fry tray. The girl devoured the greens.

'You're a little Rabbit,' said the fry lady with a smile. Such a big, warm sun of a smile. And Rabbit smiled back.

'Yes,' she lisped, 'that's my name. Rabbit. What's yours?'

'Shirley,' said the fry lady. And Shirley and Rabbit belonged then, and Rabbit knew she had a place to rest here. Never for too long. And she never told her mother about Shirley, never looked at Shirley when her mother appeared. Shirley pondered that, decided it didn't matter much exactly why the girl needed to hide their friendship.

Shirley knew, from long deep memories of her own, that sometimes children just need one friendly place, one adult who stands by. If anyone had thought to mention Social Services, Shirley would have swatted them away. Tough, stringy little Rabbit was making her way.

Shirley knew from her own life, children live through things. After her own horrors with immigration paperwork, Shirley knows that the maw of officialdom will not help this little girl. She makes fries for Rabbit. When Rabbit has money, Shirley lets her pay, but gives her back extra change. The child grows, grubby, thin, mouth-breathing and rumple haired, but she never leaves without her mother.

One day, Rabbit levels a look at her and lisps, 'Shirley, is this the right change?'

And Shirley thinks of continuing to lie, but then decides truth is always better.

'No, honey,' she says, and she takes a moment to count out the correct change. 'You should know how to hang on to what's yours.'

***

When Rabbit can say she is 16, she asks Shirley to help her get a job.

'Well, you're good with money,' says Shirley. Rabbit shakes her head.

'No,' she says, 'nothing so public.'

Shirley sighs. She also works at a call centre, from her home after hours, and she's told Rabbit this. But Rabbit lisps. As she's trying to think of a kind way to broach that, Rabbit surprises her.

'Shirley,' she says, her slight voice clear and careful, 'I have been practicing my pronunciation.'

***

Rabbit is still sixteen when it happens. She is big enough to be done with school, nobody will bother her one way or another, no matter what she does. So she follows her mother sometimes, and waits, not at the mall, but in the shadows, while her mother makes contact, makes her transactions. Sometimes, it is just words that get exchanged. Sometimes, packages. Sometimes, the men pull her mother into their vehicles.

Rabbit doesn't watch the act, never that. She just notes what vehicles her mother gets into, just marks the doorways, the dumpsters, the random angles of shelter in which her mother makes her daily bread. The men, Rabbit watches them, too. She wonders why her mother sometimes doesn't seem to recognize that hardness, that wrongness in some of them that means they will want to hurt her. She puts it together with the smell, with her mother's consumption. When she's high, her mother doesn't seem as able to sniff out evil; the sickly smell of her own self overrides her sense of caution, and then Rabbit has to be ready to pick her up, nurse her, be gentle as she feeds her instant soup and noodles, then soft fruit, then more.

Her mother must never know how close Rabbit is, though, this she also knows. While she won't protect herself, her mother holds tight to the notion that she is somehow able to protect her daughter. Rabbit never questions this. It's bone-deep knowledge, that this is all that keeps her mother alive, the thought that she is a good mother, keeping her daughter safe.

That evening, Rabbit can smell the evil radiating from the alley. The man who has taken her mother's arm smells bad, too, but he is not the worst thing. She follows, eyes huge, as her mother steps with that man into the alley. Her heart is thundering. They go behind the dumpster, that man and her mother. And she sees another form in the shadows. Hears the man with her mother say something in surprised tones. Her mother is talking too, sounding nervous. The third figure, the one that seems to radiate evil, laughs. Rabbit's hair prickles with fear.

It happens too fast. Just a sudden change in the noises, and a sudden stab of fear, her mother's voice strangled like a swift bird call. Rabbit breaks from cover, sprints down the alley, her voice a tiny inarticulate thread screaming out.

The evil figure is laughing, stepping up into a big truck.

The other man is standing over her mother. Her mother is dead. Her mother's shoes lie away from her. The man is not looking at the shoes. Rabbit does not think. She whips down a ropy arm, grabs a shoe, wraps her hand around the toe of it, still warm from her mother's feet, and, moving faster than thought, she swings.

The man, caught entirely off guard, falls. Rabbit is on him then, all claws and teeth and the heel of the shoe hammering. His blood mingles with her mother's and he slumps, unconscious.

Rabbit doesn't leave him there, though. She looks around. Nobody near. She shoves a hand into his pocket, grabs the keys, runs back up the alley. She opens his car. She drags him to it. With the last of her strength, she pushes him in the passenger door. He wakes up, bloody and terrified, as she is heaving his limbs into the car, and he starts to scream. She punches him squarely in the mouth, breaking his teeth.

'Shut up,' she lisps. He scrabbles across, catching on the gear shift, crying as he forces himself behind the wheel.

She climbs in after him, and he just shakes his head, his head shaking on and on. Night is coming on, and Rabbit, filled with a lifetime's rage, is nothing he ever in any way expected to face. His mind is utterly open, unreeling, and she is a relentless voice, telling him what he must do, where he must go. She backs out of the car, tumbling, as he drives away.

He cannot see, blood in his eyes, and his own heart thunders in time with the voice, telling him where to turn, when to hit the gas, when to wrench the wheel and let go.

***

Call me Justice. You think you want wild, but you do not consider, you do not take the weight of it. She considers. She is small. But I am not fooled. She is terrifying.

I honour Her. I catch Her, move Her now, nest out, Between, nest in, Between, her home. Ri ri ri, I sing small small. Sleep Rabbit. Sleep Abeligamuj.

I consider. Hazel is moving somewhere beyond Amiskwaciy. I slide into the piney, gnarly hills, the better to see.

HAZEL: ROAD TRIP

'Look. I never could sleep alone that easy, okay? I used to get bad dreams. They don't bother me as much when there's another body nearby.'

'So, what? All the men were just there as, as… bodyguards?'

'No. Well. Huh.' A laugh whips out of me, like a bark. 'I guess so, in a way.' I look at Shanaya, look away. How is it she can talk so easily to this woman I hardly know, when I can't even connect to my own family? True, I asked Shanaya along because I need legal advice, and I can't yet bring myself to tell her about that; but I am finding it far easier than I'd feared, to open up and talk about the visions, about the men.

'Why is it so easy,' I ask, 'to talk to you?'

'Maybe it's the open road,' says Shanaya, nodding at the countryside rolling past. 'I've always found that traveling makes me feel expansive. Don't you find it so?'

We're coming up on Big Bend, and the drumlins are giving way to the unlikely hills, the geological spur that hints of something unexpected below the surface here, pushing the land higher, making sudden heights. Big Bend, we've always called it that, is first a sweep of highway, where it swoops from East to South, if you're headed there from Amiskwaciy. Then a descent, and then another swoop to the East again and you start to climb, and the air gets piney and the hills crag up and close in Then you come through a cut bank and there is Big Bend the townsite, arrayed on both sides of the highway, but only visible on the North, at first. The South part of town is down toward the water, and a swath of trees might fool you into not noticing it if you weren't paying attention.

'But tell me,' Shanaya continues, 'where is it that we're going?'

'Out past town, here. I… we… My sister used to have a place out here. And in fact, it's right next to where we grew up. At least, where we spent some of the best years of growing up. I find it's a good place to think. And I think,' I muse aloud, 'that getting a change of scene might help make sense of what's going on.'

'And if it does not, well, I will at least enjoy new scenery.'

RABBIT: CODES

Rabbit has been paying attention. Everywhere, her long ears, her eyes, her prey-born alertness.

Once she has the codes for the call-centre job, she figures out other ways to configure codes.

She listens, reads, floats silently between the tides of communication. She has the advantage of a name. Joshua Campeau. She knows he is the one who has been protecting the men who made it their habit to feed her mother's habit, and then feed, through her, their own habit of abuse.

She is hunting now, through the most urban of means, the subway. It's a long way down to the trains here, this station built into a hill, not the river valley sides riddled with coal seams But she's not thinking about geology as she descends. She's watching the faces of people rising on the escalator beside her, the people literally at cross-purposes. She's watching for any telltale expressions that might say they'd seen or smelled or felt something down there they wish they hadn't, something they don't know how to account for, something that makes them glad to be headed for the surface, for the world of normal and streetlights.

When she emerges onto the tracks, she knows she has found another of the predators. He is leaning against the tile wall. She sidles into view, lets him see she is alone.

'What's your name?' he purrs, with a spine chilling sneer.

'Rabbit,' she lisps. She's trailing a broken heel.

A rabbit will protect her young by feigning injury, like a seemingly broken winged bird who will draw off the predator, and then take flight. But there's no flight left in Rabbit.

***

She breaks him and leaves him on the track. She is red-eyed rage. I consider, more people come on the train. Heart light. What will happen? So I move the body. Now. Between. Through coal shafts. Leave him here, and She is safe from discovery. But I consider there are more of his kind left, maybe. I consider if I leave the broken body, somewhere in sight, it is a message. I move Between. I leave this broken thing near the river.

HAZEL: GIRL TALK

'How did it start? I don't know. I guess because I was quiet. People figured that meant I was a good listener. I never meant to be one, it was just too hard to articulate what I wanted to say, and people wouldn't wait for me. They'd tell me something, and it would astonish me, and while I was trying to figure out what to say in response, they'd be taking my silence for permission to keep going. And they'd find themselves telling me things, and I'd find myself somehow tacitly bound to just listen, feel this moral weight, this responsibility to take care of their secrets. I was a wailing wall, until it began to feel too much like I was a punching bag. Do you know what I mean?'

Shanaya nods and smiles.

'One day, I said to myself, Hazel, you're crazy. You are living vicariously, letting other people bring you their traumas and dramas, and being a receptacle for all their pain and confusion.'

'Yes,' says Shanaya, 'I know. You take it on, and you try to sort it out for them. And you cry every time they walk away from you, because they've dumped the worst of themselves, and they want to leave it behind them now. So they leave you behind.'

I blink back tears, surprised to find I can't stop talking. 'So, I stopped being a listener, and I charged in to other ways. I had to. I guess I could thank George for that.'

Fuck, I think, *look at me, Sandra, speaking of my gratitude. How many years did that take?*

'Shanaya, I made hideous mistakes. The kind of mistakes that, before, I'd just be the listener for, the confessor, the wailing wall. And I did it knowing full well that it was never going to bring back those people who'd dumped and run on me. It wasn't like they were waiting for me to take a turn, to open up and show my weakness to them in turn, so we could be equals.'

I bring myself up short, look over at her, horrified. Self-pity is not my thing.

But Shanaya, she looks back, and she reaches over and touches my shoulder, just lightly, then points at the pack of cigarettes.

'Go for it,' she says, eyes twinkling. She looks so much like her mother. I light one up, and she starts talking.

'I've been there, too,' she says, 'And I thought like that, for a while—that if I listened, I would be respected. But people still like Hindu women to listen, even here, even now. I didn't get that it was about race or colour, though. And I didn't want to see the sexism, because Mom had made such a constant refrain about how I would always have to beware sexism. I didn't want her to be right. I wanted to be mad at her for divorcing Dad. I wanted my own reality.'

She smooths her sleek black hair, looks out the window for a moment.

'But she was right, of course. Men saw me as a dark muse, or some such. They wanted to be powerful, but then, they wanted to be dazzled. If they were dazzled, they had an excuse to lay their secret burdens on me. And then, they would run. And I would blame myself. How long did it take me to unravel it?'

'Mmm?' I say, just so she'll know I'm with her. I can guess the answer. 'Too long.'

'For too long, I let them get away with letting me take the blame for them running away. I actually felt guilty, imagining they felt less than me, now that I knew their secrets, and so they got vulnerable and hid away for fear that I was judging them.'

'But then I realized no, they were never giving me a chance to speak, not because of vulnerability, but out of lack of basic respect. They were simply caught up in their own story and, as regards my story, did not give even the smallest rat's ass.' She makes a rude noise. '*Rat's ass.* What does that saying even mean?'

We crack up a little, derailed from our pity party by the image of a tiny rat's behind, the rest of the rat looking quizzically around at the hands reaching out to grab his ass, to give it elsewhere.

'I guess we're all the rat, sometimes,' I say.

The road winds up, we're among the hills now, that anomaly of geology, outcroppings of mountain. I'm about to mention how weird that is, when Shanaya says, 'So what does all that have to do with Jim?'

I sigh. I really don't want to tell anyone, but I have to.

'It's simple, really,' I say and take a drag, and blow the smoke out the window. It isn't simple. I don't know where it ends. I know where it begins though—when Jim doesn't leave.

'I look at him and he's looking back at me, not at all confused, not at all guarded, none of that thing I dreaded, that moment when I know I've lost another one on the curve.' The road, obligingly, swings wide in a curve, pulling us back toward open territory. 'They find out I'm more complex and complicated than they wanted me to be, and they backpedal off like crazy. But no, he was looking square at me, same as before.'

That look was something I never expected to see again, after Gran. I had been so thirsty for that look, that understanding, that complicit ease that says, *Yes, I've been there too.*

'Yes,' says Shanaya, and she gestures anew to the pack and I flush. 'Really? God, so sorry! I never even—'

'No, I don't look like a smoker, do I?' she laughs. 'And I'm not really, not anymore. Unless I am driving somewhere with a true heart friend—

'A true—?'

'—true heart friend. My mother's turn of phrase. *Shanaya, get yourself a True Heart Friend, and every journey is a grand adventure.* I'm sorry,' she adds, 'doesn't that sound too hokey?'

'Too Mommy-ji?' I grin, teasing her. 'Shanaya,' I say, drawing myself up and hitching my imaginary professorial glasses, 'Do you really think this Hazel Le Strange, PI, is a suitable True Heart Friend? I mean,' I say, shaking a finger, 'she is a smoker, like in the worst b-movies of olden days, and here she is, encouraging you to not only die of second hand smoke, but to join her in this so very outmoded vice.'

'Now I *really* want to.' She snakes a smoke out of the pack with an elegance that speaks of practice, lights up, and cracks her own window. And we come around the last curve and down into the bright sunlight, streamers of smoke trailing behind us, and I feel like I could tell her anything.

As the fringes of town come into view, I say, 'There's more.'

'I thought there just might be.'

I start another smoke.

'You're shaking,' says Shanaya. 'But you know, whatever it is, you can tell me.'

'Not this,' I blurt.

'Hazel, we are not lovers, you are not risking that. We are friends. Adults. And I am a lawyer, to boot. I have truly heard it all.' Her tone is gentle, her presence beside me vivid and strong as an old tree.

'Not this, you haven't,' I say, as the first houses flick past. *I should slow down,* I think, but I don't, I keep to the main drag, and I know we're not stopping in town. Deep breath. How do you tell anybody? Let alone somebody who's not from your culture, who doesn't know the same stories. Why am I here with this woman, and why am I about to confess—

'That guy I live with? Jim? He's a shape-shifter. What you might call a werewolf.'

Smoke trails out the windows, the houses of the town hide behind their trees, and I have to slow down because we're coming to a traffic light. It's red. I stop. Stupid timing.

We sit there in absolute silence. Shanaya lights another smoke.

'What? Like Hugh Jackman?' I look over, jolted. She's grinning at me. She sobers up immediately. 'Just kidding.' Then she's giggling again. 'No, wait. He was Wolverine. Totally different animal.' She's laughing out loud now.

I can't say a word. I'm furious.

Haven't we just had this heart-to-heart? Hasn't she just said I could tell her anything?

And now the bitch is laughing? Her laughter sinks in pitch, roughens, sputters to a wheeze.

'Light has changed,' Shanaya says, and her voice is gruff, raspy. She clears her throat, and I am aware of an odd smell, and it feels suddenly a lot more crowded in here.

'Don't panic,' she says, her voice even more throaty. 'Don't look at me, and don't panic. Just let's get out of town.'

Something furred touches me on the arm, quickly pulls back. I am not panicking. I'm keeping my eyes straight ahead. It's hot, even with the window open, heat radiating from the massive animal presence beside me. I'm not panicking, but I am driving like the proverbial bat out of hell. We're out of town and driving on a highway I can drive by blind memory. I am way too hot. The contact with Shanaya's arm is still there, still overly hot, burning really. I want to look. I don't. Every hair on my body is standing tall.

Here, I've been before, I think, and I don't like the thought one bit.

We top a rise, swoop down into a long straightaway through open country.

Shanaya sighs heavily and slowly, the air relaxes between us.

'I'm so sorry,' says Shanaya, her voice again clear. 'I should be better at this, I really should.'

'Better at—?' I chance a look. She looks human, just… not at all normal.

She sighs, heavily, snags another smoke. 'Just turn off the highway when you can.'

I find a little road leading away to the right and, every nerve jangling, I turn off anyway. My heart is hammering like a freelance framer being paid by the joist. Even my similes are out of whack. George used to compare random things to framers.

'Now, then,' says Shanaya, 'when we reach those trees, please stop.'

The trees in question are a stubby fringe of scrub, but they're tall enough to obscure the highway. Not that there's anyone out there.

'Look,' she says, 'First of all, I owe you an apology. Back there? That was a reflex. I really haven't got the hang of this at all well.'

This? I feel a bubble of hysteria wobbling up from my guts.

I just stare at her. 'You too?'

'Not exactly,' she replies. 'Step out with me and I'll show you.'

She looks nervous, scared, and it crosses my mind what a comfort that is, and how that bastard Spider/Jim never once had the courtesy to look so concerned about my reaction. Maybe that's not fair, but annoyance at Spider/Jim feels like an anchor. My fear bubbles back down. Worst that can happen is I'll be killed by *this* werewolf, but she at least is my friend. Logic is an odd beast.

Is it logical to step out of my car with a werewolf, way out here? Nobody out here. I should know. I grew up round here. This is not what I came here looking for. I imagine myself running for the farm. I imagine her catching me. And if she doesn't?

That would almost be worse.

'Now,' she says when we're both standing in the sun, 'Could I ask you to look away for a moment? In fact, I'd be so obliged if you would walk to the edge of this copse before you look at me again.'

See that, says my mind, *she's giving you a sporting chance. She is a friend, even if you are wrong and she is about to kill you, she is giving you a head start.* Perversely though, my feet refuse to budge.

'Look,' I say, bunching my fists, 'if you're planning to kill me—'

'I promise I am not.'

She looks so sincere. I feel dizzy, but I also feel like I can believe her. So I walk away, dust luffing up from my steps. I wrap my arms around myself, then force myself to drop them. I will walk with pride. Head up. I'm creeped to shit here, but I am attempting to walk like a full grown woman of substance. I get to the edge of the copse. I could just keep walking, but I don't. Like I said, if I made for the farm and got there? That would be worse, arriving at the farmhouse, George's house now, George and Édith the Embryo. It makes me mad that they are in my potential last thoughts, so I refocus.

Curiosity has always trumped fear, for me. Does *seen one, seen 'em all* apply to werewolves? I have to know.

I turn around.

There is a tiger in the road.

This, I did not expect.

***

Turn back around, please, says a voice in my head. I turn, thinking how tigers are much more polite than wolves—who knew? I turn my back on the tiger and wait, gazing at the open, sunny fields rolling on to the shimmering horizon.

'It's okay now,' Shanaya calls, and I just turn around and walk back to her. I find it a long walk, my legs having acquired a surprising sort of rubbery feel. I make it almost to the car before they give out, and I sit myself down on the edge of the road, stretch those legs into the ditch.

'Are you okay?' Shanaya says, coming around the car. 'I really am sorry, Hazel. I just got so excited, when you said that—about the werewolf—'

She looks all shy now, her shining dark hair falling in a curtain in front of her face.

I look down, realize I've been carrying my pack of tobacco like a sacred talisman the whole time. I shake one loose, pass it up to her, take one myself. We smoke a minute, silently, as if it's the most natural thing in the world that one of us just turned into a tiger and back, out here in the back ass of nowhere.

'I did think you might kill me, you know.'

'What?' she laughs. 'Why would I do that?'

She has slipped down to sit right next to me. She punches my shoulder, and gives me that little nose crinkle she got from her mother.

'After all, you're my ride.'

We smoke a while more.

'So,' I venture, 'A were-tiger. How does that happen?'

She shrugs. 'I wish I knew. I do not know anything about the *how* of it. It just happens to me.'

'But, a tiger?'

'Why should it be that wolves have all the fun?'

'Fair enough.'

'I think this is connected to Durga.'

'Durga? As in the Goddess from the shop?'

'I think,' says Shanaya, her eyes flickering tigerishly, 'that it was no accident that we met in that place, at that time.'

'Why did we, though?'

'I don't know, Hazel,' she says. 'Why were you there?'

'I was … just driving. Running away, more like. I couldn't handle the stress. Living with a werewolf. Not knowing why he'd chosen me. My Grandmother talking to me in visions…'

I tell her the whole story, as near as I can make it make sense. And then she tells me hers.

***

'Not that there's much I can tell you, Hazel,' she says. 'I don't even remember when it started. It seemed like dreams, the earliest moments I remember. I think I thought I *was* dreaming. And I would tell Mommy about it. And she would listen. And she started teaching me about Durga puja, and for a long time, I guess I thought I was what she told me I was, an ordinary Hindu girl, second generation immigrant, wanting to connect with my tradition. With vivid dreams.'

She takes the last cigarette. The sun seems to light on the end of it along with the lighter flame.

'When I became a woman, I discovered the truth, that I really do physically change. And I have been trying since then to come to terms with it. I don't get how it fits, or not, with classical Hindu religion and culture. I've kind of given up. I don't expect to understand it. I just want to be okay with it here and now. To live as if it is normal that in Amiskwaciy here and now, I, a lawyer, am also able to become a tiger. I just am what I am. Chosen by the Goddess.' She tosses back her hair, lifts her cigarette, laughs. '*Durga's Tiger.* What do you think?'

I am past thinking. But this is getting way too easy to do, to hang around with a shape-shifter.

'I think,' I reply, getting up and dusting off my butt, 'that it's time to move on. For one thing, I don't really like this road, it doesn't lead anywhere good. For another, we're out of smokes.'

'Find us a store, and I will buy,' she says.

'You are so much classier than my werewolf.'

We double back west into town, get smokes, get sandwiches at the sub place, also chips and drinks at the convenience store where I fill up the Jeep.

'You don't want some ice cream?' I say in the 7-11, nodding at the little freezer section. 'They've got tiger-tail.'

'Have they got hazelnut?' she quips back, and we giggle like teen-agers, and the clerks exchange glances. They have no idea what's going on, but their assumptions set us off even more, and we giggle and splutter through the aisles.

'Look,' gasps Shanaya, picking up a glossy magazine, still so many on sale in the small towns, 'Here's Hugh Jackman on the cover.' Like the loonies we so evidently are, we buy that magazine, too.

'He was a Wolverine once, you know,' I deadpan to the clerk, and Shanaya reels out the door, busting an elegant gut all over. I hustle out after her. We do not need them calling the cops to report two crazed women, obviously high on something.

The giggles die away as we leave the town behind, and climb back up into the hills, now full of mysterious darkness. The moon has yet to show her face, but we've got our windows open, and the fresh scent of pines gusts in as we drive. There's nobody else on the road, nobody at all, so we slow down, talking. And when we come to another little road, I turn off. It meanders through the pines to-ward a lakeshore, minimally built up with a couple of cleared patch-es for tents, some scruffy gravelled parking area, and a picnic table perched on the grassy slope above the water. We climb up onto the table, with our haul of goodies, and eat a late dinner while the moon finds her way up into the sky, down into the lake.

We're still there, talking, when the sun sends rays over the hills to touch the trees on the lake's western edge. One night was never going to be enough to explain stories we didn't understand ourselves. But we drive away from that lake as something like sisters.

Even so, even though it's easier to tell Shanaya things than it ever was to share them with my own blood, I'm nervous, now that I've told her my worst suspicions about what's going on.

I can't afford to forget she is not just a were-tiger. She is also a lawyer.

When I told her about how George and Édith the Embryo ended up with Sandra's farm—my fault entirely, I always figured, and nothing to be done but live with Sandra's fucking unasked forgiveness (fake as the Embryo's tits) and try to keep my own kids from hating me even more than they already do—when I told her all that, she got the lawyer look, which is almost as scary as her tiger face, and started talking about how there might be a way to get it back. I can't deal with that right now. But even that feels easier than figuring out how I prove my live-in werewolf is killing men when, in the first place, I don't have proof.

I walk her through what I remember of the night at Blondie's Motel, and even though she's an experienced lawyer, she's got no easy answer.

I cannot say clearly what I actually saw that horrible night, and there's no way to tell the story that doesn't sound raving mad.

In the second place, that man, with his razor whip and cocaine? Maybe the world is cleaner without him. Maybe killing him saved a lot of other victims of his evil. Maybe my monster, not human, is humane.

MISSY: ALL-NIGHTER

They're going for sushi, again. And maybe it's that Frankie is already there with Maengan, the two of them laughing about something as Missy enters, Frankie's face catching what light is available. Maengan doesn't leap up to get her chair, and Missy scrapes it hard across the floor. Not that she's ever let him do that for her, anyway. They've gone out with Frankie before.

Why does it bother her so much that Frankie is there with him ahead of her?

'Hey, Miss,' says Frankie. 'We didn't order yet.'

She passes Missy a menu. *As if that is the issue*, thinks Missy. She flips her menu. Maengan raises a brow at her, then at Frankie. Frankie's slight moue in response just makes it worse. *How dare they understand each other so well?*

'So,' says Missy, her voice cawing in her own ear, 'no kimchi today, Maengan?'

'No, don't think so,' says Maengan, voice deliberately, provocatively, neutral and friendly. 'I'm feeling like a dynamite roll, though. Yous?'

Frankie is about to speak, but Missy cuts in, 'What is it with these pretentious names anyhow? Dynamite roll. Pfff. Don't you get sick of it, Maengan? Doesn't it bother you?' Both of them are staring at her. 'You're Anishinaabe, for fuck's sake. The Nippon Nish.'

They've called him that before, but this time it isn't funny, not at all.

'Hey, Miss—' says Frankie.

'No.' Missy shuts her down. 'Listen. Doesn't it bother you guys at all? We're in Turtle Island, for fucks' sake, and we're eating Asian food. And you,' she sneers at Maengan, 'you go on about power foods, fighting foods. What about our own? Doesn't it matter to you that there are no Indigenous restaurants?'

'Well,' says Frankie, 'there's Bannock Panic—'

'Yeah, but do we go there? No. We go here. To pretend we're in some fantasy land of the Rising Sun, some sort of Nish Samurai act. This is not *our* power food. What is it with you?'

She glares. He refuses to take offence.

'What? I like sushi.'

"But you're always going on about Japanese crap. Like some god-damned hipster. Or worse, some leftover of the 1980s. *Domo fucking arigato, Mr. Roboto!*'

'Miss!' Frankie lays a hand on her. 'Come on. Stop it.'

'No, really, you guys. Look around.' Missy hisses. 'You see any other Nish in here? We're too poor for this kind of life.'

'No, we're not,' says Frankie. 'We were once. And we've changed our situation. So what's wrong with that?'

Missy looks down, suddenly appalled at her own outburst. 'I'm… Sorry, sorry… you're right.' She heaves a sigh. 'I just…'

She can't explain the pressure she's been feeling. Hazel has gone all weird. The news has been full of that gruesome murder at Blondie's. That truck, she'd had it on her website, before Joshua asked her to take it all down. There are rumours she hears, and she can't pin them down. Missy sits and stares at her tea cup now, embarrassed that she's taken it out on Maengan, again, all her anger at the ongoing misery she can't look away from. The things she doesn't want to be central to her life.

It's Maengan who fills the awkward silence.

'Hey, listen. I grew up on the Rez, okay. People there, too many of them still figure poverty is authentic culture. It's all around them, so how could they know different? Then, even if they think they can't bring Traditional culture into a globalized city, they drag poverty behind them. That's not you, Miss. But it is the people you have to work with, the people you try so hard to serve. And we love you for that.'

We. Now he and Frankie are a team? She flushes. But Frankie actually kicks her, under the table, shakes her head. Missy is so shocked, she says nothing.

The food arrives, and as they eat, Maengan fills the silence.

'Poverty: You know what poverty is? That broken window.' He gestures at the old walkup across the street, with the one cracked pane. 'The social gentrifiers talk about 'broken window syndrome,' but they don't get it either. Poverty's when you break the window, and it stays broken because you don't know how to fix a window, because nobody ever taught you. But you don't feel you can call a glazier, if you happen to live where there is one, because they will laugh at you for your ignorance, or they'll rip you off because you don't know what glass should cost, and they'll sneer at the state of the rest of your house if they were to come to fix that window for you. So, you stay ignorant, because at least that way you have a little pride. And your window stays broken.'

'Then you patch it with wood,' says Frankie, looking at her sister, 'because you know how to hammer a nail. And maybe you don't mind it being darker inside, because nobody can see how you're hurting there, for the sake of your pride. And nobody who might otherwise reach out will know how to honour that pride, and just teach you how to fix a window. It's not too expensive, really, if you have the means to cart the glass.'

Missy heaves a sigh. 'It's not the lack of glass that keeps you in the dark, it's the knowing where to get glass, and the confidence to go in and buy it, and then, have a good way to carry the glass, and—'

'And the knowledge of what to do with it,' Maengan picks it up. 'Me, I got a friend to teach me, because I'll never forget when Dad punched out the eye of the living room, and didn't ever fix it. For the rest of the life of our house—Dad's house—we let that window be, half dark. There was always too much else that needed fixing.'

***

The three of them talk long into the night, first over dinner, then as they wander down Whyte, making eastward toward the train. As they cross the ravine bridge, flags snap in a light breeze and Frankie says, 'If you were a country, what country would you be?'

Missy shoots her a startled glance. This is their private territory, these sorts of games. But Maengan looks up at the flags, nods his head up at one. 'Nihon,' he says.

'What, just because we had sushi?' Frankie teases.

Maengan laughs. Then he stops, leans his elbows elegantly on the rail, leans out over the night ravine. 'No,' he says softly, 'I think it may be the other way around. Because I am Japan, I always pick sushi.' He smiles, tips his head a bit to the side. 'Don't I always pick sushi, Miranda?'

Missy feels her cheeks burning, is glad of the cool concealing dark. She can't think what to say.

But she doesn't have to worry. Maengan sighs and continues. 'You know, someone once told me I was 'clinging on' to Japan, because I went there on an exchange once.'

'You did?' says Frankie, and they lean either side of him, 'What was it like?'

'Like coming home,' says Maengan slowly, 'to the place we should've been.'

The girls both wait, attentive. Missy thinks wonderingly, Frankie was right to ask. He plays 'what country?' as seriously as they ever did. 'How so?' she says.

And he tells them of fire festivals and the management of forests, of shrines on all the hills, the easy acceptance that spirit inhabits everything, of the abundance of water and the ways that the hand-crafted co-exists with the high-tech.

'But what,' says Frankie, waving toward the faint sound of Mill Creek barely audible below the hum of the urban night congress, 'about the concreted rivers?'

'They still have those, it's true,' says Maengan, 'but don't we, too?'

'We brought something like old Rat Creek back to daylight,' says

Missy.

'And they've kept a lot of their wild water. And the thing is… the thing is, where they have urbanized, it's possibly as ugly as anywhere else, but there is a spirit moving always. I think it is because the land never lets them forget She is alive.'

'Mmm?' says Frankie.

'Earthquakes,' says Maengan. 'You ever been in one?'

'Around here? Not so much,' says Missy. 'Not unless you count the Fox Creek Fracking ones, back before we made UpTop.'

'I don't know about that,' says Maengan, 'but I remember the first one I ever felt. Everything shimmered, that's all. I was up in the mountains, hiking with my friend Kenji up Ooe-yama, this mountain they say is ogre-infested. It was winter, and we had just had lunch in the climbers' hut on top of the mountain. There was nobody else around, it was so peaceful. And then the air just sort of shimmered. I didn't know what it was. My friend did. He left an extra rice ball at the shrine at the top. '*Earthquake*,' he said, '*a good time to go back down.*' He just shrugged when I asked if we were in any danger up there. I tell you, I was scared. The snow was hip-deep up there, I know because we broke through once… and if there'd been an avalanche?… well, we'd have died. But Kenji just shrugged. *Shikata ga nai*,' he said.

'Meaning?' breathes Frankie.

'Whaddaya gonna do,' says Maengan in a comical voice, and pushes the railing away. 'Whaddya gonna do, sistah?' he says again, tipping an invisible gangster hat at them each in turn, and they set off eastward again.

They fall in step. Missy thinks about all the things people shrug off, the things they just let happen.

'How do you ever know what's worth fighting for?' she blurts. She expects Frankie knows what she means, but it is Maengan who answers.

'It's all worth it,' he says, 'but you learn—and this is the thing—that a lot of it doesn't need your help. The Earth is alive and she lets us live at her whim, basically. That frees up your attention, to find out what your sphere of influence really is. Who needs help, that's who you help.'

The sisters throw each other glances behind his back.

'That's why I'm here,' he adds, then falls silent. They let the silence lie, and take to the platform. The train glides in, they head north, all at ease, all somehow a little more electric. Above ground, underground, over the river, beneath downtown, the train glides into Inland Exchange, and they glide out. There are people here, too, coming and going despite the late hour. Up the escalators, they come out on UpTop, and start the winding walk down.

'It's a long way home, but we like this walk,' says Missy to Maengan, just a little challenging. He just grins, 'Shikata ga nai. Guess we're walking.'

And they glide along in companionable silence, watching the night. The sky is lightening to lemon as they turn down Missy's street.

'You guys tired?' says Frankie.

'What you got in mind?'

'Albert's,' Frankie laughs, a sparkle in her eyes as they pass under a streetlight. She has walked all night and she's still fresh.

Missy turns to Maengan. 'Do you know the pancake house?'

'Pancakes?' says Maengan. 'Those, I do not eat. But I could murder for bacon and eggs.'

'Come on then, slow poke,' says Frankie, and leads them along a small alley, heading west. 'It's a good half hour more from here, but shikata ga nai, big boy.'

In the shadows of the alley, in the stretch where the streetlights don't quite reach, they all see her. A thin woman, drawn into herself. She is carrying her shoes, they see as they come closer, and her long hair is pulled back in two tails, a young girl's hairdo, though she is clearly a woman.

Missy notices the way Maengan makes himself quiet, makes himself soft, gentles his energy.

They acknowledge the woman, all of them, with nods and murmurs. She nods and murmurs back, though her eyes flick fast over them, finding no threat but ready for one. She swings the heels, looks like she's ready to bolt. They ease by her, keep themselves quiet 'til they're well down the next street.

Missy kicks and scuffs at the sidewalk, picks up the pace. Frankie and Maengan, to her surprise, step up beside her. They say nothing, just put her in the centre, and walk on with their backs to the dawn.

SYRUP

Frankie licks the syrup from her knife. Missy cringes beside her, flicks her gaze to Maengan, not wanting to see the hunger that men always show around Frankie. But Maengan, when she looks, is looking straight back at her, his gaze kind. He picks up the syrup jug, the little glass canister with its crystallized crust around the spout.

'This stuff,' he says, 'is poison, am I right?'

Frankie puts her knife down, startled. 'What?'

'High-fructose corn syrup,' he says, 'is killing the Western World.'

'Yeah,' says Frankie, 'but who can afford the real thing?'

'Remember?' says Missy. 'Remember when—?'

'Of course I do,' says Frankie, uncharacteristically sharp. She sighs, gives Missy a little smile. 'Our uncle, the one I'm named for, used to make sure we always had a big can of real Maple Syrup, every year. He'd bring them back from Ontario, whenever he had work out there. And if he didn't, he'd get them shipped.'

Maengan nods.

'He said,' says Missy, 'that his uncle always made sure they had the real thing when he was a kid.'

'Zhiiwaagamizigan' says Frankie, 'the oldest promise. Ininatiq's gift to The People.'

'You know that story then?' says Maengan.

'Only sort of,' says Missy. 'Uncle Frankie used to tell us...' she looks at her sister, Frankie of the maple-syrup hair, Frankie with the eyes—and Frankie takes a deep breath, leans back in the booth.

They are nearly alone here. The servers are over on the other side of the restaurant, where it's filled up some. Frankie begins:

"Long long ago, the Anishinaabek lived close upon the land. And the land was good to us. In spring, fiddle heads; then *ode'iminan,* strawberries; then all the berries of summer. In the fall, *manomin,* the wild rice; and of course, the animals who also fed upon the richness of the land, in turn fed us with the abundance of their fat, rich bodies.

But the winter was hard; hard for everyone.

Geese and ducks could ride the wind south to the summer lands. Bear went out into the dreamlands. But when the snow was too deep, the cold too cutting, the moose grew thin and the people grew thinner. Separated into small family hunting camps, the people suffered, struggled, and prayed that they would survive.

The story is that one family, one time, found themselves, when winter was almost gone, wasted to the point of near death. And one of them staggered out into the snow, and prayed.

It might have been the father, too weak to track, reduced to humbly pleading; *Was there any alive who had flesh to spare him and his children?*

But some say it was the mother, her breasts too soon dry, blindly searching for some last chance to feed her frail and dying baby.

Praying, she began to weaken, her voice faltering. Her words had faded to a whisper when she fell back against the bare grey trunk of Ininatiq, the man tree, cold and sleeping like the rest of the still, grey world.

With one last whisper, there finally came an answer. *(tap tap, Frankie's fingers on the formica)*

And suddenly, softly, she heard an answering voice. *(Frankie's nails scratch the table, zithering)*

Ininatiq had heard her somehow, and somehow found words that reached through the woman's weakness and delirium.'

Frankie throws a look at Missy, nods. Missy joins in, softly:

"This, my body, like your body, belongs
to the Earth. But I am Ininatiq, and I feed on deeper things.
My roots reach deep, beneath winter's mantle, and Earth Mother
nurses me all through the cold and darkness.

All through the dark, my roots
swell with lifeblood, waiting

until spring, when again
I will unfurl my hands of green.

My hands are like your hands.
I am Ininatiq, the human tree,
and we are related.

I am full.
You are hungry.

Let me feed you
like a wet-nurse might feed her sister's babies.

My strength is yours for the asking, because
We are related. Let me feed you."

Missy falls silent. The lamp over their table feels like the only light, the rest of the diner as far as an Eastern forest, as Frankie continues.

'And where the woman's cheek was pressed against her cool grey skin, Ininatiq opened her bark for the woman and let flow her rising life's blood. And the woman, weak as a baby, drew life from this borrowed breast and grew strong.

As she nursed, Ininatiq murmured to her as a mother to a baby, softly teaching her the way to tap and use maple sap: first, to survive, to stave off starvation until the waking world brought other foods. And then, to make sweet the survival—maple tea, maple syrup, maple candy, maple sugar.'

And she starts humming, her eyes closed, and Missy joins in, just for a few bars of Ward Allen's old classic fiddle tune. Maengan joins in, their voices floating softly almost beyond time.

Then the shuffle of the server's shoes intrudes, and they all shift, spell broken.

'You about done here?' she says.

Maengan snakes a hand out and takes the little black melamine tray with the bill.

'I got this,' he says.

HAZEL: THE TIGER IN HER DEN

Morning sun lights the ribbon of highway winding back toward Amiskwaciy, back toward normal, blue glass towers, scruffy old neighbourhoods, the LRT trains that took so long to get right, Inland Station bulking dimly in the haze. I glance over at her, this woman I thought I'd chosen as a friend. Now, I have to wonder who chose who. I roll it back through my mind and it still bothers me.

'Shanaya,' I say, 'remember how we met?'

'Of course,' she says, flicking a glance out the window. 'How could I forget? Even my mother wondered after, how did that come to be? How were we there just then?'

'Durga puja?'

'Yes, but,' she shakes her head with a wry grin, 'Look at us. We are not devout, not like that. Mom's a scholar. I'm a lawyer.'

I make a noise in my throat.

'Yes, and a tiger,' she adds. 'The thing is, Hazel, we didn't even set out with the intention of going there. I'd picked her up to take her to the spice market, yes, but not that one.'

'So?'

'So. It was like…' her voice trails off, and one long hand waves vaguely toward the open pack, pulls back.

'Go on,' I say.

'We smoke too much.'

'Yeah. But you know, it is a medicine, the old people say.'

'Still, people overdose on medicines.'

She's wrinkling her nose when I glance over. I can't help seeing her other face, right there shimmering in the mind's eye. Sweat prickles out on my arms. 'Light one for me while you're at it.' I keep my voice light. 'You know you want it. I won't tell your mom.'

That brings a little bubble of laughter, and she shakes herself, pulls out a couple smokes, lights both and gives one to me. We crack our windows in tandem, drop them to the same exact height and draw smoke together. Silence reigns for a minute. Then she starts laughing.

'Look at us! We could be a synchronized smoking team.'

It's true, we're moving in unconscious unison. Maybe that's all it is, I think. She's one of my Own, those people you meet in a lifetime who just fit, for whatever the reason.

'Maybe,' she says, obviously thinking along with me, 'It's because we were family in another lifetime. We Hindus believe in transmigration of souls, after all.'

'How does that work?'

'I don't know. I am shockingly unschooled, and I don't know, sometimes, whether I really want to know.'

'Don't you think you need to know, because of … you know—?'

'Because of this tiger thing? Yeah, I think of that sometimes. But then, I think maybe it won't help.'

She crushes out her smoke, goes right ahead and lights another. I take mine without comment.

'Actually,' she sighs, 'if you want the truth, I've deliberately avoided trying to learn too much, in case I don't like what I learn. I mean… this that I am… some would say, I am a monster.'

I glance over, and her face looks stricken. I look away quick, the only privacy I can offer.

'I… I mean… Hazel… I … haven't even told my mother.'

I choke and cough. I mean, I'm good at covering, but this is a big one.

'You what?! You're kidding!' I'm horrified. We drive on in absolute silence.

Then she starts laughing and I'm laughing, too. It's a bit like hysteria, probably.

We laugh and laugh. Finally, we subside.

'So...'

'No,' she says, 'It's true. I have not told Diya. Can you imagine?'

'That's a pretty big thing.'

'Yes. And all the psychology books talk about how maturity requires developing what they call differentiation, but—' That sets us off again, giggling. *Differentiation. Turning into a tiger is pretty differentiated.*

'Still... you have to wonder... what if it's inherited?'

'Of course I wonder that. For years, I've wondered. What if she is a tiger, too? Then I think, she cannot be. Otherwise, she'd tell me. Diya is not the sort to be a tiger and not tell her child. She is such a *mother*, she'd definitely have advice for me.'

It's true and we giggle a bit, but the wave of laughter has passed. In its wake, we talk a while of the legalities of witnessing a murder if you can't say what you really saw. And does it count as abetting if the guy you drive away with is not exactly the beast that was in the murder room?

'Hazel,' she finally says, 'come on, let's go tell mother I'm a tiger. It is easier than knowing what laws apply to your case.'

So, now we're headed for Diya's house. Should've taken the LRT, I know, but neither of us even mentioned the possibility. We're driving. My Jeep smells like dog—well, like Spider, which is all the same to me, but I almost ask Shan whether she can smell a difference. She's polite. She'll never say anything about it if I don't bring it up... but God ... the smell must have been driving her crazy. No wonder she smoked so much, and no wonder she shape-shifted. Talk about your triggering events.

I look at her, she smiles at me, and there is nothing, after all, that I want to say. We just watch the streetscapes unroll, the innocuous curls of pavement leading us to Diya's place, which could be any other home in this community.

We pull up, and the door is already opening.

'She watches from the window,' says Shanaya.

***

Sitting in Diya's living room drinking coffee, we bring the conversation round obliquely, the same way we approach the snacks she has arrayed on her glass-topped coffee table. The breakfast of left-over road food feels a long time ago, so I sink my teeth as politely as possible into the most filling looking of the squares.

'Mommy-ji, do you ever feel like.. you know.. cut off from our traditions? You know, Hazel and I were talking about how strange the way we met, in the Durga puja aisle. Strange, right? Mommy-ji?,' says Shanaya, running a hand through her glossy hair. 'Do you think there is anything in it? Any chance that this is somehow spiritually ordained?'

Diya huffs. 'Spiritually ordained? What sort of lawyer says such things?! You cannot think that way.'

'Why not?'

'Look at the news! Look what Rigvedi did over there, before they got him settled down.'

'What does Rigvedi have to do with it?'

'Everything!'

'But I'm not talking about politics! I'm talking about spirituality.' Diya actually snorts.

'No. You think you are talking about spirituality, but you are dabbling in nonsense, dangerous nonsense. It has its place, but that is not here.'

She looks at me piercingly. 'It is different for you, Hazel. This is your land. You have a right to reclaim spirituality of this land, and to share it with us, but only if you wish to.' That doesn't quite make sense, given half my family were immigrants, too. I can't interrupt Diya, though.

'But we, daughter, we are best to just get on with our lives. We are not colonialists, dragging our culture and flogging all our old worn out traditions along, afraid to be where we are now.'

'Don't you regret leaving all that behind?' I ask.

'No.' Diya clicks her coffee cup down firmly to emphasize her point.

'But isn't that why you go to Diwali celebrations?' asks Shanaya.

'No! Certainly not.' Diya laughs.

'Why is that funny?' says Shanaya.

But it's me that Diya favours with a wink. 'I go because I'm looking for a cutie.'

'Ma!'

'You could stand to do the same, Beti.'

'But what does it have to do with Rigvedi?' Shanaya will not be deflected, and I am fascinated, for a moment, by the thought of how this all started between them, the two razor-sharp minds squaring off against each other. They are a closed plurality, and I'm on the outside. I feel myself struck, suddenly.

Why aren't my girls and I like this? Why do they hate me?

Okay, I know they don't hate me. *It's melodramatic to say they do, of course they don't, but look how hard it was for Missy to tell me she's seeing Maengan. At least, I surmise that's what she was trying to say. And who knows who Frankie sees. I can't even remember the last time that we sat down, we three, for any kind of serious girl talk. They probably do that with Sandra. Damn interfering busybody, why did she never have kids of her own?*

I shy away from that path, jerk my mind back to the present, where Diya is holding forth.

'Back in 1987, it was,' she says, tapping my wrist, 'Doordarshan, this is Jai Hind's first national television station. It changed everything. They broadcast the entire Ramayana over a period of eighteen months, filmed like a soap opera. People loved it. They had no idea how big it was going to be, I'm sure. But everyone watched it. You remember, Shana-Beti.'

'I do?'

'Yes, remember,' Diya peeves. 'We went to Delhi that spring, and you thought that this was normal—'

'What was?'

'The way the streets were clogged, but absolutely clogged, with people watching TV in public spaces.' She flicks a glance at Shanaya, then turns to me and puts a thin hand on my arm. 'You can't imagine, truly you can't.'

I wouldn't dare to say if I could. That much I've learned about Diya.

'Anyway, it started everything, as far as Indian mass media. Forget about Bollywood. *Ramayana* on TV in 1987, that is what started it. People gathered in their family homes, in the public places, even in the streets. They anointed their TVs with oil, flower garlands and tikkas, and they conducted *darshan*—worship by the gaze—on Lord Ram and his retinue, performed by actors for national audiences to see. And the actors! Gopil, who played Lord Ram, was never 'til now able to get any other role. He was too beloved as Ram-ji.'

She suddenly turns on her daughter.

'Why do you wear your hair long, Shanaya? You are a lawyer, not Sita waiting to be rescued from Ravana.'

It's an opening, and Shanaya takes a deep breath. But Diya springs up, shoots from the room, leaving us silent. She sweeps back in, waving a shiny business card. 'Look. Here is my new stylist. Aaron. He is great. I mean, look at this cut, won't you?' She actually spins, cupping her gorgeous pixie cut skull. 'I am thinking he may be right, that ombré would suit me. Hazel, what do you think? Shall I dare to go ombré? It's such a funny word, isn't it? Like the wild west.' She drops her hands to her approximation of a gunfighter's ready pose, then sits down, laughing.

'Oh, I am sorry, Hazel. You know I do not mean to be culturally insensitive.'

I really don't know what to say, so I just say nothing, staring at her over my coffee cup. I don't need to speak anyway, Shanaya is full of offence on my behalf.

I listen to them bickering, and know there is no way that Shanaya will tell Diya today. If ever. And I'm no closer to solving my many problems, but somehow, I haven't got the energy to care. I sink into the cushions of Diya's sofa, and drift off to the musical sound of family squabbling.

***

Soft light, warm light, golden heart, nesting, resting. Mine. Today. Ri oo ri oo. Consider.

MAENGAN: TRUTH AND CONSEQUENCES

Maengan lies still, listening to the sisters breathe, watching the light grow. Missy's lying on her back with one arm stretched above her head, and his hair is caught under her shoulder. He eases closer to her, carefully. Asleep, she moves her arm away from the pressure of his head, and Maengan pulls his trapped hair free.

What if I just don't tell her?

He can see the thin film of dust on various surfaces—a spotless house is clearly low on Missy's list of priorities, and he smiles at that. The space is not slovenly, but there's the slight disarray of a busy person. Unlike Frankie, Missy appears to care little for decoration, and the little studio's furnishings appear to be chosen for function and simplicity. She has no time for fussy things.

What good will it do to tell her?

He gently rolls over, careful not to pull the duvet away from Missy. On the sofa just above her, Frankie sleeps curled like a cat, her long hair fanned around her.

He has never felt so at peace, and now he has to destroy that.

How do you tell somebody you're a shapeshifter? He lets himself fall back into sleep, exhausted by this question that's been stalking him for weeks now.

MISSY: MORNING

Soft light, warm light, golden on them, Missy and Maengan curl on the floor, nested in the quilt dragged from her bed. Frankie lies under a lumpy afghan on the sofa, her caramel hair trailing down upon Missy's back.

Missy wakes first, her arm cramped beneath her head. Maengan has turned onto his back, and it's probably his soft snoring that has wakened her. She studies his sleeping face briefly, 'til Frankie leans down from above and whispers, in an exaggerated accent, 'Ever cute, eh?'

'Stop it,' Missy hisses, batting her sister away, and pushes herself upright. Maengan snores on.

The girls rise softly and stretch, tugging at their rumpled clothes, smoothing their hair.

'Coffee?' whispers Missy.

'Mmm,' Frankie replies, dropping into a graceful forward bend, her hair splaying over Missy's dusty floor.

Missy opens her cupboard doors carefully, aware of their squeaks.

'Huh,' she says softly, and Frankie glides over, pats her shoulder.

'How about I run down to the tienda and grab us some? Maybe some fruit?' Missy nods, turns. Frankie waves, already opening the door. 'I've got this.' She steps out, leans back in. 'I'll be gone about 15 minutes,' she grins, winking, 'but I can take longer if he wakes up.'

'He's awake, now,' says Maengan. 'Bring him coffee.' A cushion sails through the air, and Frankie dodges, laughing. 'And stop embarrassing your sister.'

***

Ti-en-da. Nest. Caw fee. Black bitter. Roots them to day and this where. Frankie brings caw-fee.

Ti ti ti, tienda is nest for caw-fee. Ti ti ti, Sun loves Frankie. Consider. In coffee and sun, Maengan can tell them, they will stay safe in nest.

***

'So,' says Maengan to Missy, 'there's something I need to tell you.'

'Okay,' she says, leaning back, palms wrapped round the edge of her countertop. She tilts her head slightly, nervous. He paces slowly around her apartment, as if trapped in its open-concept single room.

'Um… could you not look at me for a moment?'

Missy looks at her floor. *He's going to say he's gay.*

'So, last night, Missy,' he says, 'I really had a great time with you and Frankie.'

'Mmm,' she says, small and tight. *He's gay, or he's got a girlfriend. Or kids. A wife.*

'I mean it. I really felt at home, you know?'

'Mmm.' *He's going to say she feels like a sister to him.*

'Safe.'

'Mm.' *Yup, it's sister-zone, whether he's got a girlfriend or a boyfriend.*

'Okay. Missy. Stop. Stop saying *mmm*.' He stops pacing, in front of her. Her arms are wrapped tight around herself.

'Missy,' he says, 'This is really … um… look… Can you look at me?' She brings her head up, then, shoulders squared. He looks deeply into her eyes, and she looks back, guarded, ready for whatever she thinks he's going to say. He loves how her chin juts forward, her whole jaw, like a pugnacious she-pirate.

'I really like you.' She blinks. 'I mean, I really like you.' She turns, brushes past him, strides to a kitchen chair and sits.

'Okay,' she says, 'I'm sitting down. You really like me. What's the 'But'?'

He spins away, bends over the countertop, like he's going to be sick in the sink. He groans.

'Hey, come on,' says Missy. 'How bad can it be? So, you don't want a relationship, just say it—'

'No. No! No!' He thumps the counter top, pushes himself upright. She springs to her feet, really alarmed now. 'It's not like that!'

He holds out his hands to her, pleading, 'Sorry. Sorry. Look... phew... um...'

Now she is wondering whether it is a disease.

'Is it a disease?'

He actually laughs, a strangled little bark of a laugh. He's shaking.

'Hey,' says Missy, unaccustomed to the need to soothe. 'Look. Maengan. Whatever it is, you can just say. I mean, I've seen it all, okay? Some nights in Emerg—'

'Oh!' Maengan interrupts her, looking out the window. 'Here comes Frankie.' He sighs, straightens his shoulders. 'Maybe that's best. I'll tell you both when she gets here.'

Missy frowns, forces herself to soften. His distress reminds her of the girls who come in, beaten, terrified. Whatever Maengan is trying to say terrifies him, and her heart goes out to him.

'Okay,' she says.

***

'So,' says Maengan, as they sit together around Missy's table, her little kitchen bright with late morning sun. He takes a deep breath, blows it out, puts down his cup. The sisters look at him, heads tilted in unconscious unison.

'I need to tell you something.'

'Okay.' They speak as one.

He looks from one to the other. A little breeze slips in the window, faintly acrid. His lip curls reflexively. He shakes his head, blows out his breath. They are still, alert, focussed on him.

He takes a deep breath and blurts it in a rush: 'I'm a shape-shifter.'

DEVIN: FINAL SCORE

The priest opens the door to find Devin bent over, puffing a bit.

'Father,' he says without preamble, 'I've found another one.'

'Slow down,' says the priest, 'Another…?"

'Another tally mark. It's fresh.'

'Huh,' says the priest. 'Come in a minute, have a drink of water. I'll get Mitts and we'll go see.' He uses all his calming force, all his years of training in projecting calm and surety. He waves Devin toward the kitchen, deliberately taking his time to find his hanging vest, pat through the pockets for his smokes. 'Mitts,' he calls gently, and the little dog looks up. She's already at his feet, protruding eyes sparkling. She knows there's a walk impending. He smiles indulgently at her, ruminatively dresses her in the small harness and snaps on the leash. 'Dog bags,' he murmurs to her, rummaging in the little storage bench.

'Devin,' he calls, 'could you bring me a plastic bag from the back? We're out of dog bags.'

These easy, familiar things have calmed Devin when he comes out, and the two men set out, little dog ranging happily ahead, into the evening air.

It's there, almost blazingly fresh, the jaggedness of it contrasting sharply with the other marks on the wall. This one looks almost brazen, the top of it well above the potentilla, easily visible from across the street if you know what you're looking for.

The priest idles to a halt casually in front of it, and Mitts proceeds into the underbrush as the priest languidly pulls out the smokes, lights himself one. Narrowing his eyes against the rising smoke, he takes a drag, looks a question at Devin. 'It wasn't there this morning, Father,' says the kid.

Shit, thinks the priest.

'The thing is,' says Devin, bobbing his head, tugging at his hair, then planting himself solid, responsible, 'My friends say they saw what happened.'

Shit, thinks the priest. *He gives too much to those friends.*

'They say, Father—and this just doesn't make sense—it was a rabbit. LeWayne left me a text. How could it be a rabbit?'

Devin has worried this thought over, and he doesn't like the answer. The Boys have told him they are clean, but he also knows they just say stuff like that to appease him. It's written all over their bodies—oxy, blitz, meth—the stuff they use to get by.

He shows the priest the text.

'I called LeWayne, Father, and he sounded... well, he sounded high, Father. He said something about going after this rabbit. That the cops told him to get this rabbit. That's crazy, right?'

The priest does not know what to think. Then again, he's not sure he's ever cared less for thinking. Something wild is hammering through him, and he almost grabs Devin and swings him around gleefully. Efren knows he is absurd. Efren wonders if he's high.

He just can't believe what has happened.

Shit, thinks the priest. *Why does worry about the world never leave Devin alone long enough for him to just be a normal boy? To fall in love.*

'Listen, Devin. I think you need to let it go now. Your Auntie has those files. Send her the text, if you think it's anything more than LeWayne on a trip. And I'll text LeWayne's group home manager to check up on him, okay? You've done what you had to do, okay?'

The kid looks doubtful, slightly hurt. *How can I explain?* Efren wonders. Then he breaks his long discipline, and grabs the startled youth around the shoulders, not even worrying that the kid might be alarmed.

'Devin,' he says without artifice, 'If I had a son, I'd want him to be like you. In fact, you're the closest I'll ever come to being a real father. And I'm telling you this because I love you: leave it with the professionals now. You need to put the burden down, and let yourself be young.'

If the priest has a prayer for Devin, it is that he can be young while he's got time. As for himself, Efren Mannfredsson can only pray that this wild thing is real, and that there is time for a tired, middle-aged, cynical priest to still be just a human, just a man. He prays for time for love.

He'd been walking Mitts, thinking about Devin, about the mystery, about all the mysteries and aches of his parish, and he'd wandered over the Creek, up into Norwood, and was coming home, the little white dog pattering wearily, well-exercised by keeping up with the priest's long-limbed stride. And then, he turned a corner.

Just that. Turned a corner, and there she was. *Cendrine.*

She stood in the fall of light, slightly dappled by leaf shade. As he drew nearer, he saw that she was not at all Cendrine, she was her own self, a plump middle-aged woman at the foot of his stairs about to ascend to the rectory porch. Mitts gave a tiny yip and she turned, and her face was the face his soul had searched for all his life. Or something stupid like that.

Logically, it was because she was Devin's aunt, and he knew Devin's face so well. But his heart still hammered illogically, and he stopped stock still, just staring, a smile of wonder on his face.

'Sandra,' he said, 'you must be Sandra.'

Her look of astonishment that he knows her name makes him laugh, and she marvels at how young he suddenly looks, how tall, how vivid. She stares back, open-mouthed.

'Devin's Auntie, yes?' he saves her. 'He told me you would come by for his book.'

Mitts has tired of waiting and is bouncing against Sandra's knees, yipping approval.

Efren invites Sandra in, and as she steps over the threshold, he feels a physical shock, as if all his decades of restlessness have come to ground in her. She glows in his view, like a live, life-saving copper line.

MAENGAN: I LIKE YOU...

There. He's said it. And they are stock still, staring. Then they look to each other, blowing out their breath in unison. They take a deep breath, still looking at each other, and then they both turn to him.

'Really?' They both ask.

He nods, looking down.

'Well, I'll be,' says Frankie, sliding out a chair and melting gracefully onto it. 'We were just talking about this the other day!'

'What?!' Now he looks up.

'No, no,' says Missy, 'not about you being one—'

'Although maybe in our hindminds, do you think we knew or something, Miss?'

Frankie sounds like a little kid with a new toy. Now it's Maengan's turn to stare. Missy pulls out another chair, and Frankie gets up, steps in, and takes him gently by the arm.

'Come on, Maengan, sit down and spill, before we have to tip you.'

He lets himself be set on the third chair, and listens, dumbfounded, while Missy and Frankie tell him everything they know in theory about shapeshifting, and badger him with questions about how his personal experience matches with the theoretical.

The sun climbs into the sky. They drink their coffee and examine, in the bright light of morning, this newfound dimension in Maengan. As for Maengan, for the first time in his life, he's told the truth, and he can't quite orient himself.

'I thought,' he says finally, 'it would be so much different. So much harder. Impossible, really, to just tell people I'm a shapeshifter.'

'What about the one who … you know…' Frankie hesitates, '… made you?'

'That's different.' He colours up. Missy glares at her sister.

'Sorry,' says Frankie, 'It's too soon, eh? We don't need to know.'

They haven't asked him the other obvious question, so he asks them.

'You want to see me shift?' They nod, speechless.

'Well,' he says with a thin, wry smile, 'That's the thing. I can't just do it whenever. I have to be really upset or something. And…' he looks around the bright apartment, heaves a sigh, 'It is just so hard to be that upset with you two.'

'What?' quips Frankie, 'You telling us we just have to take your word for it?'

Missy has turned red and silent. She pushes her chair back and shoots upright.

'Maengan Nolan!' she shouts. '*I Like You But I'm a Werewolf?* That's the worst break up excuse ever!' And she stomps away to the bathroom, slamming the only available door in her house. Maengan is staring at her, mouth open, when Frankie winds up and slugs him, hard. He folds over, winded.

And comes back up, snarling, shifting.

'Missy!' shouts Frankie. 'He's doing it!'

And Missy storms back to the kitchen, then stops short.

There stands Frankie, and there stands a wolf. The wolf shoots yellow glares at both of them, then gallops, skidding a bit on the dusty floor, into the bathroom, somehow contriving to push the door shut behind himself.

The sisters are still looking owl-eyed with shock when Maengan pokes his head out the door.

For a long moment, they all look at each other.

Frankie breaks first.

'Okay, then, Maengan,' she says, 'we believe you.'

'Thanks.'

'Sorry I punched you.'

'Thanks.'

'But seriously, that is a crappy excuse to break up with my sister.'

'I wasn't—' he objects.

'We're not even—' Missy blurts.

'Well, you should be,' says Frankie, the social convener. 'For the adventure if for nothing more.'

'Come on, Maengan,' she adds, 'you might as well come out here.'

'My clothes—' he stops as Frankie starts laughing.

'Miss! You should've seen it! Just like those old Hulk cartoons … rrrrip!'

Frankie's laughter ripples through the tension and pushes them through the waves of confusion toward shore.

In a world of wonders, what's one more, between friends, or between people who are more than friends?

'Borrow a towel or something,' calls Missy, and when he emerges, clad in her old blue bathrobe, she starts giggling along with Frankie.

Maengan takes a deep breath, flings out his arms dramatically, and lets loose a tiny, falsetto howl. He bows to them each, in turn, and comes back to the table, his eyes bright with tears.

'Thank you, thank you very much,' he says, still in falsetto, wiping his eyes on the bathrobe sleeve. Then he sighs. 'Seriously,' says Maengan Nolan to these women who have brought him home, 'Thank you.'

EFREN: ALL CHANGE

Efren drags himself back to the present, watching Devin turn the corner.

Rabbit. Devin said something about a rabbit, in connection with the marks on the wall. He smiles, wondering if those friends of Devin's have hit upon the notion of hunting urban hares. Jack rabbits? Snowshoes? Whichever. *Good luck to them*, he thinks, bemused and unconcerned for the hares. They are wily, the rabbits of the inner city, and ought to easily outmatch Devin's friends. The priest knows he's not being uncharitable, just honest. Those kids were not the brightest lights, even without the growing damage of their addictions.

Devin, now, Devin would never hunt for fun. If Devin ever needed to hunt, he would just get on and do it, and it would inexorably be done.

Efren smiles as he brushes his hair, leaving it loose. In the foyer mirror though, he catches sight of himself and long habit wins. He retreats and finds a hair tie. He supposes that the pony tail and hat, same as always, hide the fundamental change that is carrying him out the door, down the street, toward an invitation to dinner and the door to a whole new world.

MISSY: FIGHTING FOODS

'So,' says Maengan, from the kitchen, 'I've got some kimchi. Want some?'

'Kimchi?' says Frankie, 'Isn't that Korean? Aren't you supposed to be Japan-man?'

'The Nish from Nippon, the Nippon Nish?' quips Missy. They've walked all the way back to Maengan's place, talking about it. The girls took it surprisingly well, his revelation about shape-shifting. Maybe they're just pretending it's normal to know someone who can turn into a wolf. It's not something they've seen before. But after his initial tears, their blank shock, all three of them address it for what it is, a fact of life that may be new to Missy and Frankie, but with which Maengan has simply had to live.

'So,' asks Frankie, as they turn into his street, 'Is it anything like your period?' Both Missy and Maengan stare open-mouthed. 'Come on, you guys. Seriously. Isn't shape-shifting supposed to be controlled by the moon, too?'

They walk and talk, and Maengan unburdens himself of his own ignorance. He doesn't know when it started. He doesn't know why. He isn't triggered by the smell of blood, not anymore. The moon is just the moon. He can't wear electronics near his body, or they fry. He isn't super strong, super smart, super fast. He just turns into a wolf, sometimes. And now, he's a young man standing in his kitchen, waving a jar of pickled cabbage at women who have made him feel, for the first time, fully seen and accepted.

Maengan offers each of them the bright orange condiment; each waves it off. 'More for me, then,' he says, and finds a spot on the floor, leaning against an awful leatherette pouffe chair. It sags, and he wriggles up until he's sitting on it.

'The thing is, this is Fighting Food,' he says, holding aloft the little plastic tub. 'When we were talking about maple syrup, I thought of this. See, Korea and Japan survived colonial incursions because they had their power foods.'

'Oh yeah?' says Frankie, eyes brightening.

'Yeah. And we,' says Maengan, 'have them too. But the difference is, somehow we lost a lot of them, for a while there.'

Frankie counters, 'At least we kept zhiiwaagamizigan. Maple syrup is not at all like high fructose corn syrup in how it acts on the body.'

'Because we're adapted to interact with it,' says Missy. 'I've been thinking about that, too. How that story matters, because it carries real information.'

'Absolutely,' says Maengan, 'about how to tap trees, when it happens, why it matters, the spiritual truth of it.'

Missy scoffs. 'But only the freakin' hipsters can afford the real thing now.'

'I've been thinking about that, Miss,' says Frankie. 'And I've decided, I'm only going to eat the real thing from now on.' She shrugs and her long hair ripples, 'Kind of a tribute to Uncle Frankie, and to The People.'

'Pfft,' says Missy, '*The People* are the ones who can least afford the real thing.'

She thinks of the thin woman they'd passed in the alley, her dangling shoes, her scant blouse, the stringiness of her altogether.

'Sorry,' she says, 'it just pisses me off that we're reduced to eating the crap of the crap, while our 'power foods' as you call them, are all in the hands of colonial elites who don't give a rat's ass about us. Who don't know the story of Ininatiq. If they think of maple syrup's origins at all, they think it's French-Canadian, for fucks' sake.'

'That's so true,' says Maengan, waving his tub of kimchi. 'Exactly the point I was going to make.' Missy stares, surprised.

'Same thing happened to Manomin.'

'Manomin?'

'Wild Rice, as they call it. Now that,' he says, 'was a power food of our people. And,' Maengan continues, 'do you know the stories of how we got related to Manomin?'

'No,' says Frankie, 'do you?'

'I wish,' says Maengan, shaking his head. 'I just know there are people fighting really hard to protect our harvests from multinationals. It's been a long fight. We've had to work really hard not to lose the spiritual connection in it, because we had to industrialize our production to a certain degree to fight them off.' He finishes the kimchi, licks the spoon. 'That's another reason I love Japan, actually. It was Japanese tech that helped us win the fight to keep control of our Manomin.'

'Oh?'

'The little Hino harvesters. Nobody was making those here,' says Maengan. 'All the agricultural equipment here was gigantic. Monster-sized. Japan had perfected smaller harvesters for the scale of rice fields there.'

'Like those little Hino trucks,' says Missy.

'Hino Elf,' says Frankie, laughing. 'There was one in Mom's neighbourhood, for some reason. Who knows why?'

'But we used to see it around there—'

'And we even made up a little song. Remember, Miss?'

'Oh God, no. Don't let her start, Maengan. You will regret it.'

Frankie begins to croon softly, 'Hino, Hino Elf…' and then she leaps to the middle of the floor and strikes a disco pose, 'I want to drive a HINO ELF!'

'No,' says Maengan, laughing. 'Not the Village People. I can accept many things in my house, but please, no Village People!'

He stands. Frankie laughs, settles back into the sofa.

'My point,' says Maengan, again in the kitchen, 'is that we had to break the Noble Savage idea that we are only authentic if we don't use technology. That's what Japan did so well.' He comes back with a glass of tap water. 'Now Korea, they did pickles. Kimchi,' he declaims, 'kept them healthy and strong.' And he settles back into the pouffe, with a discreet burp. The sisters drift over and settle against him, all of them just quietly resting.

And then, Missy's phone chirps, and the spell is broken.

'Stay with a lonely werewolf?' he croons at them as they rise and gather their things, but he walks them to the door as he says it.

Frankie steps out, pushes Missy back. 'At least give a lonely werewolf a kiss!' she says, and turns her back on them with a flourish, hands over her ears, tapping a foot while they kiss. Then Frankie turns back, leans in herself, and pecks Maengan on the cheek. 'Smooth,' she says. 'I guess kissing doesn't bring on the Change, either!'

And she grabs Missy by the arm, pulls her laughing down the hall.

***

At home, Missy finds her mind racing, looking through her cupboard. *All very well,* she thinks, *for them to talk about traditional foods and how they were key for health. How eating traditional foods is healthier, cheaper, cleaner in every way. All great. But what would they do if the global trade networks collapsed? What foods belonged here only? And how would the people who most needed them get them?* She knows what goes into the hampers for the Food Bank. The worst sort of crap. She'd done a project about that as a student nurse. Another thing that burned her up, how fucking ignorant people could be about how global economics play out on a local level.

She sighs. Pulls out a tub of chocolate spread. 'All hail Chocolatl,' she says to the empty room, and grabs a spoon. She kissed Maengan Nolan, and it was good. But what does it mean to be involved with a shape-shifter?

Her mind reels.

HAZEL: CARDS ON THE TABLE

A lower lip you could hang your purse off of gives him a look of permanent disgruntlement. His eyes, lopsided and thyroidal, are no help to his face.

How is Nell August sprung from this? I wonder. *Guy is a natural born cuckold. We are so suspicious of the ugly, when really, it's just one more mystery of natural selection. But that face. Has it always looked this bad? Is it a medical condition? How did—*

I blink. He's been talking, and I've been distracted by my revulsion. What did he just say?

'Some guy from down East.'

'James something,' adds Mrs. August. 'She was always going on about him, for a while there. Whenever she would talk to me. James says this, and James says that.'

'What was his last name?' Ugly Guy inquires mournfully of the ceiling.

'How would you know?' scoffs Mrs. August, and they stare at each other for a minute. I can't tell whether they're going to say more, or start fighting. Something contentious there, all right. But when isn't there, for people like them?

People like them. I hear it. It's the sort of thing Big Frankie would say, when he wasn't being piously Traditional. God, I miss that silly asshole. But that is not the point. The point is, they are finally telling me that Nell had or has a kid, whereabouts currently unknown. They saw this kid when she—*ah, a daughter*—was tiny, and Nell brought her up to visit.

So, this is it. Mrs. August is getting agitated, her pitted, puffy face darkening. I listen to what she says, what she doesn't say, the way she hardens toward Ugly Guy. The probabilities flash through my mind:

Ugly Guy trying to assert his status as man of the house. Ugly Guy pointing out that Nell is obviously a whore. Ugly Guy on her. Or maybe he went after the little girl—Mrs. August knows, but can't prove, or is scared to try to prove, because people will blame her, she blames herself, she isn't sure Nell didn't come on to Ugly Guy, who—one small mystery solved—is not her natural father; and there's a relief, a very small relief.

I hate people sometimes. Reminding myself that these sorts of ugly things happen to the rich and 'respectable' too doesn't help. For two cents, I'd—I feel my fists bunching, and keep them down below the desk edge. I swallow hard, not knowing what to say.

And just like that comes a scratching, quickly turned to a tapping, at the door. I make a show of looking at the clock.

The Augusts have stayed too long anyhow.

I let Jim in, and he nods briefly, keeps his eyes to himself as he moves over to the window and looks out, waiting for the Augusts to get their stuff together and get gone.

'You could've waited in the hall.'

He turns to face me.

'Hazel.' I really look at him then. 'I remember it now. All of it. I can tell you why I'm here in Amiskwaciy.' He's crying. 'I couldn't remember...'

So I go set up a pot of coffee, let him gather himself and begin again.

'I have a family, you know, back east.'

'I know, your sister who transferred your accounts.'

'No, I mean a wife.'

'Oh. Kids?'

'Her kids. She wanted to have more with me. God knows why. I was a shit. I'd go out drinking...' he coughs, shakes his head. 'Mar—

my ex, told me she was pregnant, and I went out for a pity party about what a burden that would be for me...'

I try not to think how he sounds like Ugly Guy.

'There are so many ways I fucked up my life. Mostly ordinary fuck-ups, selfish moves. But the thing is...I don't even remember when it happened.'

'When what happened?'

'Whatever made me *this*.' He runs a nervous hand through bushy hair. 'Look,' he holds up his long-boned fingers shackled in silver rings. 'I started wearing these in case they might stop me turning. Huh.' His hands are scarred beneath the silver. 'They do nothing. I bought them. I lost them. But I was already used to buying things, then losing them in stupid ways. Gambling, fighting, waking up someplace without my things.'

My lip curls. I look away.

'I was no different than any person who treats their life like something they can just abuse and push away, and have it come back to them, like a dog.'

My dog. How did I ever think of him that way, even for a second?

'I was an asshole. I never beat my wife, but I wasn't good to her or her kids. They had to deal with the aftermath, over and over. After I became...*this*...it got worse. I'd come home bloody, and I knew... not details...but I knew I'd done...wrong things. Mar tried to stop me. But she had no idea what a monster I was. Her kids started hiding from me.'

Screaming. 'You'd better run!' Fists on the bathroom door. Splintering. Pain. Mar, belly swollen, swining back the cast-iron pan, her teeth bared, eyes red and and streaming.

'I left them. To protect them from me.'

Teeth. Claws. Shaking the body.

'I tried to heal. I stopped drinking, learned ceremonies and songs and how to hold meetings, and how to be a mentor and a role model. But nobody, anywhere, ever mentioned how to be sane if you happened to be a shape-shifter.'

The coffee gurgles its readiness, and I jump up, pour us cups.

'I wrote to Mar, to the kids. Apologized, told them I couldn't come back. But I could never tell them this.' He lifts his hand again.

'Oh, bull *shit*.'

He snaps upright. I slam the cups down, sloshing coffee.

'You left your wife pregant? Didn't tell her you're a shapeshifter? That she might have *puppies*?'

It's a ridiculous thing to say, but he recoils like I've hit him, then slumps.

She lost the kid.'

I can't even muster an *I'm sorry*. He's more than sorry enough for himself.

'And I went out and tried to die.'

Roaring, pain, pain, rolling down rocks, and then lying, human and broken, at the water's edge. Water, so cold so clear so near such a simple way out of this pain. And then, the smell of sage, a soft wind swirling, warm breath, a voice telling him to stay, stay quiet, stay still, his body wrapped in softness, his pain ebbing and surging, his blood loud in his veins, and in this close, dim warmth, a shadow, and then out of the shadow, a slim long-legged figure.

I stand there, watching this man, this wolfish dog, this infinitely strange creature, confess his sins—the ones I hadn't been part of. I've walked through some really dark nights with him. So I sit back with my back to the door, and drink my coffee for a while. My gaze drops down to the open files.

'Her name was Nell August.' His voice is so soft.

'What?!'

So he tells me the rest of the story. He'd made the most of his 'geographical,' and got a job in Treaty Six. He'd seen Nell at a confernece, and he loved her the second he saw her. 'She was so beautiful,

Hazel, you can't imagine.'

I think of her drug-ravaged face on that last evening. No, I really can't quite.

And tells me of the Nell he knew—hard-working, quiet, with hair like flags of darkened grass, kind eyes, and a rare smile. How she sat in the front of a workshop he was leading on recovering traditions. How she'd smelled of sage and lonesome spaces, and how he couldn't believe his luck when she turned her deep brown gaze on him.

His wild and sudden love, his fear, all the moments she shared with him, how she hopped and trusted...

'And then?'

'I ran away.'

He was making no excuses. My every hackle is going up. I want to lash out at him, to call him all the names for men like him, who run from entanglement to entanglement, who never see it through. I knew I hated him when I met him, now I understand why.

But then he stops talking and looks up at me. 'I wouldn't blame you if you wanted to kill me, Hazel. I've wanted that sometimes, you know. I even thought maybe I was brought here so you would do me in—'

My lip is curling

'—some days I hoped for it.'

I stare.

'But that would be wrong. Not your job to take me out. Not humane to make you clean up my mess. Not your fault I am what... *who* I am.'

I fumble for my smokes, held by something in his gaze. *No excuses.*

He looks around, gets an ashtray, holds out a hand. I know he doesn't smoke, but I give him tobacco.

He lights one, sets it in place in the ashtray, washes his hands in the smoke, then his head, his eyes, ears, heart, smooths the smoke along his body. I do the same, in my turn, and then light one just to smoke, while he tells me more.

'Anyway, there was this one Elder out in Mi'kmaki, when I was training. He told me about how this nun almost killed him when he was tiny. And how it took years of hell before he realized he had a gift. He survived, and he had seen enough of suffering to know the power and importance of being gentle, of overcoming suffering with love.'

Smoke flickers between us.

'Also, he could fly. He didn't say that. I saw him. The day I left his mawi'omi, he came as an eagle to see me off. Landed on the pier and gave me one long look, then flew away. Ever hear a bald eagle sing? It's sweet and pure, just like he was. That eagle sang for me then I knew that I wouldn't see him again, that he would walk on before I could find my way back to him.'

Jim touches a small blue tattoo I've never noticed, a feather faintly etched along the inside of his left wrist. 'After that, whenever things were really bad, I would remember him, his stories and his smile, and this one morning we sat and drank tea for four hours, after tending the fire all night...' He stops, gazing off into memory.

'And so I had something to hold onto. Sometimes, I'd even catch a glimpse of an eagle, and imagine I felt his spirit. But then, you know,' he shrugs, 'I'd feel kind of ridiculous about it; such a stereotypical thing.'

I nod, sitting in my office with a shape-shifter in jeans, his blue shirt, his hair pushed back, his face looking kind of scholarly in glasses. His hands are wreathed in silver rings, his wrists too, like shackles. No, silver doesn't kill Indigenous werewolves. Why would it?

Anyhow, he keeps talking, and I deal cribbage hands. He picks his up and we play, the *slip-click* of the cards punctuating his story, the pegs creeping obediently along their paths.

'So, then' Jim says, looking away from his hand 'one night last fall, I read somewhere that she's dead. *Nell. Dead.* I don't know what to do. I thought I had a handle on it. No more drinking, no more random shifting, no more nights I didn't dare remember. But she's dead, and I start to sink. And I start to shift randomly.'

He pokes with an angry finger at the printed pages detailing her grotty little life and death. 'Nell. They got her name right. But the rest of this, it's all bullshit, Hazel. She wasn't like that, not at all.' He brushes a fingertip across the police picture of Nell, as if he can rub it all away. 'Not when I knew her.'

He shuffles, deals, throws his two in the crib without seeming to see them.

'I went out to kill myself, but I found I didn't have the guts to do it. I kep thinking about that Elder, turning his suffering into service. Thinking about Nell, how brave and beautiful she was. My biggest fear, when it came down to it, was that, if I went ahead and killed myself, they'd be waiting on the other side.'

I must have looked puzzled, because he sighed and went on. 'If I hadn't made amends here, dying wouldn't fix things, would it? So, I walked.'

I suddenly want to walk myself. I draw breath to suggest it to him, but then I don't. This story belongs in the frankly ugly room where I pretend to be a professional, where I first got involved with this whole situation. A situation I do not, it is abundantly clear, understand at all.

And so, I deal the cards in my turn and I listen as he describes the night he went looking for death and found a vision of Nell. Not Nell broken, not the dead hooker Nell, but the young beauty he had loved and abandoned. *Human and broken. Stone and breath and water.*

'She was standing in a field of tall grass and smelling of sage and flowers. You don't think you're going to be able to smell in a dream, right?'

I nod. I know what he means.

'But I can see that this field is rolled up against a wall, and there's that Eagle/Dragon mural on the wall.'

He is ahead of me, I notice, glancing at the crib board. 'So I know I'm in Amiskwaciy.'

I nod. I know the mural he means, flaming blues and reds and golds, looking out on Giovanni Caboto park.

'And she turns and points—'

She turns, graceful as the grass, her arm extended towards the snow-shoe hare dancing slowly along the top of the landscaped hill. The hare slips from view, behind a luminous blue boulder, and a young woman rises in her place. She turns, her dark eys huge. 'Mama, mama, mama—' she softly chants, darkness swirling around her. Dim light sheds down on her from hulking pines above her.

'This is your daugher, James.' I heard Nell's voice. *'Come and find her,'* she said. *I cannot help her. She needs you now.'*

The dark wind rises, grass runs red with blood, stars fall from tree brances, the smell of sage becomes a reek of blood, drumming, thrumming.

'She told me to let myself be caught, to call myself Spider...You know the rest...'

I really don't. But my heart is hammering and every hair is up.

'Jim,' I say, grasping at straws, 'why Spider?'

'Oh, that was just Nell's little joke.' He colours up a bit. 'She knew spiders freak me out. One time I tried to kill one and she stopped me and told me about, you know, the Dream Catcher.'

I nod. We've both shuddered over the cheap, mass-produced dream catchers you can find just about anywhere. *Hokey.*

'Hokey story, right? Only, when she told me, it wasn't hokey at all.' His face softens in the fading afternoon light. *'Spiders are our relatives. Spiders are our friends.* She made me repeat it, over and over. Silly, right?'

Tears slide down his cheeks, and silly or not, I want to wipe them away, but that's not what we hold between us, Jim and I.

'So, that's how you knew it was real?'

He nods. 'That, and I heard this little song that only Nell ever sang.' He pauses, as if listening still

I gather sage on the wind
I gather cedar, gather pine
I gather sweetgrass, and wild willow tang...

'Anyhow, I woke up here, a dog. I didn't try to change. I don't re-member much of what I did the first couple times I slipped and turned human. I...well, I emailed my sister one day when you were out. She says I gave notice at work, all proper and stuff. She assumes I moved out of my apartment. She didn't even blink about me start-ing a new bank acount out here, just helped me transfer everything. She's good that way.'

At first, he tells me, he didn't know if he wanted to find Nell's daughter. 'One thing to know what's right when you're dreaming. But when you wake up?'

'Even after I got used to changing back and forth, knew I could be reliably human, I had no idea whether she'd want me to find her. Why would she? The father she never knew? If I did find her and she did need help, would she want it?' He had no idea where she would be. 'When I read what happened to Nell, though, I didn't think her kid would be anywhere good. I prayed hard. Begged Nell to tell me more. And I followed you here and waited outside and,' he ducks his head in embarrassment, 'I eavesdropped on your meet-ings with the Augusts. I realized there was no use telling them.'

'Yeah, but why couldn't you tell *me*?' I am annoyed at the slight whine in my voice. I'm not one of those kinds of girls. This is not that kind of situation. I really hate when people get all selfish at moments like this. I do. But there I am, doing it. I'm in shock, okay. I'm trying to take in what he's telling me.

He shrugs, looking at me with his head tipped on one side, con-sidering.

'I am telling you now.'

'Thank you for that.'

'We sit quiet for a while more. He picks up the deck of cards. I go turn on the light. He shuffles and deals while I reset the crib board. For a while, the comforting slip and the click of cards, the cadenc-

es of the game—*fifteen two, fifteen four*—settle over us. It feels like
we should be urgently doing something, right? But we don't know
what, so we sit and wait for knowing.

Finally, Jim huffs out a groaning sign. 'So, *that* night?'

I know why my skin is crawling. I don't want him to tell me this.

'Yes. That was her. My daughter.'

'Oh my God.'

My lip is curling into a snarl, hands into fists. Steady. I mark my
hand, mark my crib. We're neck and neck, past the double skunk
line now, into what I think of as 'the backstretch,' curling up the
bottom of the 9. I see her. Him, naked in front of her. *What kind
of monster—?* Cold rage runs in waves up my spine. I don't know
whether I want to smash his face or run. Steady. Mark the points,
peg by peg.

His deal again, his hands are shaking.

'I...Hazel...' he puts down the cards, his hands wrapped tight together on top of the cards, his face a mask of grief.

'I don't know what happened that night. That is, I...'

*His daughter? How could he have gone into that room? Once in,
how could he have hesitated to destroy the man with his daughter?*

'*I don't want to be a monster,*' Jim says, and it echoes in my mind.
Around us, the light seems to flicker. I catch a whiff of sage. Jim
turns his head, his sad eyes searching, as if he smells it too.

I remember her. The man had called her Doll, her lank two-tone
hair, her strange eyes, her slight figure walking away swinging her
shoes...

'But you—' I choke.

'I was a wolf. And the door opened. And I was human and naked and terrified. And I didn't know what to do. I tried to change. I
didn't want her to see me like that...' His voice is a whisper.

'I just babbled, tried to stall him. I couldn't change. And I looked
at her. She looked so much like Nell. All the things Nell suffered
because I ran out on her. And the girl...my daughter...looked at me
and despised me. And I hated myself too. How could I not? My fault
she was a whore...

'I couldn't change. I tried to figure out what to do. I played for time, kept him talking. I kept waiting for the horror, the rage, to kick in, to let me switch back to wolf. But it failed me. I don't know why, because I've never been more scared or angry, and I was running out of time. So finally I did what I could as a man. I grabbed her, pushed her away from him towards the door. And then it all went...'

Blood, Screaming, Shaking the body. Cedar boughs thrashing. Teeth and claws. Justice.

MISSY: ROOT WOUND

Missy is dozing on her sofa when someone bangs on her door. She bolts upright. 'Missy?'

She springs across the apartment. How did he get in the building?

'Missy,' he's trying not to be too loud. She opens the door, and Devin shoots in, incongruously fast, puffing a bit. 'I slipped in past some guys who were going out partying,' he explains, before she can ask him out loud how he got into the building. For a big guy, Devin can make himself surprisingly easy not to notice.

He bobs his head, runs a hand through his hair. 'Okay,' he says, and follows her into the living room, sits down, like a bear lowering onto his haunches. 'So, you know that case Auntie—your mom is working on?'

She nods. That dead hooker, Nell August—but he doesn't call her hooker, he says *dead lady*, typical Devin. He tells her what he's found out about the case he gave her mother, which he hasn't been able to let go himself. How these three men, men Missy has never heard of, can all be traced back to the same school.

'Why would you think of that?' she asks. And he colours up. 'It fits the pathology of recidivist violence,' he says, the formal language rolling oddly out of his owlish face. 'North Oaks School,' Devin says. And Missy remembers Big Frankie, her uncle, getting together with some other parents and running off this shady educational advisor, whom they'd realized was grooming the kids for whom he'd designed this special inner city school program, grooming them for abuse. Devin's school was one of the ones where he had insinuated himself.

Missy remembers the adults sitting stiff as trees, listening to Big Frankie tell how he had been there one day, volunteering to read to the kids, and heard this big shot was scheduled to come read, too.

'It's like I heard Dad's voice in my head, telling me to wait and see this man they were all talking about, this supposed champion of education. And then I saw him. Dressed in his best suit, reading to the kids. Fine.

'But then after, he puts them in a line in front of him, like he's a priest, and he makes them take a piece of candy from his hand, like some kind of sick communion rite.'

Missy hadn't understood at the time what was going on, though she'd perched on the edge of earshot and listened, riveted by the adults' quiet, seething rage, and how they organized. In the end, a group of parents talked to that man, merely hinting at the threat they posed. How they knew he'd covered himself so it would be hard to prove, but how easy it would be to disappear in the maze streets of UpTop, or down a rewilded ravine... and he crumbled, tucked his tail, and left the community.

She remembers her mother was relieved. She remembers Big Frankie was still angry, still holding on to the injustice of how they'd never be able to actually prove everything. That man was gone, but his victims, the uncounted damaged survivors of his evil, would still have to live with what he did. Maybe Big Frankie would have done more about that—if he hadn't gone and gotten sick, and died. And nobody else had the heart to do anything more about it.

'Recidivist violence,' says Devin.

It's plain enough that he suspects that these men, all schoolmates at another school grateful for the program and the predator's attention, were all victims of sexual predation, and that that is what twisted them into predators themselves. That, he is saying, is the root wound.

He thinks one of them killed Nell August. All of it possible and making sense to him, and to her. But none of it can be proved, so he just says the school name, knowing Missy will remember and know what he means. She nods. 'Like the Action Boys.' They would be guys like Devin's friends with their hopeless name—Action Boys—so broken they never got out of the drugs and street life, and got mixed up in Nell August's murder, and died because of it.

And then he says, 'Look, I'm going to go talk to the Action Boys. They seem to have gotten some crack-brained notion that it's this kid called Rabbit who's killing those men. It's not true. I don't know who it is, but it can't be her. She's around our age, maybe a year or two younger, just a kid.'

Missy looks in wonder at Devin. He's nothing like Big Frankie, his father, her uncle, who was always whip thin, even before he got sick and wasted away. Nothing like him physically. But she sees the core of strength in him, now that he's too concerned for his community to hide his powerful nature behind bumble and humble.

'What do you want me to do, then?' she asks.

'Would you get Little Frankie, and go talk to your mother?'

She nods. 'I'll go with Frankie, and we'll get Maengan Nolan too. You know that guy, Jim, that mom lives with?' She stops herself from saying, *'He's a werewolf, and maybe he's the killer.'* She'd have to tell him that Maengan is a werewolf, too. *Now is not the time.* Instead, when he nods, she simply says, 'He may be involved somehow. And Maengan knows him, so maybe he can help us figure out what's going on, and who killed those three men.'

'And one more,' says Devin.

'One more?'

Devin nods, bobbing his chin. 'A police officer. From Joshua Campeau's unit.' He pulls a paper from his pocket, smooths it on the table for her; just a name and barest facts, but her skin crawls.

Damn.

He gets up. 'Got to catch the fast train back over, go talk to the Boys before they do something stupid.'

'I'll go talk to Mom.'

She is reaching for the phone when it rings Frankie's tone. 'Hey,' says Frankie, 'Can I come over? I have this feeling we should talk more about Maengan.'

'I was just going to call you.'

'Good. So let me in?' Frankie laughs and hangs up, and Missy buzzes her in. *Sister sync*, they used to call it, how their thoughts would fall in line, how they'd finish each other's sentences, how they'd sense each other coming down the street, or decide to visit just before the other invited them.

'I'll call Maengan,' she says when she opens the door for Frankie, but Frankie just winks.

'Done. *Sister sync.*'

Maengan buzzes the door a couple minutes later and when he walks in, they exchange an awkward hug.

He wraps his arms around himself, then, and instead of sitting, leans a shoulder against the bookshelf. Frankie has gone straight to the window and opened it, letting in the spring air, which seems to carry a slight sharp reek. Maengan curls a reflexive lip, stifles it, addresses them.

'So...'

'First things first,' says Frankie. 'Yes, we are still okay with you being a shapeshifter. Right, Miss?'

A flash of thunder crosses Missy's brow, but she nods.

'Okay, then,' says Frankie. 'What's going on?'

As Missy explains what Devin told her, Maengan begins to pace. Then, without warning, he howls, 'Nooo!' and hurls himself onto the sofa, punching it, sobbing. Hair bristles from him, his shape distorting and resettling like a flickering image.

In sync, the sisters shift into defensive postures. Missy's hand closes around the pole of her standing lamp. Frankie grabs a kitchen chair. Then, as one, they exhale. There is no harm for them here, just a young man wrestling, literally, with his demon. He has turned his rage and terror away from them, as if he'll drive himself into the sofa. He's riding the change like a seizure, and within a minute, he's pulled himself back together. He sits up, staring at nothing, his lips moving in a chant just below their hearing.

'Is that what happened to—' Frankie begins, but Missy silences her with a glare.

'Sorry,' says Maengan. 'I thought I … was okay with it… '

He sets his hands, palms up, on his thighs, and breathes. Frankie drops elegantly to the floor, facing Maengan, and brings her breathing in line with his. Missy sits down beside him, not too close. It seems there is a voice at the edge of hearing, singing softly.

'So—' says Maengan, opening his eyes, but not looking at either sister.

They tip their heads to the side, in sync, exchange glances. *Do we press him to tell us?* The thought seems to hang on the shimmering edge of visible between them.

'You can tell us,' says Missy, softly.

'I came here,' says Maengan, because I found out the man who... changed me...had come here.'

'You mean, he bit you?' asks Frankie.

'Bit. Punched. Kicked...and...worse.' Maengan shudders. 'We were in on a Youth Leadership conference in Ottawa. And after...I just went home. And then I ran.' He shakes his head.

'Fucker tried to make it up to me. I couldn't even tell anyone why I didn't want to even see his fucking face. So, I got on that internship thing, went to Japan. He couldn't reach me there. And nobody there knew what I was, so I stayed until I could be okay. Came home, found out he'd come here...'

His dark hair, unbound, hangs in ragged hanks around his face. . 'I didn't know what I'd do about it if I found him.'

The girls huff.

The thing is, before...what happened...he was a good guy. And I want to believe he's trying to live with it, and not be a monster.

He takes a deep breath, rocks back, straightens.

'I have to beleive it's possible to do that.' He looks into their faces, seeking acceptance. He sees fear and love.

'I try to understand it as a trauma response.'

'Like multiple personality disorder?' says Missy softly.

'*Reorder,*' says Frankie. 'Like, under duress, DNA gets reordered and you can access another physical form. It's a shamanic thing.'

'Maybe,' counters Missy. 'But it's not that simple. Or hospitals, streets, prisons...everywhere would be full of shapeshifters.'

'And people would be deliberately messing themselves up, just to activate the power,' says Frankie.

Maengan laughs.

'You guys are amazing,' he breathes, but his breath goes ragged. 'Look, I have to tell you—it was your mother who helped me when it happened. That's how we met.' He shakes his head. 'She didn't know. Didn't ask.'

But Missy remembers the first day at her mother's house, how Hazel said his name, Maengan. *Wolf.*

'And now I don't know how to tell her...that dog she has...it's *him.*'

Frankie jumps up, eyes blazing. 'Miss! come on!'

HAZEL: THE HAND DEALT

He's dealing the cards. He looks like an ordinary man. But he's not. He's a shape-shifter, a confessed abuser, and either he killed a man, or... it is unthinkable, that that slight and delicate girl... but that's my problem. I remember seeing it, but not seeing it. I remember seeing red. I remember somebody screaming, and it is a sound I want to bury so deep. I definitely don't want to talk about it, draw out the threads, force him to tell me what *he* actually saw, what he did, what actually happened. It is horrible enough, that he followed his daughter into that place, with that hideous man. *David Lancaster.* A man with a name. And a family. And some sort of deep-rooted evil, such that I could not find it in myself to be upset that he was dead.

That stills me, that certainty, and I just sit back for a moment, looking at Jim. Who is he, really? Just a guy, mid-sized, could be Nish, could be Asian, could pass without notice into crowds in several countries—mid-tone skin, dark eyes, modestly dressed, his hair pushed back. He's wearing glasses, even though I'm pretty sure he's never needed them. How can a werewolf be short-sighted?

I won't ask him again about that night, but there is something else.

'Jim,' I say, 'the other day, I passed a crime scene. Down in the valley. I didn't stop. I don't know if it's being around you for so long, but whatever the case, I felt like... I could smell it. You know?'

I am rooted in place now, aware that my back is to the door.

He looks up, and his eyes are red. Not with rage, with tears. I don't have to be asked. I get up, go to the kitchenette. Pour some water, refill the coffee pot, it's still warm. Bring him water, a beer stein full to drink while the coffee perks.

Sit down opposite him, waving him back into my chair when he makes a move to give it up for me—finally, a whiff of manners, but we don't have time for that.

He gulps the water, scoops the cards back into a pile, picks it up, taps it into place, shuffles once, puts the deck down square, and looks straight at me with a sigh.

'So, tell me, what haven't you told me yet?' No answer.

After a while, we start to play again. But only for a few minutes. He can't concentrate. I can't blame him. But, though I don't know why, I *can* tease him.

'You trying to get out of getting skunked here?'

He gives me a tiny smile. I've grown accustomed to his face, his middle-aged skin getting rough along his throat, the way his hair has a life of its own, in whichever form he appears… and then, I make a big mistake.

I show him the other file, the original one Devin gave me, including the kid's texts from today that I printed out and added. It doesn't seem like a mistake. It feels right. I gather up the cards, deal solitaire while he reads through it, ready to answer any questions. I'm not ready for it when he leaps up, growling.

'It's him! It's him!' he roars, leaps over the desk like some superhero in a movie, and he runs out the door into the last sullen dregs of the light.

***

Zabeh: My Sister

He is hunting now. Rage and anger. I did not come here to make more killing. I came to make it stop. I considered I could bring Justice for Her. And for Nell. And for Hazel. For all of their heart-lights lost in the human forest of Amiskwaciy. I consider broken. But Nell would sing. And Abeligamuj, Rabbit, She would sing. Ri ri ri. I love them in song. Mother and Daughter. Root and branch. Root and branch with whom I grew will say, Zabeh was foolish. But how could I be wise? Root and branch, my mother stepped Between, and they told me I must leave her there.

Who can stop loving a mother? I looked Between. I did not see my mother. I saw Her. I saw her alone, missing her mother. I saw her try to save her mother. I saw her lose her mother. I am Zabeh and She is human, but we are sisters, Rabbit and I.

Root and branch, I was only trying to help. Now Man/Maengan hunts. And She is out there, my sister. Her heart-light is in storm. Hard to see her. I will find her.

RABBIT: THANKS GIVEN

Rabbit, when she can say she is sixteen, finds Shirley one day at the food court. Shirley knows, without the girl saying so, that Rabbit is looking for work. She has tied back her fine, lank hair, into a smooth low ponytail, and dressed in a cream-coloured polyester blouse over dark leggings. In the hollow of her throat, the little silver bunny charm catches the light.

'You maybe,' says Shirley, as Rabbit surveys the application Shirley hands her, 'can't call yourself Rabbit.'

'Too weird?'

'Too weird.'

Rabbit nods, writes down her name as Abbie, and Shirley notes the last name, August, without surprise, having long since filled in the blanks about her background. It's a common enough name, a common enough story, August, Paul, Cardinal, all the names rising out of same global tide that, somewhere, gave her Johnson. Not that she says anything, nor would she necessarily expect it to be something about which she'd be asked to comment.

She just nods.

Abbie August of Amiskwaciy gets a job at a call centre on Shirley's say-so, and uses her first pay cheque to buy Shirley a fancy box of tea, a round box in an appealing shade of blue, and the individual packets laid out in a wheel inside. For a moment, when the girl holds it out to her in her slim honey-toned hands, Shirley pauses to take in how expensive she knows this gift to be, with its biodegradable, plastic free, and fair-trade logos. She doesn't make the mistake of commenting, though, just meets the girl's sombre gaze with her own, allowing a smile to glimmer in her eyes, holding the look until Rabbit begins to smile in response. Gradually, a grin of successful conspiracy lights up both their faces, as Shirley tucks the wheel of tea back into its gift bag. Rabbit allows her a brief hug round the shoulders, then spins like her namesake and disappears as swiftly, into the maw of the mall.

Once she has an identity code, Abbie August makes swift work of learning how to slip between the commercial networks and the dark web, hunting for a man in a position to make calls that aren't rightfully his to make. Abbie August sends Joshua Campeau a message, to meet her in UpTop, she has information vital to his inquiries. He asks her the question she's been expecting.

'Yes,' she types, 'I am family.'

HAZEL: COUNSEL

Jim has run out into the night. And so I call Shanaya.

'I'm on my way,' she says, 'like my name.'

I can't even raise a mocking *pfft*.

While I'm waiting for her, I think back to that night…

I walk and I walk, and I smoke.

The light has bled out of the sky.

The wind wipes my face, but it can't dry the tears. Why should I try to solve a whore's murder when I couldn't save my brother, whose life actually meant something?

'Why the fuck do people throw themselves away like that? And why should I have to try to pick up the fucking pieces?'

Mrs. August—if she loved her daughter, why couldn't she save her?

Something looms ahead, the big ragged pine in the hospital parking lot. Up in the highest branches, there's enough wind to make it shake and move.

Shinguak. Pine. Pine means wisdom, supposed to be Anishinaabe tradition. This shitty, shifty, skinny remnant. And I run at it as if beating on a tree can make it cough up answers.

Of course, it hurts to run into a tree.

It hurts all the way down as I slide into a heap in the dust and grime and gravel. I lean my head against the big bare wound on her side, this awesome, awful, lonesome thing. And we just lean like that together, in the dark.

Shinguak. Shinguak was the man who saved my father from the schools, taught him things.

'Go home, little daughter.' I think I hear that, really clear.

I am not dying here. I'm just mad and weary, and I should go home. So, I do.

And I go to bed.

And that night, in the wind and the creaking darkness, I get that dream. Grandma, standing there, firm and strong, telling me what to do.

***

I was not alone there. That's the thing. We are never actually ever alone. The world is made of dimensions beyond our knowing, and we vibrate things in those dimensions. I don't know how it works. I don't know, now, if it was actually my Grandmother's spirit. I believed it was, and I—rebel in the real world Hazel—listened to what she told me to do, and now? Now, I wonder what my next move is.

I have to review what I know:

Nell August is dead, and her family want me to find out who killed her. For some reason, Joshua was trying to figure that out, too. Jim has circled his name—*Joshua Campeau*—all the places I never noticed it—or if I did, never realized it meant so much, all the tiny web of things I hadn't put together.

I had looked at Nell August and not seen her. I'd believed what I was told, that she was a prostitute and a drug addict and nothing else. Her family had told me that too, and I hadn't understood that all I was hearing was her mother's guilt and fear, her step-father's guilt and fear.

I hadn't seen Jim clearly, either. Shape-shifter, yes. But also human, man, lover, father; and not some generic version of any of those things, but a person, just one person, trying to do what he could with the hand dealt him. He is a killer. But it is clear he figures Josh is the bigger danger. And if Josh is after Jim's daughter, Jim is right.

Now he's gone out into the thickening night and I am scared. I don't know what I should do. I need counsel.

'Here's the thing,' I say, pacing the office. Shanaya sits curled in the visitor's chair, her golden eyes tracking me. I've brought her up to speed on the rest of it, it being remarkably easy to tell a shape-shifting tiger about inter-dimensional prayers, and werewolves in love, and even to admit that I'd totally fucked up by letting other people tell me who Nell was, and never once asking Jim, when all along, he was looking for her, too, and her daughter. Why hadn't I found out about the daughter sooner? And even if I didn't know who she was, why didn't I try to find the obvious other witness to David Lancaster's murder—the woman they'd called Doll?

'Why didn't I just open my eyes all along?'

'Well, to be fair,' says Shanaya, 'It is rather a lot to take in. Look at me, I can't even tell my mother I'm a tiger. I think you should give yourself a break and admit you had your plate full, living with myths and monsters.'

'You're not a monster, Shan.'

She waves it off. 'We're not talking about me. I mean Spider/Jim.'

'It's not even him, Shan. I mean, it's not *just* him.'

Not just opening my home to a werewolf, becoming his accomplice in some weird vigilante version of Bear Clan work, not just throwing out—

'—It's Joshua, Shan.'

She crinkles her nose. 'Go on.'

'He never told me he had any connection at all to the case, see? He just *never said*. And all the time, he was just getting closer, you know? Building trust.'

I have to get this timeline right, have to understand it. The August family bring me Nell's case. I start working on it. I interview them, and that is the very day I meet Joshua.

'He must have been staking you out,' she says, nodding. I hate hearing that. I can't believe I fell for it, the oldest trick in the book. I hate how my skin crawls remembering him now, and how I felt about him. Then again—

'What's funny?' says Shanaya.

'What's funny is, the very morning I got Spider? I woke up with him, with Joshua, and I took one look at him and I threw him out! Just couldn't stand him anymore. Couldn't stand his face.'

Shanaya looks at the picture on her phone. 'Not exactly a bad face, though,' she says. 'Not Hugh Jackman. More… George Clooney?'

'Phfft. I don't see it,' I wave her off, but I'm grinning back. Shanaya has such a gift for light in the darkness. Frankie would love her. Deep breath. This is serious. I look out the window, down at the side-street I think of as mine.

'So?' I say, 'What do you think? What do we do? And before you ask,' I hold up my hand, 'I don't know if I'm asking you as a lawyer, as my friend, or perhaps as a tiger—what do we do now?'

'Well, let's look at the facts,' she says, straightening up and assuming her lawyer face. 'Joshua Campeau struck up an acquaintance with you in a public place, in a public manner, and developed a friendship with you right out in the open. Yes?'

'Yes. Come to think of it, he was very deliberate about that, approaching me in a liquor store—Hey! If I were paranoid, I'd make something of that, and of the way he loved to tell the 'six-pack' story. You know, establishing that I might be a *drunken Indian*—'

'What do you mean?'

'I mean, we met in a booze shop. Evidence that Hazel is a drunk, if we ever go to court.'

She nods sadly. 'I should be able to tell you that's bullshit, but it fits. And of course, the same doesn't apply for him. He's a man.'

'A White man.'

'You look as White as him.'

'Maybe I am. I never asked his parentage, actually. But he's still got the Man advantage.'

We heave a simultaneous sigh. We didn't invent the double standard, but we cannot be oblivious to it. It's as persistent as prostitution and poverty. If we choose to ignore it, we always know we are making a choice. Yet, it never even really struck me with Josh, at the time.

'How did I not see it?'

'Because not all Whites are bad, not all guys are bad, and maybe you don't live in a Feminist fortress?'

'Bully for me,' I crack back, both of us mimicking Diya, 'I live in the personal, not the theoretical. But, how did I not see it, Shan?'

'My friend, you are not all seeing, not all knowing. I on the other hand, am a lawyer, and a tiger, and we are inclined to noticing.'

'I pretend to be an Investigator, for fucks' sake!'

'Plus, it didn't happen to me. He turned those Clooney eyes on you, not me.'

That's the thing, always. It's hard to see if it is happening to you. But laid out for Shanaya, it becomes miserably clear. Bad enough he seduced me—though really, that wasn't all bad—

'—But Shan, he went after Missy! He weaselled his way into her life, and now I have to figure out what danger she's in, because sure as shit, she's at risk!' My spine crawls, saying it. I want to roar out into the darkening day, like Jim, but I cannot track by smell. Me, I need a plan.

'Why don't you text her, Hazel?'

I text Missy. I text Frankie. I text Jim (not that he's going to answer.) '*Call me.*' Just that.

MISSY, MAENGAN, FRANKIE: GATHERING

Bikes are often the fastest way through Amiskwaciy, thanks to the valley trails and the greenways. Now, racing through the valley trails, Missy thinks about Devin. He said he'd be okay, he was going to talk to Father E, and to his friends. He's known them all his life, he'd said, he knows how to talk to them.

'Just make sure your mom's okay, okay?' he'd said, and she'd blinked, wondering how the clumsy, overlooked boy had grown into this suddenly powerful young man. She realizes anew that she simply likes her cousin. She smiles in the dark. The rising moon glints on the water below them as they flow across the bridge, the three moving in the same harmony as a flock of birds, shifting, turning as one thing.

Frankie is thinking, too, as she works to keep up with Missy and Maengan. She is thinking that they cannot afford to be distracted tonight. The thing that matters, she tells herself, is to see, clearly, what is actually happening.

Not what stories say must be there. Not what your fear tells you, but whatever is really there.

After all, she doesn't know if her mother is a werewolf, too. None of them have exactly mentioned the possibility, but Frankie chugs up the hill carrying that heavy thought. *She must be prepared to see what her mother is, whatever she is.*

And Maengan? He feels clear, feels empty, feels zen. Tonight, he knows, one way or another, he will make peace with the monster who made him a wolf. He is sure, riding with the sisters in the moonlight, that he is a wolf, but he is not a monster. The white moonlight bathes him, and shines on these women, who have brought him home to himself.

RABBIT: TWANG

The Boys have her cornered now. They form an uneasy hedge against departure. Rabbit, her back to the wall, looks oddly monochrome against the mural. She does not seem to belong here. But there is no place else to go, no place to be. They look at her. She looks at them. All of them are breathing hard, unsure what comes next. What do they do now? What do these young men do with this strange young woman?

It's not like they don't know her kind. She is their sister, their mother, their Auntie, their ragged female dreams. She is not the woman they have been raised to see as valuable, as queenly, as magnificent. But they are held at bay as much as she is. It is the wall that stops her, and it is her thin magnificence that keeps them still. They will keep her here, at least a moment more, but they are not sure how to advance on her.

Rabbit feels their confusion. She sees they are as young as she is, and in some ways, they also carry her agedness.

There's Tomlin, used to carrying the weight of his parents' prescribed addictions, and the weight behind that, of the tragedy that cost them first their other children and their bodily health, then their will to act, and slowly, their dignity. Tomlin carries what little hope they have left in life.

And there's Cody, who picked up his brother's shorts that time he came home from the drag. The blood, the single word, 'Please,' repeated, brokenly, and Cody nodded—never tell Mom, never tell the uncles, never tell anyone, never the pretty girl his brother admired, never tell a soul about the blood and the shame.

LeWayne, now, he's floating. He's never quite connected like the rest. He resonates to the other Boys and he will follow their lead, unless his own internal tension overbears it. They are held still, vibrating with tension and uncertainty. He twangs, amped up on meth, close to break or spring. He is the one Rabbit has to fear.

DEVIN: BEAR CLAN MAN

Devin barrels into the park, running like he never knew he could. His big body fairly flies, pulling him forward.

There. There they are.

They have Rabbit backed up against the wall, the dim light from the park lamp posts just enough to transform the mural's daytime rainbow hues into a seething mass of shapes, inchoate and angry behind them.

He sees a glint, LeWayne's arm rising, the blade.

'Nooo!' he screams, his voice as empty as in nightmares, not enough breath to voice it.

LeWayne lunges toward the woman, slashes at her, connects. She grabs her torn arm and screams in his face, a high, eerie sound, and LeWayne stumbles back. Too late, he understands his mistake. She kicks him, hard and high, in the big muscle of his thigh, and he lurches, half-falls, scrabbles back to his feet. Rabbit bolts. LeWayne, crazed with pain, high and unhinged, staggers around the corner after her as she runs out beyond the throw of the light.

Cody and Tomlin gather themselves to launch after LeWayne. Devin spreads his arms wide and bowls into them, all three going down in a flurry of limbs and grunts. Around the corner, in the packed dirt alley, the hollow, out of rhythm running stops.

An eerie shriek splits the night, in tandem with a sharp-pitched wail, abruptly silenced.

None of them can move. Cody and Tomlin stare at Devin, who

sprawls, heaving, eyes closed, face pressed to the cool sour grass. He hears them begin to rise and pushes himself up on his elbows, stills them with a word.

'No.'

Tomlin starts crying first, and then they are all sobbing, quiet, devastated boys. They help each other to their feet and stand, embraced and shattered, crying for everything. How do they know what they'll find when they gather themselves and go round the corner? Their whole lives dictate this. They are veterans of loss, without a shred of illusion regarding the invulnerability of loved ones. They just look at each other now, and press closer to Devin, the soft boy who has become the hunch-shouldered mountain in their midst. He finds himself patting their backs, muttering, 'Okay now. Okay.'

It is not okay.

But then, for the Action Boys, it never was. Devin though, has found a kind of clarity. He closes his eyes, sees it again, the long instant when LeWayne's root-damaged, pitiful life of drifting into one kind of trouble after another, came into focus. LeWayne's hand, the knife in it, raised against the thin and pitiful little woman, LeWayne choosing rage and despair, choosing death.

They are still snuffling and hiccuping as he takes a deep breath, mutters a soft sad growl and sets them walking. He guides them, his arms clamped firm around them, their own upper arms slack in his grip. As they step into the dark, he takes in a deep breath. The air reeks of blood, fear, the earthy dung of extremity.

In the dark of the little lane they stop, leaning into Devin, heads down. He mutters another soft growl, and they all raise their heads and witness. LeWayne's body lies face-up, vacant. His knife sticks up from his throat at an angle, one hand folded up as if to seize it, one arm loose at his side.

Tomlin sinks to his knees, retching, then curls down on his side in the dirt, creeling softly, 'Momma, Momma.'

Cody huddles down and holds him. 'Hey, Tommy. Hey, Tommy,' he croons, his words muffled by his own tears.

Devin stands over the body.

Where, he wonders, *do they bury kids like LeWayne? What is a pauper's grave in this day and age?* He is stunned, considering it. *Why doesn't he know the answer? How can he not know this?*

He looks away, down the dusty lane, his anger building. The sweat has chilled on his back, and he wants to move, to do something. There is nothing left to do here.

'Momma. Momma,' Tomlin's voice echoes oddly.

Then Devin realizes it's not just Tomlin crying. There, where the lane opens out to parking lot, the little woman has squeezed herself into the gap between an old power pole and a dumpster. Rabbit's voice too is repeating over and over, brokenly, 'Momma.'

'Hey—' he says, and she raises her head. In the dark, he cannot be sure, but he feels like her eyes lock on his. He feels like he sees her eyes, red, round, frightened, the red of a rabbit in the headlights. Then she squeezes out of the gap and runs, barefoot, further into the night, her shoes swinging, her eyes shining with tears.

She did not want that boy to end. But more than that, she did not want Rabbit to end. Not until it is finished. And it is so nearly finished.

***

Devin wants to follow. But more than that, he wants to make right what he can.

'We've got to take care of Tommy,' he bends down to Cody. 'Come on.'

Cody looks up, bewildered and terrified.

'Help me take Tommy to the church rectory. To Father E. Come on.'

And Devin lifts Tomlin up, wrapping an arm around him. Cody wobbles into position, his arm around Tomlin's waist, though he's leaning as much as Tommy. They turn away and walk.

Devin finds it hard to see, but he still smells blood and the faint fading reek of feces. There was so little dignity for LeWayne, in death as in life. Devin stumbles, blinks, overwhelmed for an instant. He shakes his head and lumbers onward, relentless as a bear. LeWayne's body lies dead in a pool of blood and piss and rank extremity. But he cannot help that, and it's not for him to follow Rabbit's trail.

Take care of Cody and Tomlin, help them take care of what's left of LeWayne. As Devin burls onward, shoulders rolling like a grizzly, Rabbit lopes with purpose, once more on the trail of her intended prey. Two other beasts roll through the night, hunter and hunted.

EFREN: VINES

And Efren Mannfredsson sits in Sandra's kitchen, shyly drinking tea.

How did this happen? He did not plan on this. He looks around, wondering. How can it be that, having spent decades counselling other people about the perennial mystery of love, he forgot that it could happen to him?

How, having schooled his heart to love platonically, as a spiritual act of service, is he sitting here in this woman's kitchen, his big bones settled against her furniture as if it were made just for him, his skin warm with the memory of touching her, his hands cradling a chunky mug, just idly watching the steam rise? How, this pinpoint accuracy, this feeling that here and here alone, he is at home? He lets his gaze go to her kitchen window, thinking of his own windows at the rectory. He's come to love those windows, their recalcitrant quirks seeming entirely appropriate in the context of the community he serves.

The community he will leave.

He feels buoyant, incredibly light, and yet in the dizzying lightness, he feels some new connection vining around his heart. Her window frame is obscured by vines, some sort of houseplant.

It's like that, he muses, *love. Green, twining, vines that feed and bind the heart.* He shakes his head.

When his phone rings, he just looks at it. Who could need him more than he needs to be right here, right now? He glances dreamily down at it in the act of switching off.

    'Devin,' he breathes, and hits call-back.

HAZEL: PACK

It's been half an hour, and no text back. I'm getting frantic, and I'd have left long since if Shanaya weren't sitting there, implacable, exuding confidence. She must be a hell of an opponent in a courtroom, I think. She flicks me a smile now, just an edge of one.

'Hazel, do you—'

and just like that, a banging on the door. It bursts open, and it's Frankie and Missy and Maengan Nolan, all breathless, wild-eyed.

'*Mom!*' the girls chorus. '*Thank God! You're okay!*'

'*I'm okay?!*'

They talk over each other in a jumble for a moment. Then they notice Shanaya, sitting there so quietly, golden eyes watching them. They all draw breath together, in perfect sync, staring at her. I almost laugh. But I keep my mouth shut, for a miracle. They stare.

Shanaya gives it a beat more.

'Hello,' she says, soothingly. 'I'm Shanaya. Your mother's legal counsel. You must be Hazel's daughters. And,' she smiles her own mother's beaming grande dame smile, 'you must be Maengan Nolan, yes?'

'Legal counsel?' Missy lasers me with her gaze.

'Yes,' says Shanaya smoothly, 'and friend. Let me sum up here, to save us all a lot of time we don't have. Your mother has taken me into her confidence as her dear friend—'

'*Friend?*' Missy again, this time with that edge of anger and suspicion turning another direction. She is startled when Shanaya throws it right back.

'Yes, *friend*. Not euphemistic, as in lesbian couple-hood.'

And she chuckles, and the girls and Maengan all colour up, just a bit.

Kids, I think, *they still think they're the ones who invented any manner of experimentalism in regards to sexuality. Whatever the norms of the day, it is always expected to be the youth who push the boundaries, the older generation who react, who slowly accept.* It flashes through my head that my girls have probably hung on to my heterosexuality as at least one spar of conservative, properly older generation character. They've got friends who are all over the map of gender and preference, and that's okay. That, at least, they can dare me to accept. I don't really give a shit myself, but I realize that I've been letting them hold on to *'at least Mom is straight,'* in order for them to have room to maneuver me. *No wonder the hippies' kids I grew up with were so damned angry—their parents had hogged all the fun experimentalism, all they had left was Reaganomics in the USA, Mulroney here, cocaine and crass materialism.*

I snap back to the present, where Shanaya has summed up the human aspects of the situation for the kids.

'Your mother was worried sick about you,' she says.

The girls stare with a disappointing amount of skepticism at me. I look away. What am I supposed to say? *Focus.*

'Anyhow,' I manage, 'we're all here now. And Joshua is out there, looking, we think, for you, Missy. And Jim is looking for him.'

'*Spider* is *hunting* for him,' says Shanaya. Her eyes rivet me. 'You have to tell them.'

'Tell us what?' Maengan blurts.

I'm an asshole, okay? It's that look of his that gets me, and that little phrase—'tell us'—*us?* Like suddenly he's an inseparable part of my daughters' lives? Like he's the insider, I'm the enemy? Fucking pup. I gave them life. I raised them. Without even thinking, I turn on him.

'You!' I snap. 'You of all people ought to know what! Maengan! *Wolf!*' I don't give him a chance to speak. 'Don't you know your traditions? Your stories? Your shamans and your shape-shifters?'

I'm in his face, and he steps back. I swear his hair is going up, literally.

'Mom!' the girls chorus.

'He's a werewolf!' I spin, pinning them with a glare.

They stare at Maengan, over my shoulder.

'Not *him*,' I snarl, but their eyes don't track to me. They're wide open, and my girls, who don't step back from anything—my fault, and my pride—have both taken one big step back. And now their hands are coming up, Missy's curled in fists.

'No!' they shout, and grab me, push me behind them. I hit the wall and spin around, and there is Maengan, pressed back against the opposite wall as if he's trying to escape from himself, and he's half-shifted, and Shanaya, still human, stands between him and us.

She raises one hand, and a nail flicks into a claw.

'Stop, please, everyone,' she says firmly, throatily. 'Deep breaths please. All around.'

I've pushed past my girls—*my girls!*—my eyes are all blurry with tears. They were about to take on a werewolf, for me.

I give my head a shake. *Focus, Hazel.* Maengan has hackles back down, has mastered himself and is once again just a lanky Nish boy, though he looks like he'd melt through the wall if he could. Again, not like Spider/Jim, at all. Jim is an asshole. The kid is fundamentally kind. *Damn it.* I want to hug him. But I am an asshole, too.

'Well, well,' I drawl, 'Maengan Nolan... *et tu, Wolfie*?'

He just tips his head to one side, like a curious pet dog. I can't help it. I laugh out loud.

Shanaya chuckles too, and Maengan looks at her still up-raised hand, then at me, and he starts laughing, too, nervously. We look at each other, the three of us laughing—'*What the Hell is going on here?*' shouts Frankie over our cackling.

That stops me. Frankie doesn't yell.

'Mom! Stop laughing! Maengan is a werewolf, and that the guy who... hurt him... who turned him into this... is your *dog*, Mom! Your *werewolf!* How can you be calm, when *you've been living with a werewolf?!'*

She draws herself up. Little Frankie, always so silken, so elliptical and gliding, stands in a pose that's pure Missy—pure *me,* I realize with a start—and demands I look her in the eye.

'Mother. You need to come clean. Are you a werewolf, too?'

She's rooted there, like a tree, so still. I turn to them. Suddenly, I feel calm in a way I've never felt in my whole life.

'No.' I say, just that. My heart is bursting with pride in her terrified courage.

And then I sit myself down on the floor, pat the floor beside me. Shanaya folds herself elegantly to the floor, nods to Maengan.

***

It takes the kids so much longer to shift gears this time, for this, but they slowly do and by the time Shan and I have lit smokes, they're all three of them sitting in a circle with us. I put the ashtray in the middle, like a ceremony. I offer the smokes around. Maengan takes one. Missy takes one. Frankie takes one, too, but she just cups it in her beautiful hand while we four light up.

I go first. It is easier than I thought it would be, to tell them now.

I had a dream, in which Grandma LeSage came to me, and advised me to go get a certain dog from the Humane shelter. Spider. Who is also Jim. Who is a shape-shifter. I find myself thinking of him as Spider/Jim now, one word, like Shanaya calls him.

'He was Nell August's lover, and fathered her child,' I say, looking to Shanaya, 'and he came here looking for her, he says. But he also came here hunting Nell's killer.'

I ask her with my eyes to pick up the narrative, but it is Maengan who speaks.

'And I came here hunting him.' We all stare.

And Maengan goes on, tells us the barest version of it. Himself, a youth looking for direction, looking for guidance; Jim, the Traditional guy, taking the youth group on the land, teaching them old skills, teaching them language. The girls hold him in their gaze. It dawns on me that they've already heard this story.

'Maengan means Wolf, you know?' he says to Shanaya. She nods.

'So, he named you?' I blurt. Missy shifts beside me, uncomfortable.

Maengan shakes his head, face still dark with emotions. 'No. It's just my name.'

'Hazel,' he says, straightening up, 'I'm sorry.' He looks at my daughters, and at Shanaya, who is just sitting quietly. 'I was… kind of a mess when your mom met me. And she… helped me out…' he's gathering breath for a big confessional moment. I can't be having that.

'Look, less said the better. It happens. Shit happens, hair grows.' I crack wise, but he tries to go on.

'No, look. Hazel, I need to say, you saved my life, and I—'

'You came all the way out here to thank me. You're welcome.'

But he told my daughters, not me.

'But why did you tell them, not me?'

'I didn't know why Jim came out here. When I found out he was living with you… I didn't know if you were part of it. So I waited, and watched.'

All the time, the little bastard was torn between wanting to thank me, and worrying that I was a monster, too? And so he set himself up to protect my girls?

My girls. They're looking pretty shaky. I pull on my smoke, sink into this grounded feeling. I am their mother, and I've got this. We all have to get clear, and it has to be now.

Maengan is a werewolf. Spider/Jim is a werewolf. Joshua is involved in some very questionable deaths: three men, all connected to Nell August. Nell, whom I'd seen and thought I recognized in life; Nell dead, turning out to be so much more than I'd been told she was.

Shanaya is my lawyer. I may need one because apart from Joshua, the people I have been investigating are dead. Brutally dead like Nell August, whose death somehow started this whole chain of events. I am an accessory to murder, or maybe just a witness, but I don't know how to prove what actually happened. Don't know anymore if that is the point. Proof. *To whom? Of what?*

I lay it out, plain as I can. They nod, owlish in the smoke. For once, they don't get on me about how cheap cigarettes make me smell, about how b-movie it is to smoke, about how bad for my health. For once, the smoke hangs like it's properly schooled traditional smoke, bridging the worlds of human and spirits, a blue haze in which we see clearly in ways not normally available.

Here and now, sitting in this circle, they can take it in, and they do.

There are shape-shifters right here among us, and that is just reality—not magic realism or some cultural myth trotted out like a trinket to assuage all the centuries of poverty and humiliation. We are all Anishinaabek, a word that just means The People, *real people*. We sit on my dingy grey broadloom carpet in my dim-lit office as real as we would be in any lodge.

As real as my lawyer, who also happens to be a part-time tiger.

Do I go into this with them now? Do I save that for another time?

I'm saved from deciding by my phone, shrieking from the desk. I never turn it on that loud, but it's clanging out Jim's particular ringtone, and my head is buzzing with a voice trying to speak. Then the smoke alarm asserts the laws of physics and joins the shrieking.

We all clamber to our feet. Missy opens a window, Maengan cracks the door and Shanaya steps under the alarm.

'Is this thing wired to the Fire Station?' she asks. I shake my head. Tiger-swift, Shanaya springs up and punches it into crumpled plastic silence.

I press the button on the phone, and the buzzing in my head becomes Jim in my ear. 'Speaker' mimes Shanaya, and they all hear him fill me in.

***

He's in UpTop, hunting Joshua. 'Someone else is out here too,' his tinny voice rasps. 'Stay where you are and wait—'

We're out the door before he finishes, like avenging angels—no, like a pack of avenging mortals, which is worse. We have skin in the game.

***

Five of us packed in tight, the Jeep surges like a wild horse up the street, north toward UpTop. The Inland station lights glow balefully in the dark, looming like a beacon of doom. We roar past the Humane shelter, turning and climbing into the weirdest part of Amiskwaciy. Of course they're going to UpTop, where else would a werewolf and a killer cop have a showdown?

'*Someone else is out there, too, and we're not to come after him...*'

'Then why did he call?' I ask out loud the question we're all chewing on as the jeep winds higher into the night.

***

Zabeh, we don't get bothered by linear time the way you do. So, a lot of the things you solve mechanically, we don't need to. Distance. Talking to the mind. Knowing how to tune into souls and spirits and shape an image—a ghost—of someone held in the mind or heart light. We can do that. Turns out, we can also use the phone. I could have just gone into the tobacco haze, joined in their circle of prayer. I consider they had so much to consider. But truly, I wanted to try. First Zabeh on cell phone! I made a call. I consider Hazel would probably say I'm an asshole.

HAZEL: INTO THE DARKNESS

We drive on.

'Slow down,' says Maengan from behind me. He's got his head out the window—*I will not laugh, but why does the absurd always show up in a crisis ?*—He's half-shifted, wolf-snout searching for Jim's scent. Now Shanaya opens her window, pokes her head out the other side. I drive on in the dark, down the weird little alleys of UpTop, and a tiger and a wolf have their heads stuck out, searching the breezes.

I remember that first morning, when I almost got hysterical, and Spider grabbed my arm to steady me. *Not always an asshole.* Pretty brave, really, considering how scared he must have been himself. I never thought about him before, not like this, not as a person every bit as vulnerable as any other, who just happened to be a wolf sometimes, but more importantly, who wanted to make amends now for the mistakes of his life, who wanted to save his daughter, if not himself.

Why can't I hear him? I realize I'm holding my breath, trying to hear him in my mind. Nothing.

Then a faint whisper.

Left.

And the damn Jeep sputters, stalls, stops.

We all stare at each other. This isn't how stories go. Not how the chase scene plays out. But the Jeep is dead. The gas gauge reads empty. Nothing mysterious. Just me, so occupied with everything else I forgot to gas up my car.

We stare at the gauge. Nobody says anything. And we all hear it, clearly, through the window.

'*You!*' Just that one word, echoing.

Here behind Inland station, nobody lives. UpTop's all physical plant for the City, the arrays that make everything run. Quiet, automatic. At night, not even maintenance people. All quiet.

We jump out of the Jeep, and leg it toward the sound of voices, now lower, indistinguishable.

It's dark, but Maengan and Shanaya move like hunting beasts in their natural environment, and we just follow them.

'As long as they're talking, we don't do anything rash,' I say to the tiger and the wolf—and my girls, who might be more trouble than either beast. They've shifted too, into something I never really saw before, either: women. Full-grown powerful women. I don't have time for the rush of absolute mother love and pride to slow me down. Good thing it lifts me and deepens my breath. The five of us stride through the dark like mythic heroes.

Step light, I think, but I don't need to say it. They are all light on their feet, even Missy. Frankie has always been able to glide like an old-fashioned Indian, but Missy, she was always a thumper. 'Feet mad at the world?' I'd tease her, back when. Now, she's slipping along on quiet feet, the smart kind of hero, a woman who won't give herself away in the clinch.

We stop still, in the dark, in a half- circle.

They stand in the only light: Josh, plain clothes, evidently big and strong, but I can't tell, is that all him or is he wearing his kevlar? Jim, facing him, human.

He's thin. He's not big.

He's faded looking, all his colours diminished. A middle-aged, mid-toned man. Put a ball cap on him and he'd pass for any number of men, Nish or otherwise; just a northern man, not particularly good-looking, not unattractive. His dark hair brindled with grey. His age indeterminate in the indeterminate light. But it's the way he steps, slowly, lightly, circling. And it's his eyes, locked on Joshua, eyes that seem to flame even in the dark. *I know those eyes.*

I love those eyes. I hate this asshole creature who's turned my life upside down, who's never made anything better… but it hits me then that I love those eyes. They seem to pulse along with the river of my own blood. *Not fair. Not fair. Not fair. Justice. Just Us. Justice. Just us.*

He is circling, and I'm rooted in place.

And then she steps out of the shadows, into the light.

***

Now! It is now! I go there now. Sister, I am coming!

***

She looks like Nell August, but her body is young. Her hair is ombre-washed, brown to pinkish, shimmering in the light. She is barefoot, her heels in her hands. Her eyes are red. Her lips are red. Her face is a mask of grief.

Joshua and Jim stop moving. Everything in the night seems to come to a still point of light. In the middle of that, this woman. She looks hard at Jim, then turns her back to him.

'You and your men,' she says to Joshua, 'you took her from me. She was a good mother. Even when you were breaking her, were using her 'til she came home empty, she remembered to be a good mother. She tried. You would not let her be.'

'Who are you?' It's Josh who asks. Jim says nothing.

'I'm the collateral damage.'

She takes a step closer to him. He's frowning, his peak-browed look of concern and puzzlement. He clearly doesn't know what to make of her. She is small, slight, insignificant. But her eyes burn with luminous rage, and she has all his attention.

'I'm what you never considered. When you started her working for you, you could have let it be okay for both of you. But you and your men, you had to break her. You had to beat her and drug her and make her depend on you. You knew she had a child to care for, but that didn't matter to you, did it?'

Joshua knows her now. 'Nell August's daughter.' He tries to defuse the situation. 'Of course. Look, kid—'

'My name is Rabbit.'

'Abeligamuj,' whispers Jim, behind her, so soft maybe only I hear it, the Mi'gmaq version of her name.

'Well, Rabbit,' says Josh, 'she never mentioned you to us.' A beat later, he realizes he's admitting he knew Nell August, and he continues. 'We picked her up so many times for soliciting, and she never said. Guess she named you after the way she—'

'Noooo!' Jim roars, startling Rabbit. Joshua grabs Rabbit, spins her, pulls her in.

'—fucked,' says Joshua, spitting the word out. 'She was a whore, kid.' He sneers at Jim, frozen in a crouch. 'What's this whore's kid to you?'

'She's my daughter.' He says it soft and clear and deadly. 'And you need to let go of her if you want to live.'

Joshua feels Rabbit struggle against him, and he shifts one arm into a choke hold.

And Rabbit twists, slips sideways and low, swinging her heels blindly against him. For the crucial instant, she has all his attention. Jim shifts, a man leaping, a wolf in flight, and bowls Joshua down to the ground.

The wolf stands over him, snarling. Joshua Campeau, eyes bugged out in terror, pisses himself. We all smell it. He scrabbles backward in the dirt, and he claws a taser out of his concealed holster, presses it up into Spider's snout.

A sizzle.

A smell of burning.

Spider's head snaps back and up, and the taser arcs away.

Joshua reaches for his gun. *Of course he has a gun!*

But another roar splits the night, and Maengan leaps in over Jim's inert body. He seizes Josh's arm in his jaws, wrenching it to the side, holding him. Officer Joshua Campeau faints.

Now Jim stirs, weakly pushes himself up. Human again, his face looks a mess. Shreds of his human clothes hang haphazardly on him. He turns to Rabbit, who stands pressed up against the wall of a dark, silent building. She is staring at him horrified.

'Daughter,' he whispers, holding out a hand. 'Abeligamuj—'

'My name is Rabbit.'

'Abeli—Rabbit. My girl.'

'Not your girl.'

'I loved your mother.' She stares on, red-eyed and shaking. 'I came here… to find you…'

None of us can move.

'That night—' she whispers.

'That night,' he sobs, 'I couldn't believe it. Couldn't believe it was you.'

I reel from the sudden hideous memory of that night.

'Naked,' her thin voice rasps, 'What kind of a father—'

He recoils as if struck. 'I was—' his head drops in shame.

'He was a wolf, Rabbit.' I find my voice suddenly. 'He tracked you as a wolf. He knew you were in danger, and he came as a wolf to save you.'

'I was there,' she says to me, her little voice shaking. Her red eyes turn back to Jim, who is looking up at her in abject pain.

'I was there, *Father*,' she scrapes the word in her teeth, 'to destroy the man who killed my mother. You? What good are you?' He crouches in the dirt and lets her speak. 'If you had loved her enough, you wouldn't have left her to raise me on her own. If you had really loved her, you would have protected her from those evil men. But you didn't.'

She steps away from the wall, plants her bare feet firmly on the earth.

'Those evil men destroyed her, but only because you hadn't the humanity to stand by her.'

He bows his head to her, nods.

'So, you are my father by blood. But she gave me life, and she protected me, all her life. She was all the family I had in this world.' Rabbit's wispy voice cracks for a moment, then she swallows and goes on. 'And I have done what needed to be done.'

Jim and I both stare. '*You?! You* killed Dave Lancaster?!'

There is a sudden reek in the night. A wind. And a shadowy form steps from the darkest of darkness. It's huge. We don't move. There's nowhere to go. It fills our view.

'Sister,' creaks a voice like wind in pine branches.

'Sister,' whispers Rabbit.

The shock has shifted Maengan back to human, and he and Jim speak as one. 'Zabeh!'

And I am standing in an alley with my daughters, two were-wolves, a were-tiger, and a sasquatch. *Zabeh*. The inter-dimensional being known across Turtle Island for their ability to appear and disappear, never proven to exist, but always known by The People. Zabeh, protectors of the waters, who live in darkest forests. Not in cities. But this is Amiskwaciy, and there she stands, a bonafide zabeh, hulking by Rabbit's side, holding Rabbit's thin hand in her massive one. Rabbit speaks.

'My sister came, when I had nobody else. She sang me songs when I was sick and my mother had to work. She witnessed when my mother died.'

The zabeh croons at this—*ririrri*, a birdlike song from her massive face.

'And she helped me make justice for my mother.' She looks at Jim. 'Yes, my sister and I killed that man.'

I'm an asshole, I had to interrupt. 'And the others?'

'They ended themselves,' says the zabeh, matter-of-factly. 'But we were there to tell them it was time.'

And because we are all staring at the sasquatch talking to us, none of us notices that Joshua has awakened. He has not come to his senses. But he grabs his gun, and with a wordless howl, points it at Maengan. Jim lunges against him, the shot flies wild. Rounding on Jim, Josh fires again, his hand bucking back.

'No!' cries Rabbit, her thin arm thrust out. Do all assembled see the resemblance flashing between them, and the recognition? Does the wolf leap, and fall at her feet?

There is a zabeh beside her, surging in perfect counter to the flare of fire.

There is a third gunshot in the night, sound echoing in lag behind the movement.

Rabbit, for a moment, appears to be wearing a ghost dance shirt. A wind blows, as if from a long way away, a southerly wind with a scent of dry grass and sage, of clean things and open spaces, a wind of long ago, unstopped by road, fence or boundary, unbent by living skylines, a wind that carries chanting voices...**Abeligamuj... waabooz...jistu...quetshadee...mastinca...ometochtli...mehtoqehs... abeligamuj...abeli...abeli...**

And Rabbit is lifted in the wind, whirled, and dropped back, against the wall. She stands in a blue shimmer, the ghost shirt flickering, red, brown, blue, yellow, roan against her thin body, trailing down her arms ribbons like veins...

It flickers and fades. She shimmers for a moment, seems to disappear. And then she becomes as real again as the rest of us. She swings her mother's heels in her hand and they smash against Joshua's face, and light explodes around him, and the reeking wind, and he falls.

And in the ordinary light of the alley lies a dog.

And next to him, a broken policeman. Joshua's hair, taffy brown, looks so soft. His eyes will nevermore look upon anything.

Spider! Spider!

It is me shouting, me screaming, me leaping into the circle of light, me falling on him like a warrior, like there is some bomb yet to fall and I can protect him. Like it's not already too late.

I press into his heavy fur, into his flat slabbed ribs. I bury my face in his heavy ruff.

Mama! Mama!

***

I cannot understand who is calling me. Even when I feel Missy's arms locked around me, even then, I cannot take it in.

'Mama! Mama! Mama!' she wails, holding me as hard as she can. And Frankie's voice comes in, and I feel her slight body, and the staggering weight of their love combined. We crouch there, pressed together, pressing a dead black bastard of a dog into the dust, for untold eons.

And then, because there is nothing else to do, we loosen our hold on each other, and just get back up again.

Rabbit stands waiting, the zabeh by her side.

***

Shanaya stands with her sternest lawyer's face on, facing the zabeh. Maengan stands beside her, straight-backed, stiff-legged.

'Zabeh…' Maengan growls the word, his voice shaky. He's bristling, half-shifted, but immovably between the zabeh and my girls.

'Zabeh is what I am, but that is not my own name.'

'I advise you,' says Shanaya, her voice half lawyer, half velvet-striped death, 'not to move. Whatever and whomever you may be, if you hurt my friends, there shall be consequences.'

The zabeh looks at them with her strange mouth open, then purses her lips. For a moment, she radiates pure gentleness.

'I am a zabeh. I have not come here to harm you.'

She trills like a bird, a strange sound from such a large creature. The reek of her swirls around us, mingling with lingering sage.

'Ri ri ri. I consider you. I hold you in my heart light now. You are strange people, but you sing well together. You have made each other family. Family must help family. I have come for my family. For my sister.'

Rabbit looks gravely into each of our faces.

'I'm sorry,' she lisps. 'I'm sorry for your sorrows. I'm sorry for your pains. It had to end. When the story gets too bad, sometimes your only strength comes from knowing you are in a story, and you can choose to bring it to an end. My sister and I are going now.'

She looks into the zabeh's face, then back to us.

'Family is everything,' she says. 'Hold on to what is yours.'

And they walk away from us, a barefoot girl with pink ombré hair and a sasquatch. They walk into the darkness, then step into light, singing as they go:

I gather sage on the wind, ríríríri
I gather cedar, gather pine rí rí
I gather sweetgrass, and wild willow tang rí ríríri
And all the healer's flowers…ríri riri riri…

NOKOMIS: DAYBREAK

So, that's what happens when you listen to your Nokomis, your Grandma. If she comes to you in a dream, and you've got the guts to do what she says when you wake up, who knows what you can get into?

Look at that Hazel and her bunch:

The night is ebbing, a golden green blue light etching the edge of the world. Rabbit walks into the edge and disappears from your view. But you can see her, if you're looking, in all the food court babies, formula or breast fed, poorly grown or thriving, all the tatter-minded sons of toxicities large and small.

These are Rabbit's family, and she will fight for them. You may not think she's worthy, or strong enough to win the fight, but Rabbit goes on fighting. Let her go, over and over.

Promise you'll see her courage in the real faces you are given to see. Know that she goes by many names: Wapos, Waaboos, Abeligamuj, Mehtoqes, Jistu, Quetshadee, Mastinca, Ometochtli... some say she lives in the Moon, and that the Moon alone knows all her children.

The light is growing now, a warm spreading stain. Stain, yes, we all carry some part of it. We all carry some measure of light, and the bloody birth of the sun reveals renewal every ordinary day.

Look, Hazel and her daughters stand together, and they're crying now, at last, for Spider/Jim, but also for Big Frankie. If you want to imagine that flickering green in the dark just above the top edge of dawn is Big Frankie's soul, imagine it. If you imagine that, you will have to know, he's in such good company—all the souls gone so suddenly and soon, all the ones who didn't make it, the ones who fell too soon, fell short, who couldn't believe it could end like this, so sharp and so soon, Frankie is dancing with them, The People. He belongs. And of course, he is trying to lead the line—bossy is bossy, down through the cycles of creation.

But look back now. The alley is empty.

Hazel and her family have carried Spider/Jim away.

In another part of Amiskwaciy, Devin, the boy who has become a Bear Clan man, a protector, walks with Sandra and Efren and Cody and Tomlin.

They will do their best for LeWayne, and for all the broken kids who never had a chance.

When you look at them, really see them. They're a lesson in breaking boundaries. You have to put aside your puny laws and understand the spirit of things. However broken and feeble they are, if they bind and heal, and that makes them healers. And this world needs healers.

They've got hard times coming. So do Missy and Maengan, and beloved Little Frankie. But they will find their way. I know this. I'm a Grandmother.

But wait.

What about our lawyer, tiger, true heart friend Shanaya? You didn't think a lawyer was going to give an invisible epilogical narrator named for an ancestral abstraction that last word, did you?

Here's what Shanaya does next:

HAZEL: COME THE SUNRISE

Shanaya walks very carefully, her velvet paws practically silent.

'What does Anishinaabe legend say it takes to kill a werewolf?' Shanaya asks Maengan, as they walk. Her voice is burrs and blurs, but it's clear enough to understand.

Her back is broad, and she walks on velvet paws.

Together, the four of us lifted Spider/Jim's inert form onto Shanaya's back, and we're all walking home through the early morning light, down the silent alleys of UpTop. On Shanaya's left, Maengan holds Missy's hand. Frankie and I walk on the tiger's right side. All of us keep one hand on the inert body sprawled on Shanaya's back. It feels correct, ceremonial even; it's not necessary. She's huge, and he's deadweight. I cannot look at his face, though the smell of burnt fur from the tazer shot rankles my nostrils.

'I don't know,' Maengan says. 'We're not European, and our stories go back long before there were guns, so there has to be something other than silver bullets.'

Frankie chimes in. 'I wouldn't have guessed it would be a plain old police bullet.'

'I would not be surprised by that,' replies Shanaya, 'but I would be surprised if a werewolf were any different than a human with respect to the fact that it ought to at least be a bullet that has pierced a vital organ.'

I stop, startled. 'What did you say?!'

And we all stop. And I run my hands feverishly over the big

dog's body, its ridiculous shards of man-clothing draping it, feeling for an actual bullet hole.

'How did we not—?'

***

'Ah,' purrs Shanaya, 'Do not blame yourselves for not checking more closely for wounds. There was a lot going on.'

We just stare at her.

'I only noticed because I am, as I told you once, a lawyer and a tiger, and as such, doubly inclined to very careful noticing.'

We stop, in the alley in the dawn.

There is no wound on him, other than the terrible burns on his face. And then his yellow eyes open, staring at Maengan. Breath rasps out of him. 'Maengan,' he gasps. 'I'm sorry.'

'I know,' whispers Maengan, smoothing one hand through Spider/Jim's fur. His other hand holds tight to Missy's. 'And it's alright now.'

The softest of breezes moves Spider/Jim's brindled fur, his tattered clothes like ribbons. And as the light dims out of his yellow eyes, a song echoes in the bright new morning..

I gather sage on the wind
I gather cedar, gather pine
I gather sweetgrass, and wild willow tang
And all the healer's flowers...

THE END

THANKS & ACKNOWLEDGMENTS

First of all, thank you so much to Netta Johnson. I hope this book is worth your faith in it, and in me. Thanks to Lisa Murphy Lamb, Anne Brown and everyone at Stonehouse, a powerhouse of literary endeavour. Your guidance, support and expertise have made writing this book a rare delight.

Thanks to trishsewell.com for the cover art. It's like we heard the same stories growing up or something... Thanks to my Beta Readers for your input; special thanks to Zdeña Sewell Sattler for incisive insights on key narrative moments.

Thanks to Edmonton Arts Council, whose Edmonton Artists' Trust Fund enabled me to draft this book. Thanks Darrin Hagen, for nominating me—and for the accordion jam!

Thanks to MacEwan University, whose Writer-in-Residence position enabled me to finish it. Special thanks to Dr. Mark Smith and Dr. Lynne Honey, for getting me there and for keeping me there.

Thanks to all the scholars formal and informal who create a body of knowledge that honours the histories of Turtle Island. Thanks to those who kept stories secret when it mattered, and those who bring them forward when the time is right.

In particular, thank you to Dee McCullay, whose excellent film Sasquatch on Lake Superior deserves a million views, at least.

Thanks are also due to whoever had the brilliant idea to have

The Six Million Dollar Man encounter a sasquatch, back in my impressionable childhood, and to have Andre the Giant play the role.

This book is for my family.

This book was written in Amiskwaciy Waskahigan, known as Edmonton since 1904. This is the heart of Treaty 6 territory in present-day Canada. Humane is set in a place also called Amiskwaciy, which is not meant to be a factual representation of the real Edmonton.

I make no warranties that the opinions and perspectives of any of the characters in this story represent actual authentic Indigenous knowledge, lore or traditions, nor the cultures and beliefs of any other peoples... Likewise, world events presented as context in this story are not in any way warranted to be true history, though they are inspired by actual events, trends and possibilities in history. If any reader finds information that feels resonant and true, I encourage you to seek factual histories related to that moment.

This is a work of fiction.

With the greatest of love and respect for all my relations,

Anna Marie Sewell
Marigold House, Amiskwaciy, Canada, 2020